The Liberators

The Liberators

James Pattinson

ROBERT HALE · LONDON

Robert Hale Limited
Clerkenwell House
Clerkenwell Green
London EC1R 0HT

www.halebooks.com

2 4 6 8 10 9 7 5 3 1

Typeset in 10/13.5pt New Century Schoolbook
Printed in the UK by the MPG Books Group,
Bodmin and King's Lynn

1

THE PROPOSITION

HARVEY LANDON STOOD watching the traffic sliding along Fifth Avenue. He was wearing a black oilskin coat and no hat. In his pocket was the sum of exactly six dollars and forty-five cents in good American money. In his left forearm there was a shallow bullet wound, four days old and healing fast, in his left side the more recent graze of a murderer's knife. Across his stomach was a wide, humped scar, but that was old – a war wound caused by a bursting shell in a corvette. It was older, but sometimes it hurt him more; he believed there were still some pieces of shell splinter embedded in the flesh, and sometimes the iron seemed to turn inside him like a sword.

He was forty-one years old, and he had six dollars and forty-five cents and nothing else in the world except a few cheap clothes and the watch on his wrist. In New York he had expected to collect five thousand dollars for delivering a letter. Five thousand dollars would have been enough to set him off on a fresh start, but he had never collected because a man named Delgado, who was to pay him for the letter, had been shot dead in a barber's chair. So here he was, washed up in New York with scarcely more than the price of a meal and maybe with the police looking for him in connexion with the deaths of three men in a cabin on board a Panamanian oil-tanker lying in a dock in Philadelphia.

Whichever way you looked at things, the prospect was not good, not good at all.

There was a cold wind blowing up Fifth Avenue between the sheer cliffs of the skyscrapers. It flapped Landon's oilskin, slapping it against his sinewy legs; he could feel the sting of it even through the thick seaman's trousers that he was wearing. The wind came up under the coat and wrapped him in a sheath of ice-cold air; it seemed to press upon his chest, squeezing his lungs, so that to breathe was a pain.

He turned his back on the wind and began to walk down Fifth Avenue with the wind flicking at the edges of his ears; it was like a whip flicking at them, metal-tipped.

'Rock bottom,' he said bitterly. 'Hard rock bottom, and you can't go lower.'

He was speaking aloud, but no one took the least bit of notice. If he had plunged a knife into his chest and had died on the spot in a pool of blood he might have caused a momentary flutter of interest, but in New York eccentrics were six for a dime, and a man talking to himself was not worth a second glance. The cars flowed past – the yellow cabs, the chequered cabs, the buses; people on foot, wrapped up against the weather, pushed by him. In this, the greatest city of the western world, there were eight million other human beings swarming round him and he was as much alone as he had been on board his yawl in the middle of the Atlantic; he was completely and utterly alone with the problem of his own survival.

He looked at his watch and saw that it was past noon. With that glance at the watch his mind seemed to start working again, to recover from the shock of learning that Mr Delgado was dead and the dollars gone. Now he had to make a plan, a new plan, any plan. He must get away from New York, that was certain. But which direction should he take? Northward to Canada? It was winter, and Canada was frozen under a blanket of snow. Westward to San Francisco or Los Angeles? It was a long way – maybe three thousand miles. South to Florida and the sun? On six dollars and forty-five cents? That was a joke, but not a good one. It failed to raise a laugh.

Well, at least there was the watch. It was a good one; he could sell it; it should be worth a few dollars. And he would have to travel cheaply; maybe he could thumb a ride; maybe he could work his way westward or southward. Maybe.

But the watch would have to go. He had lost it once before. Garcia had taken it in the gaol in Santa Ana and for a while had worn it on his own fat wrist. But now Garcia, the policeman, was dead on board a tanker in Philadelphia and the watch was back with its rightful owner. He would be sorry to let it go again, but he needed the dollars. It was no use being sentimental about a watch, even one that he had carried through the War and through a hundred other adventures, a hundred journeys into danger.

He went into the first jeweller's shop that he could find. His feet sank into the thick pile of the carpet as though he were walking on a sponge, and the heated air met and enveloped him like a promise of the soft climate of Florida; it was a tropical pool imprisoned in a shell of concrete and glass and iron.

Landon felt out of place in that pool. His black oilskin, stiff with the cold, rustled as he walked; his lean, bony face with its thin, hard mouth, seemed to have nothing in common with the soft lighting, with the decorous glitter of precious stones. He was like a dark excrescence, a blot on a clean page. And he knew it.

A salesman, dressed as impeccably as an actor in a society play, his collar and cuffs spotlessly white, came forward warily. Another hovered in the background. One corner of Landon's mouth drooped sardonically. Already, so it seemed, they were bracing themselves for emergency action. It could be that somebody already had a finger on the alarm.

'Is there anything I can do, sir?'

The man who had come forward had a soft, sleek oily voice. It seemed to flow over Landon like the superheated air. He disliked the man on sight.

'I want to sell a watch.' He held out his wrist to show what it was that he was offering for sale. The salesman looked at it with distaste. Landon might have been a leper exhibiting his sores.

'We don't buy watches. You've come to the wrong place.'

'It's a good watch,' Landon said.

'It could be the best watch in the United States of America. We still wouldn't buy it. We don't do that sort of trade.'

'You don't know what you're missing.'

'Might be we don't want to know.'

'Might be,' Landon admitted. He turned and walked back to the door, the carpet sinking away under the pressure of his feet. He looked back once before going out into the cold wind. The two men were watching him, not trusting him an inch.

He spread wide his hands and gave his crooked, sardonic grin.

'Nothing up my sleeves, nothing in my pockets. You could search me if you wanted to.'

They said nothing. He went out of the shop, and they watched him go.

The wind slashed his face and the folds of the grin stiffened into the fixed grimace of a carved goblin. A man was looking into the jeweller's window. He was a fat, squat man, hunched into a thick overcoat, the collar turned up. On his head he wore a pearl-grey felt hat; muffs like old-fashioned headphones protected his ears from the cold.

Landon glanced at him, and the man turned his head with a slow, deliberate motion. He had cold, stony eyes set deeply in the folds of a pudgy, unhealthy-looking face. The eyes reminded Landon of Golbek; they were killer's eyes, devoid of feeling. But this was not Golbek. Golbek was dead, with Captain Garcia and Able Seaman Green on board the tanker *Gloria del Mar*. Golbek had killed Green and had tried to kill Harvey Landon also, but it had not worked out according to plan, and now he would never kill anyone else.

The man with the ear-muffs gave Landon a long, hard stare and turned again to his examination of the window. Landon felt the cold biting into him with renewed venom after the warmth of the shop. He moved away, and the cold seemed to slow down the working of his brain, so that he could no longer think clearly, could make no more than the blurred and hazy outline of a plan.

He wondered whether the police were on his tail. Perhaps already they had his description, the description of an English seaman in an oilskin coat, five feet nine inches and one hundred and fifty pounds of bone and sinew and muscle, fair hair clipped short and ice-blue eyes. It could be.

He saw a uniform and a peaked cap ahead of him, and was assailed by sudden panic. He jumped on to a bus, and the man in the ear-muffs got up behind him, watching him without appearing to do so.

When Landon got off the bus he knew that what he needed above all else was a drink. He went into the first bar he came to and ordered whisky.

'Make it Scotch.'

The barman poured from a square bottle and pushed the drink

across. Landon brought out a dollar bill. There were only five more where that one came from.

The barman was not busy. He moved a cloth in circles on the bar-top and watched Landon pour whisky down his throat.

'You look like you needed that drink.'

He had drooping shoulders and a sorrowful face. His eyes were like mud.

'Want to buy a watch?' Landon asked.

'You got one going cheap?'

Landon extended his arm, baring the wrist. 'This one.'

The barman looked at the watch. It was the kind of look he might have given to a toad that had crawled up on to the counter.

'That's an old watch.'

'It's a good one.'

'Maybe it is, maybe it ain't. I just don't have no use for an old watch. I thought you meant new stuff. You're off a ship, ain't you?'

He stared at the oilskin coat.

'What difference does it make?' Landon asked.

'Nothing. No difference at all. I just thought you might have a new watch to sell – cheap.'

'I've got an old one.'

'No good, pal. I just don't have no use for an old watch. Sorry, but that's the way it is.'

He moved along the bar to serve another customer. Landon drained his glass, and saw the fat man with the stony eyes.

The man took his drink and shifted closer to Landon. He had pushed the muffs away from his ears and they hung on the sides of his forehead like fungoid growths on the trunk of a tree.

'You don't have to sell no watch, Mr Landon.'

He had a harsh, grating voice; it could have been an old model that had been driven too hard and was ready for the scrap-heap. The sound of his own name made Landon swing round.

'What did you call me?'

'Mr Landon. Mr Harvey Landon. Could be wrong. Don't think so, though.'

'I don't know you.'

'You could know me. Wouldn't hurt you.'

'What's the game?'

9

'No game at all. Business.' He moved closer. 'You can call me Gregg; everybody does. It's my name. What you drinking? Scotch? Hey, bartender!'

Landon said: 'What do you want with me?'

Gregg rubbed his chin with a fat white hand, his eyes staring unwaveringly into Landon's.

'I got a proposition to make. Could be to your advantage.'

'I doubt it.'

'What have you got to lose?' Gregg said. 'Drink your whisky and listen to me. You don't have to sell no watch. I told you. Good things to have around – watches. You want to know what time of day it is, you need a watch. That so?'

'Go on,' Landon said.

The barman had moved away. Gregg rested one of his fat white hands on Landon's arm.

'I know a man who would like to meet you. He's got a job for the right guy. A nice, easy, well-paid job. You interested?'

'There aren't any nice, easy, well-paid jobs.'

'It's well-paid anyway,' Gregg said.

'What is it?'

'Not for me to say. Maybe I don't even know. I'm just the go-between, hey? Just the go-between. You coming?'

'What have I got to lose?' Landon said.

He poured the whisky down his throat and followed Gregg out of the bar.

Theodore Cranefield opened a box of big, fat Havana cigars and pushed the box across his desk towards Landon.

'Have one.'

'I'd rather smoke a cigarette,' Landon said.

'As you wish.'

Cranefield took back the cigar-box and slid a silver cigarette-box into its place. He picked a cigar for himself, sniffed at it, held it to his ear, snipped the end, and lit it. His cheeks went in and out like bellows as he puffed smoke, and he stared at Landon through an overhanging tangle of grey eyebrows.

'Glad you came, Mr Landon. Got a job of work. Think it might suit you.'

Landon nodded. 'So I understand.'

'Gregg told you. Good man, Gregg. Trust him.'

Gregg was sitting on a chair pushed back against the wall on Cranefield's right. He had taken off his overcoat and his hat and ear-muffs, revealing black hair that had been subjected to the worst crew-cut Landon had ever seen. It looked as though a lawnmower with half the blades missing had gone over it, leaving a kind of ridged effect.

Gregg caught a cigar that Cranefield threw at him and bit off the end. 'Sure, sure. You can trust me.'

Landon judged Cranefield to be about sixty-five. He had thick white hair, parted on the right, and a heavy, pouchy face, with a dewlap that disappeared into the secrecy of a stiff white collar. His grey suit had obviously cost a deal of money, and the watch on his wrist would have paid for three of the kind that Landon had attempted to sell. Everything about Cranefield gave the impression of wealth, everything about the room, with its quiet opulence of carpeting and furniture.

Landon drew smoke into his lungs from the cigarette, and it came out again with his words, blue-grey, drifting lazily until it was caught by the air extractors that kept the atmosphere clean and fresh.

'What made you pick on me? How do you know I'm the right man? You don't know anything about me.'

Cranefield gave a booming laugh, and the dewlap quivered. His voice had a rich, gravelly quality, as though it were being dredged up from a deep pit.

'But there you're wrong. I know it all.'

'What do you know?' Landon kept his voice level, but there was a feeling of tension inside him. Just how much did the man know?

Cranefield seemed to be enjoying himself; he leaned back in his chair, holding the cigar between the thumb and fingers of his right hand.

'Just to get things on the level I'll tell you a piece of recent history – very recent. A man was sent to New York by a South American revolutionary leader, who has since been executed, with a letter to deliver to a Mr Delgado. Delgado was to pay the courier five thousand dollars on delivery, but before the courier could get to him

Delgado was most unfortunately shot to death while he was having his hair trimmed. And so the poor courier had nothing for his pains but a door in the face. Do I interest you?'

'Go on,' Landon said.

Cranefield took a puff or two from the cigar. Gregg was looking at the ceiling.

'The courier travelled from Buenos Aires to Philadelphia on board a Panamanian tanker called the *Gloria del Mar*, having been signed on as a member of the crew. Early this morning three dead men were discovered locked in one of the after-cabins of the tanker. One was a South American police officer named Garcia, travelling under the pseudonym of Torres, one was a Pole named Golbek, and the third was a British seaman whose name escapes me for the moment. Garcia and Golbek had been shot, the seaman had a knife stuck in his back. Do I still have your interest?'

Landon nodded. He could feel the throbbing of the wound in the side that Golbek's knife had inflicted and the irritation of that other scratch in the arm that the bullet from Golbek's gun had made. He remembered very clearly the shock of finding Green's body on his bunk, killed in mistake for him, and the final bloody struggle in the cabin when he had shot Garcia and Golbek.

'Go on,' he said.

'The South American and the Pole were trying to prevent our courier from delivering his letter to Mr Delgado. This courier must have been a very tough baby. Wouldn't you agree?'

Cranefield stuck the cigar in his mouth and smiled at Landon. It was a friendly smile, but there was a hardness in Cranefield's eyes that gave warning of the iron in the man. In his way Cranefield was a tough baby also.

'What has this to do with me?' Landon asked.

The smile dropped away from Cranefield's face. He put his cigar on an ashtray and leaned towards Landon, his white veined hands resting on the edge of the desk.

'Come now, Mr Landon, let us not make any pretence about the matter. You are that courier. Let us agree on that point. Now you're in a spot, you really are.' He coughed. 'But maybe that is no new experience for you.'

'Maybe not,' Landon said. 'And I admit nothing.'

Cranefield picked up the cigar and leaned back again. 'No matter. I am not a policeman. But I think the officers of the law would be very glad to interview you if I cared to tell them where you could be found.'

'Why don't you?'

Cranefield made a gesture of impatience. 'Really, Mr Landon, you are not a simpleton. Please don't try to give the impression that you are. It must be perfectly clear to you that the sole reason why I have had you brought here is that you are the kind of man that you are.'

'A tough baby?'

'That, among other things.'

'What other things?'

'You know how to sail a boat?'

'Pretty well.'

'Of course you do. No modesty please. You sailed a yawl single-handed from England to Brazil. Isn't that so?'

Landon nodded.

'Not an unparalleled feat,' Cranefield said, 'but nevertheless, it argues considerable skill in the art of sailing and navigation.'

'What's the job?' Landon said.

'One that should particularly appeal to you in present circumstances, since it will take you out of the United States, where your presence at the moment is, to say the least, not unattended by certain hazards.'

'Let's have it.'

Cranefield smiled. 'The job is simple. All you have to do is take a small sailing-craft – a ketch, I believe it is – from its moorings in Florida to a point on the coast of Central America.'

'Mexico?'

'No, not Mexico. Anagua. Do you know the country?'

'I have never been there.'

'That is immaterial.'

'So you want me to deliver this ketch to a buyer in Anagua?' Landon said, feigning obtuseness.

Gregg gave a sudden barking laugh, but remained leaning back in his chair and staring up at the ceiling. He seemed to be questioning the standard of the plastering.

Cranefield still smiled. 'You do not, of course, believe that I have picked a man like you to carry out so simple a transaction as that. You will be carrying a passenger.'

'A passenger who cannot get to Anagua by the more usual methods? One who may not be welcomed with open arms by the present government of Anagua? Correct?'

'How did you guess?' Cranefield said.

'And what do I get paid for this job?'

Cranefield blew out a cloud of smoke and watched it disintegrating. He stared at the cigar in his hand as if the price were written there.

'Wouldn't it be worth your while to go – just for the trip? Sea-voyages are good for the health. At least, so I've been told.'

'Without some financial incentive I might lose my way. I might never get to Anagua. Empty pockets make for bad navigation.'

'I could maybe get somebody else to do the job.'

'If it was as easy as that you wouldn't have bothered about me.'

'Perhaps, perhaps. I don't deny that you're unusually qualified. You are a skilful sailor, you speak fluent Spanish, and you have had experience of revolutionary work both in Central and South America. You see, I know a good deal about you, Mr Landon.'

'So this is revolutionary work?'

'I didn't say that. You mustn't put words into my mouth. However, I didn't pick on you for cheapness. The labourer is worthy of his hire. It says that in the Bible, doesn't it, Gregg?'

Gregg's gaze came down from the ceiling. The cigar rolled to one side of his mouth to allow for the passage of words. 'Sure, sure. In the Bible. That's right, Mr Cranefield.'

'As if you knew. Never read the Bible in your life.'

'I did too, Mr Cranefield, when I was a kid.'

'That doesn't bear thinking about – you, a kid.'

'Nice kid too.'

'Only your word for that.' Cranefield finished with Gregg and his gaze swung back to Landon. 'Five hundred dollars – two-fifty in advance, the rest when the job's completed. How does that appeal to you?'

'I could use more.'

'Sure you could. Who couldn't? But don't forget this is for your own good. You get clear of the States. In Anagua they can't touch you.'

'What's your interest in this, Mr Cranefield?'

'Never mind my interest. That's no concern of yours.'

'It might be,' Landon said. 'I don't like doing things in the dark.' He looked at Cranefield's dewlap; it hung over the edge of his collar, loose and heavy. There was something vaguely disgusting about it. 'You've told me a bit of the story; why not the lot?'

'I've told you all you need to know – so far.'

'Suppose I told the police what you've told me. Haven't you taken a risk on a doubtful character?'

Cranefield did not look worried. Landon had never seen a man who appeared to be more confident of being fully in command of the situation.

'We have ways of looking after our interests. We have ways of keeping people quiet. Isn't that so, Gregg?'

Gregg gave his barking laugh again. 'That's so, Mr Cranefield.' His right hand disappeared momentarily inside the jacket on the left side of his chest. 'That surely is so.'

'The idea of a man in your position, Mr Landon, threatening to go to the police,' Cranefield said, chuckling. 'You have a sense of fun, if you'll allow me to say so.'

Gregg chuckled too. 'The cops'd love it, just love it.'

Cranefield cut off the laughter as if shutting a door. 'I don't think we need worry about you, Mr Landon. You'll take the job?'

'I'll take it,' Landon said.

2

A RIDE WITH GREGG

LANDON RODE OUT of New York with Gregg. They travelled in a big Studebaker convertible. Gregg drove. They headed south.

Landon had a new outfit of clothes; he had a zipper bag in the back of the car. Cranefield had paid. Cranefield had found a passport also, made out in the name of Henry Cannings. Landon's hair had been cropped even closer and he was wearing glasses.

'You look a different guy,' Gregg said.

'I feel different.'

'That's the way it needs to be.'

Landon was to receive the first two hundred and fifty dollars when he was safely on board the ketch. 'You won't need any for the run down to Florida,' Cranefield had said. 'Gregg will pay for everything.'

'Are you afraid I'll walk out on you? Don't you trust me?'

'Maybe I do, maybe I don't. Either way you get the dollars when you're on the boat, not before.'

'I have to take your word for that.'

'You wouldn't expect a signed contract, would you?'

'No. Not on a job like this. Will dollars be good in Anagua?'

'Dollars are good anywhere.'

'I hope so.'

'You'll get your money,' Cranefield had said.

'I'd better.'

Gregg was a good driver. The Studebaker travelled fast; there was plenty of power under the bonnet.

'Good car,' Landon said.

Gregg lifted his shoulders, let them fall again. 'It's okay. Me, I'd go for one of them little English jobs, them Jags or Astons just to play with. Do a hundred and twenty easy. More.'

'You're too old for that,' Landon said.

'Ain't nobody too old for a fast car.'

They drove south through Philadelphia and Baltimore and Washington, through Virginia and North Carolina, stopping here and there at filling-stations and snack-bars for petrol and food, but not staying long. They covered five hundred miles on the first day with the Studebaker going well. Landon offered to take over the wheel for a time, but Gregg refused. This thick, stumpy man seemed to be completely unaffected by fatigue.

'I could drive in my sleep,' he said. 'I could do it with my eyes shut.'

'I hope you don't,' Landon said. 'I want to reach journey's end.'

'You will, Mac, you will.'

They spent the night in a motel in South Carolina and were on their way early in the morning. They went down through South Carolina and Georgia, and came in the late afternoon to the state of Florida that pushes a long arm between the Atlantic Ocean and the Gulf of Mexico.

'All according to schedule,' Gregg said. 'The sunny south. Everything as it should be. What you think?'

'I'm in your hands,' Landon said. 'I do what you tell me.'

Gregg laughed, wiping the sweat off his forehead with a white silk handkerchief.

'That's the way. You do just what I tell you; then we don't go wrong. We make the right moves. Okay?'

'Okay.'

Gregg had bought a newspaper at one of their stopping places. He had tossed it over to Landon.

'Seems like the homicide boys are looking for a guy might be around your size. There.'

He jabbed a finger at the paper, and Landon read that the Philadelphia police were anxious to interview a British seaman named Harvey Landon in connexion with a triple murder on board the tanker *Gloria del Mar*. Landon had apparently jumped ship and disappeared.

It was not a big news item. Perhaps there would have been more in a Philadelphia paper.

'Don't even give you a classy headline,' Gregg said. 'Just the same, if I was you I'd be good and ready to leave the hospitality of dear old Uncle Sam far behind me and never come back. What do you say?'

'It'll suit me to be going.'

'You bet it'll suit you,' Gregg said. He shot a glance at Landon as the car started off, then gave his full attention again to the road ahead. 'You sure get mixed up with some trouble, don't you? I guess you're just one of them guys who can't keep their fingers out of mischief. That so, Mac?'

'Look who's talking,' Landon said.

Gregg laughed, so that the folds at the back of his neck quivered. 'Sure, sure. I never kept my nose clean either.'

They had only one moment of serious worry on the way south and that was early on the second day. They came suddenly on a line of cars, bumper to bumper, stretching away ahead. The cars were inching forward slowly.

'What is this?' Landon said. 'A jam?'

Gregg shook his head. 'Road block. The cops. Looks like they're checking up.'

There was a police-car half across the road, leaving only enough room for one car at a time to squeeze through. Three or four uniformed policemen were examining licences. Gregg drew up close to the car in front and another car came up on his tail. There was no going back.

'Nice situation,' Landon said.

Gregg took a cigar out of his pocket, bit off the end, and spat it out of the window. He lit the cigar and rolled it to the corner of his mouth.

'I'll do the talking. You answer questions. Just the straight answer and no more. Remember you're a guy named Henry Cannings. Just remember that.'

'I've got a good memory for details,' Landon said. He looked through the rear window of the car ahead and saw that it contained a man, a woman, and two children, about four or five years old. A family party. One of the children, a boy, pressed his nose against the rear window and stared at Landon. He had red hair and a mass of freckles. His tongue came out and made a wet pattern on the glass.

'That kid,' Gregg said. 'Thinks he's a window-cleaner.' He puffed smoke. 'Relax now, just relax. Maybe it's only routine. Them cops, they got to do something. Don't have to mean they know you're heading south.'

'Nobody said it did.'

'But somebody might have thought it.'

'Let's just suppose it's the other way,' Landon said.

'Okay, let's do that.'

The Studebaker shifted forward and halted again. The boy with the freckles gave a last lick and turned round to stare at the policemen.

The one who came to attend to the Studebaker had a craggy, humourless face and disbelieving eyes. He looked at the New York registration number on the car as though it were a dirty word chalked on a wall. He looked at Gregg with the same expression.

'You from New York?'

'You guessed it,' Gregg said. 'Maybe you're psychic.'

The policeman looked sour. 'You better not try to be smart, feller. Don't get you no place. You came a long way.'

'That's what automobiles are for. One day you're here, next day you're some place else. Science.'

'Some folks like that,' the policeman said. 'They think it's good for the health.' He took Gregg's driving-licence and read the name. He handed it back.

'Okay?'

'Could be.'

'You bet it could.'

Landon had the passport in his hand. The policeman took it, staring at Landon's face.

'What's your name?'

'It's down there,' Landon said.

'Suppose you tell me.'

'Maybe he don't read too good,' Gregg said. 'He's only a cop.'

'Maybe you better shut your trap,' the policeman said. 'Now, let's have it, son.'

'Henry Cannings,' Landon said.

'English, huh?'

'Yes.'

The policeman stared at the passport, stared back at Landon. The photograph matched; Cranefield had seen to that. And it was a genuine passport. At least, it looked genuine. Landon wondered whether there had ever been a real Henry Cannings, and if so what had happened to him. Cranefield had been reticent on that point, had told Landon not to trouble his head about such matters. The passport was there, it had his photograph in it; what was he worrying about?

'You got business in this part of the world or just here for pleasure?' the policeman asked.

'Pleasure,' Gregg said. 'I'm showing him around.'

'I didn't ask you; I asked him. He can talk, can't he?'

'Sure, he can talk.'

'Let him.'

'I'm on a sight-seeing tour,' Landon said. 'I'm enjoying the hospitality of your great country.'

The policeman thrust the passport back at Landon. 'That so?' He took his hands off the car and stood back. 'Okay. Get moving. Don't block the highway. Step on it.'

The Studebaker moved forward, past the stationary police car. The road stretched ahead, long and straight and smooth. Gregg took the cigar out of his mouth and spat carefully through the side window.

'Damn cops!'

'Why did you try to needle him?'

Gregg looked genuinely surprised. 'Me try to needle that bum? I was being extra polite.'

'You riled him,' Landon said. 'Did you see the colour of his neck?'

'They rile easy,' Gregg said. He let the Studebaker work up its speed and the fence along the side of the road was a blur of posts rushing past. There were cars ahead, cars behind, cars slicking past in the opposite direction, all, it seemed, going flat out, as though an extra minute spent on the highway would be as regrettable as the loss of a thousand dollars.

'What's the ketch like?' Landon asked.

'What ketch?'

'The boat I'm to sail. Cranefield said it was a ketch. Remember?'

'I don't remember anything. Don't know nothing about boats. All

I got to do is get you there. I don't go no farther than that. Don't want to.'

'You're not coming for the sea-voyage?'

'I'll say not. That ain't my idea of a good time.'

'Know when the passenger comes on board?'

'As soon as I fetch him.'

'Who is he?'

'You'll find out soon enough.'

'Where's the ketch?'

'In Florida.'

'That's a big state. What part?'

'Don't ask questions,' Gregg said. 'Guys that ask too many questions get a bad name. You got it nice. Let it stay that way.'

They came to the house late on the second day; it had been dark for some time. Landon thought he could hear the sea, could smell it. They were away from the traffic now, following a dirt road. The headlight beams swung one way and then another. Trees cast black shadows on the road.

'You've been this way before?' Landon said.

He could sense the shrug of Gregg's shoulders. Gregg was as shadowy as the trees.

'I ain't guessing,' he said.

He swung the car off the dirt road on to a rough, bumpy track. The car bounced, flinging the glare of the headlights up into the sky and down again. They came to a gate, painted white, seven-barred. Gregg stopped the car.

'Open up, will you?'

Landon got out of the car and walked to the gate. Beyond it, against the skyline, he could see the outline of the house, no light was showing. The smell of the sea was stronger now; or perhaps it was not truly the smell of the sea, but of the sea's edge, a harsh, weedy smell that was lost when you got away from the coast. It was a clear night, starry, warm, with scarcely any wind. The air was as soft as velvet. Beyond the house would be the foreshore, beyond the foreshore the Gulf of Mexico.

Landon heard Gregg's voice, fretful. 'What you waiting for? You gone to sleep?'

21

He unfastened the gate and swung it open. The car surged through and stopped again, blowing exhaust fumes at Landon. He fastened the gate, went back to the car, and got in beside Gregg.

'You dreaming?' Gregg asked.

'I was taking a look round. It's new ground to me. I'm interested. Is that criminal?'

'Depends what you mean by criminal. I got no time to admire scenery. We got plenty to do before the night's finished. Plenty.'

The house came nearer. Gregg sounded the horn once, briefly. A light came on, illuminating a timbered porch, two smooth, white-painted pillars supporting an apex roof. The rest of the house was shadowy, with a hint of windows staring blindly at the night.

It sounded like gravel under the tyres. Gregg pulled up in front of the porch, stopped the engine, switched the lights off. He got out.

'Bring your grip, Mac.'

Landon pulled his bag out of the back of the car, turned, and saw that the door of the house was open. There was a black man standing in the doorway, hair going grey, bent at the shoulders. An old man. He was wearing a white cotton jacket, black bow-tie, black trousers. He stood with one hand on the door-knob, peering out towards the edges of the light that came from the porch lamp. His voice quavered.

'That you, Mist' Gregg? That you, suh?'

'Sure it's me, Mortimer. You didn't think it'd be somebody else, did you?'

'No, suh. Didn't think so.'

He came down the steps from the porch to help with the luggage.

'Glad to see you, Mist' Gregg, suh. And you too, suh, you too.'

He looked at Landon and then dropped his gaze, as though abashed at his own presumption.

Gregg said: 'Let's go inside. I need a drink.'

They went up the steps, between the two pillars, into a spacious hall, dimly lighted and shadowy. Mortimer closed and bolted the door. He flicked a switch, extinguishing the porch light.

'Nobody else coming tonight,' Gregg said. 'So we hope. You hungry?'

'I could eat,' Landon said.

Mortimer rubbed his hands together; they were dry, skinny hands, veined and fleshless.

'Susan done fried some chicken. You like fried chicken, Mist' Gregg? Apple pie 'n' cream. You like that?'

'Fried chicken, apple pie and cream. You never use any imagination?'

Mortimer looked as though he had been whipped. 'I done thought you like fried chicken.'

'I gotta like it. That's what you got, so I gotta like it. Okay, okay; fetch it.'

'Mebbe could cook sumpin' else,' Mortimer said. 'Mebbe I tell Susan – she think up sumpin'.'

Landon said quickly: 'Fried chicken and apple pie sounds just right to me. You can take my order for that dinner.'

'Me too,' Gregg said. 'I ain't got time to wait for nothing else.'

He led the way to a door on the right, and Landon followed. Gregg switched on the light, revealing a big room, high ceiling, the electric light diffused from a glass chandelier hanging in the centre. A polished mahogany dining-table was set out for dinner – two places. There were heavy mahogany chairs and a mahogany sideboard covering almost half the length of one wall. Over the sideboard hung an oil painting in a gilded frame; the painting was so cracked and dirty that it was difficult to tell whether it was meant to depict a man on horseback or a woman seated in an armchair.

'Old master?' Landon said.

Gregg looked at the painting. 'Old master, old mistress. I don't know. And if you want the truth, Mac, I don't care. I don't go for all that painting crap. Okay?'

'Okay,' Landon said. 'But it could be worth a few thousand dollars. You never know.'

'Anybody that gave a grand for that would want his head testing.' He went to the sideboard and uncorked a bottle of Bourbon whisky. 'You want a drink?'

Landon nodded. 'I won't say no to that.'

Gregg filled two glasses with neat whisky, gave Landon one, poured half the contents of the other down his own throat. Landon tasted his. It was not Scotch, but for Bourbon it was good enough. It was drinkable.

'This place belong to Cranefield?'

'No questions,' Gregg said. 'Ask no questions and you'll be told no lies.'

'You've been taking lessons from a clam.'

Mortimer served dinner. Gregg snarled at him now and then, grumbling at the way the meal had been cooked.

'You tell Susan – you tell her she couldn't cook a can of beans.'

'Yes, Mist' Gregg, suh, I tell her.'

'Tell her it's a first-class dinner,' Landon said. 'Give her my compliments.'

He had not seen Susan. He guessed she would be Mortimer's wife. He supposed Cranefield owned the house and left Mortimer and Susan as caretakers when he was not using it. It had the smell of a house not often occupied, a smell of furniture polish and damp. There was something incongruous about this dinner shared with Gregg in the big room under the cut-glass chandelier, the silver glittering on the table, and the grey-haired man shuffling in and out. It was like a scene conjured up from the past.

Gregg scowled at Landon. He seemed to have settled into a dark mood, and the whisky had done nothing to relieve it.

'You don't know what good food is.'

'Have it your own way,' Landon said. He was getting sick of Gregg. Mortimer glanced nervously from one to the other and left the room.

'Damn servants,' Gregg said. 'You got to keep them in their place. And their place is underneath.'

He was eating fast. Whatever he had said about the food, he was piling it into himself as if he were preparing for a long siege. He was a noisy eater.

'I take it that this is where we spend the night,' Landon said. He wondered whether Gregg would refuse to answer even that question, but the answer came fast enough.

'You don't. Tonight you'll be on the boat. You won't be coming ashore again.' He belched, wiped grease from his mouth with the back of his hand. 'Soon as we've finished eating we'll go aboard. Then I got other work to do. Maybe I don't ever see you again. Who knows?'

'You break my heart.'

'Mine too. We'll be a pair of broken hearts. You got a gun?'

'No.'

'You had one once. So you lost it. Careless.'

'You think I'll need one?'

'I never saw a guy who looked more like needing one. You don't know what you're in for. But you don't have to have your own gun. You'll find the armament on board the boat. That's all been seen to.' He drank some more whisky and smacked his lips. 'Maybe I'm wrong though; maybe it'll go as quiet as a rubber-soled shoe. Maybe it will at that.'

'I hope so,' Landon said. 'I'm a peace-loving man.'

'That wasn't the way I heard it,' Gregg said.

They went out through the back of the house, Landon carrying his bag, Gregg pushing on ahead. Gregg had a torch, but he was not using it. The stars made a pale glow, and on either side were vague shadows that might have been stunted bushes or clumps of grass or men crouching. There must have been some kind of path, although the ground looked pretty well featureless to Landon. Gregg seemed to know the way.

The smell of weed became stronger. Gregg called back over his shoulder: 'Better watch your step here. It's tricky.'

There was a smell of mud too.

The path swung away to the left and dipped suddenly. Landon's heels skidded in loose earth or sand, and he went down on his back. Gregg flashed the torch on him briefly and switched it off again.

'I told you you gotta take care.'

Landon got to his feet and picked up the bag. He said nothing. Gregg turned and went on, half walking, half sliding down the slope. Landon heard the ripple of water; then he saw a reflection of the starlight. He heard a voice coming suddenly out of the darkness to the right, urgent, apprehensive.

'Who's that?'

Gregg answered. 'Okay, Pete, relax. Where in hell you got that boat?'

'Right here, Mr Gregg. Just along here.'

They went in the direction from which the voice was coming, the ground under their feet uneven, slippery, treacherous. The water was on their left, and they were close to the edge of it. And then there was the shadowy outline of the boat and a little jetty.

'All okay, Mr Gregg?'

'Okay so far.'

Landon could see the man as a pillar of denser darkness in the gloom of the night. He was black from the ground upward; even his head was black except for the momentary glimmer of white teeth.

'We're ready to go,' Gregg said.

Pete came forward, took Landon's bag, and dropped it into the boat. It was a small dinghy with an outboard motor clamped to the stern. Gregg got in clumsily and the dinghy dipped one gunwale.

'Steady, Mr Gregg,' Pete said.

Gregg, sitting down in the boat, snarled up at him: 'You don't tell me what to do. I tell you. Got that?'

Landon heard Pete's breath whistling through his nose. It was an angry sound. But all he said was: 'Sure thing, Mr Gregg. I got that. You the boss.'

'Remember it then.'

Landon stepped into the boat and sat down. Pete loosed the painter from the jetty and lowered himself into the boat also. He hauled on the starting cord. The outboard motor coughed, spluttered, and relapsed into silence. The dinghy drifted away from the bank, turning lazily in a sluggish current.

'Maybe you better try again,' Gregg suggested with heavy sarcasm.

He tried again. The engine coughed again, spluttered, stopped.

'You got any gas in there?'

'Plenty gas. She's cold. Mebbe the plug got damp.'

'Maybe we'll get damp too if you don't hustle. You think we came here just to go drifting, for Chrissake?'

Pete spat over the side. Landon could hear the spittle drop into the water with a gentle *plop*; he believed he would have liked to spit at Gregg, and this was the next best thing. The night was very still. He took a grip on the cord and pulled it fiercely. The engine burst into chattering life.

'About time too,' Gregg said.

Pete steered the boat round in a wide curve, and water streamed away on either side, gurgling. The stern dipped lower under the thrust of the outboard, and the chatter of the engine disturbed the quiet of the night.

'You know where you're heading, I guess,' Gregg said.

'I know, Mr Gregg.'

Landon wondered how he knew; perhaps by instinct. There were no lights showing, only the reflection of the stars dancing in the wash of the boat. Ahead was a dark mass of foliage that might have been a wall standing up against the sky; beyond that perhaps the sea. Landon had put himself in other men's hands; for the present he could do nothing but let things take their course.

The dark mass came closer; it became a dense shadow hanging over them. They went into the shadow and it closed around them. He seemed to be following a channel of some kind, and the overgrown sides of the channel were like walls containing the boat and the men in the boat. They had to gaze directly upward to see the sky and the stars; there was no horizon. The dank odour of rotting wood and mud and water-weed was strong, stirred up by the churning of the small propeller.

Pete slackened speed; the engine chatter became less strident. Landon could see nothing; it was like floating on a stream of black ink into the folds of a black velvet curtain. Perhaps he could see in darkness; perhaps he had cat's eyes.

He announced suddenly: 'This is it. We got here.'

The engine died away into silence. The boat lost way, drifted a few more yards, and bumped gently against something solid.

Gregg flashed his torch and the white beam splashed on white-painted boards, travelled upward to a cabin top, a mast, furled sails, rigging.

It was the ketch.

3

GETAWAY

WHEN LANDON AWOKE it was already day. Light crept through small portholes and the skylight into the cabin of the ketch, revealing a table screwed to the deck, a book-rack, lockers, settees. The light had a greenish tinge, as though it had been filtered through a sieve of leaves. It was peaceful. The ketch was motionless, silent.

Landon was lying on one of the settees with a blanket over him. His mouth felt like the inside of an old boot. That would be the after-effect of the Bourbon. The bottle that Gregg had left was still standing on the table, but there was not much whisky left in it. Gregg had had one drink before going back with Pete in the dinghy; the rest of the shrinkage had been Landon's work.

He licked his lips, trying to moisten them with a dry tongue. He ought not to have drunk so much; it was a bad thing to drink by yourself; that was the way alcoholics did it. Better watch it, Harvey, better watch it.

He wondered when Gregg would be back with the passenger. He hoped it would not be long; there was no pleasure in lying up by yourself in an anchored ketch. Too much time to think; too much time to imagine policemen drifting down from Philadelphia, detectives nosing out the trail of a man who had jumped ship, leaving three dead men in his cabin. Explain that one, Mr Landon; just give a full, coherent explanation, and see if anyone believes you. No, he wanted no time to think; he wanted to get away to sea, away from the United States.

Gregg had seemed to guess as much. When Landon had asked him for the two hundred and fifty dollars advance Gregg had shaken his head, a lop-sided grin creasing his face.

'Not yet, Mac. What's your hurry?'

'I was to have half the money on embarkation. Well, I've been embarked.'

'You think I'm green?' Gregg said. 'I give you two-fifty and tomorrow no boat, no Mr Harvey Landon neither.'

'You don't trust me, then?'

'Why would I trust you? Trusting people don't get you no place, except maybe in the poor house. But don't you worry; you'll get your dough as soon as Mr Alvarez steps on board.'

'Alvarez?'

'Your passenger. Señor Ramon Arturo Alvarez. The Liberator.'

'El Aguila?'

Gregg looked surprised. 'You know him?'

'I know of him. El Aguila – The Eagle. So that's the man I have to take to Anagua. I can see why it has to be secret. The Generalissimo would hardly welcome him with open arms.'

'With a gaol more likely. Iron bars and chains. A prison yard and six men with rifles. Bang, bang, bang, and no more Mr Alvarez.'

'I have the nice job,' Landon said. 'I always have the nice jobs.'

'That's the way it is, Mac. You're getting paid.'

Gregg had gone away then with Pete in the dinghy. Landon had waited on deck until the sound of the outboard had faded away into silence, and then he had gone back into the cabin to the bottle of Bourbon.

El Aguila! He might have guessed that this would be the man. But he had not realized that Alvarez was in the States. He wondered what Cranefield's interest in The Eagle was. Cranefield did not look like a devoted liberator, even if Alvarez was. But the American was a businessman, and there might be big business in Anagua for somebody who had a pull with the government – the new government, under Ramon Arturo Alvarez.

Well, that was all very nice for Mr Cranefield. No doubt he had his tracks well covered, and if anything should go wrong, if other people should be killed or be thrown into prison, nothing in the faintest degree unpleasant would happen to the occupant of that gleaming, air-conditioned office in New York. But for the man who was to put Alvarez ashore in Anagua things might be a little more sticky. Gregg had mentioned a firing-squad. That was the usual way in which Pancho Valdez, the Generalissimo, sometimes known as The Sergeant, dealt with his enemies. It saved trouble. And Alvarez might not be the only one to face the rifles. For five hundred dollars Cranefield was getting a cheap agent.

Landon had done a lot of thinking after Gregg had left, and the level of the Bourbon had sunk steadily lower.

The morning air was warm. Landon rolled off the settee and stretched himself. He pulled on his trousers and shirt and went barefooted to find a drink of water. No more whisky this morning, no liquor at all. The water was lukewarm and tasted vaguely of tar. Landon decided that coffee would be better – black coffee, and something to eat. But first he would have a look at the position of the ketch in daylight.

He climbed out of the cabin into the cockpit. The ketch was in a narrow waterway with trees on either side and a lot of tangled undergrowth. A haze of mist or steam hung about the trees, dimming the sun's rays. The channel curved away sharply in both directions, so that the ketch was completely hidden from sight at any distance of more than about fifty yards. The water appeared to go in among the trees, and there was no clearly defined bank. Big, twisted roots stood up, slimy with mud and hung with green weed.

The ketch was in the middle of the channel. Landon went for'ard and saw the cable slanting down from the bows. He looked down into the water, but it was dark and muddy, and there was no sign of the anchor. The cable looked new, and though he could see that the ketch was an old craft, it had obviously recently been overhauled, and the rigging was in first-rate order.

He wondered who had brought the ketch to this anchorage. But it made no difference. Someone perhaps who was not willing to do the other job, or who could not be trusted to do it. Someone whom he, Landon, would never meet. It did not matter.

There were bird noises in the trees. He could see a pelican resting on a stump. There were furtive water noises, nothing else. Otherwise it was a still, quiet morning, with no wind to stir the tops of the trees or crease the surface of the channel into ripples. Only at the bows was it possible to notice the sluggish current that kept the anchor cable taut. There was no sign of human life. Even the house in which he had dined on fried chicken and apple-pie was invisible. He had never seen it in daylight; it was something that might never have existed.

He shook a cigarette out of a packet and lit it. The flame of the match did not even waver. He dropped the stick over the side and watched it float slowly towards the stern and away downstream.

'A nice quiet spot for a nice quiet life,' he mused. 'I wonder how long I've got to be here.'

He found provisions and a pressure-stove, and cooked breakfast. The smell of coffee and of frying bacon chased away the dank odours of the anchorage; the coffee drove the memory of the whisky from his head. He felt better, more alive.

When he had washed the breakfast things he went over the ketch with the keen and practised eyes of a skilled yachtsman. He could find no fault, no reason here for cursing Cranefield. There was an auxiliary engine and spare cans of fuel; that might be useful in an emergency, for getting out of a tough spot. In the cabin he found charts, navigational handbooks, instruments, a sextant – everything that he would need to guide this small ship across the wide expanse of the Gulf of Mexico. He did not know yet where he was to make his landfall, but no doubt Alvarez would tell him that. Alvarez would be able to tell him much – if he felt so inclined.

One discovery was particularly interesting. Under one of the settees was a long drawer. It was locked, but he found the key with some others in a smaller drawer. He unlocked the long drawer and pulled it out. It contained the armament.

Landon blew softly through half-closed lips. 'Pretty. Very, very pretty indeed.'

There were two sub-machine-guns, a rifle, two revolvers, and a heavy automatic that looked like a Mauser. There were several boxes of ammunition and also about half a dozen magazines for the sub-machine-guns. Landon picked one up and saw that it was fully loaded.

'Businesslike. Nothing left to chance. Somebody believes in efficiency. Could be Cranefield.'

He put the drum back in the drawer and took out the automatic. It was, as he had supposed, a Mauser of 9 mm. calibre. The revolvers were Colt .45s, and the sub-machine-guns had been made by the company that had given the tommy-gun to the bootleggers and gangsters of the prohibition era, before it had become respectable in the hands of soldiers and the cause of freedom. You could do a lot of damage with a tommy-gun; you could liquidate a stack of enemies.

The weapons were all in top condition, clean, oiled ready for use. 'No chances. That's the way it should be.'

Alvarez might not be expecting trouble, but if trouble came his way he was certainly ready for it.

In a tin at one end of the drawer were four metal cylinders, rather like short lengths of water pipe with the ends closed up. At one end of each was what might have been a fuse and detonator. You could do quite a lot of damage with things like that also.

Landon closed the tin, pushed the drawer back, and locked it. He went out on deck and found that the sun had chased away the last of the mist. It was warm, becoming hot. He yawned and stretched himself. There was nothing to do but wait.

He started the auxiliary engine, just to check up; not because he had any doubts now that everything had been well checked before he had come on board, but because he wanted something to do. The engine started, as he had expected, without hesitation. The sound of it seemed startlingly loud in the quiet backwater; it was as though he had proclaimed his presence to a listening world. He cut the engine and the sound died. The ketch relapsed into silence. Landon went back to the cabin and lit a cigarette.

The day drifted away and nobody came. He felt the old pain grumbling in his stomach, but nothing came of that either, no agony, just the sullen hint of the old trouble. He touched the scar lightly with his fingertips and felt the ridged skin where the iron had ripped him open. He passed a hand over his bony, angular face; there was bristle on the chin; he had forgotten to shave. The bristle made him feel dirty. He boiled some water and shaved, and felt cleaner.

The light began to fade; shadows and darkness crept over the anchorage. Landon did not like it. He wished Gregg would come back with Alvarez; he wanted to get away; this backwater was like a trap; you could be caught here.

But when night came there was still no sign of Gregg; there was no sound but a faint rustling in the trees and the murmur of water sliding past the ketch.

Landon thought of lighting the lamp, but decided against it. He lay on the settee and smoked, waiting.

At some moment of time he fell asleep, and there was nothing to waken him – nothing until the sound of the shot. He was awake then, quickly; awake and alert. For a few moments he lay where he was, staring up into the darkness, uncertain whether he had in fact heard a shot or whether it had simply been a dream from which he had awakened.

Then he heard three more shots in rapid succession, and then a fourth, and then silence. They were not very loud – some distance away, he judged. A heavy sleeper might not have been awakened by them, but Landon's existence had so often depended on the quickness of his reactions that he had acquired the habit of sleeping as a dog sleeps – lightly – ready to wake upon the instant.

He got up and went on deck. The stars were just beginning to pale as a grey hint of day came in from the east, but the water and the trees were dark. Objects were visible only as vague black shapes; overhead, through the slit in the trees were the paling stars in a grey sky.

Landon waited for another shot, and none came. He thought of the guns in the ketch's armoury; it might be advisable to have one ready. He went below, fumbled in the darkness for the key, pulled out the drawer, and picked up one of the tommy-guns and a drum of ammunition. He went back on deck and fitted the drum to the gun. He laid the gun down beside him on the deck. He waited and listened.

The sound of the outboard motor came faintly at first, then gradually louder. Landon cocked the tommy-gun and held it ready in the crook of his arm. The sound of the outboard came nearer. He watched the point beyond the stern of the ketch where the channel swept round in a curve, the point at which the boat must appear.

His eyes were becoming accustomed to the faint light of early dawn, but the dinghy was invisible to him until it had approached to within a stone's throw from the ketch. He watched it, holding the tommy-gun ready.

But it was Gregg's voice that came from the boat. 'Hey there! That you, Landon?'

He lowered the gun. 'It's me. Who did you expect it to be?'

The boat bumped against the side of the ketch. Gregg threw a painter and Landon caught and secured it. Gregg climbed on board fast. He was hatless and in the faint light it appeared to Landon that he had a dark stain down one side of his face. It could have been a smear of mud, but Landon did not think it was that.

Gregg saw the tommy-gun. He said: 'You found the hardware. You know how to use that baby?'

'I know,' Landon said.

'You may need it.'

Another man had climbed up after Gregg. He was tall – head and shoulders above the American. He had a hat pulled down low over his forehead, and Landon could see nothing of his face but the end of the nose. The man said nothing, gave no greeting.

The last to come on board was Pete. Landon could see the flash of his white teeth. He threw some baggage on board and came up after it. He loosed the painter, gave the dinghy a push and sent it drifting away from the ketch.

Landon caught his arm. 'Why did you do that?'

'We don't need it no more. Never no more.'

'We're coming with you,' Gregg said savagely. 'We're coming right now. We better get this barge moving.'

'I thought you were staying behind,' Landon said. 'That's what you told me.'

'Plans are changed. Some guys changed them for us.' He turned and spat over the side. 'Hell, you don't think I wanted to tag along. No help for it now. We better hurry.'

'If we start in this light we could run on to a mud bank. We'd be in trouble then.'

'No fear of that. Peter knows this channel like the back of his hand. He'll get us out; he's the pilot. When we get to sea that's navigation – your job. Okay?'

'I suppose so. I'd better start the engine. You had trouble?'

Gregg's voice was bitter. 'Plenty. Some other guys had trouble too. One of them won't have no more – not in this world.'

'I heard some shooting,' Landon said. He turned away from Gregg. 'I'll see about that engine.'

Pete was already hauling up the anchor. Landon heard Gregg say to the tall man: 'You better go inside, Mr Alvarez.'

The engine started sweetly. Pete came aft and took the tiller.

'Think you can get us out of here?' Landon asked.

'I know so,' Pete said. Landon caught the flash of his grin, heard the throaty chuckle. 'You trust me, Mr Landon. I get you out to sea. You don't need to worry just one little bit.'

Skilfully he eased the ketch about. The water began to ripple gently at the bows and Gregg came aft.

'I don't think they got a boat,' he said. 'But you better keep your eyes peeled.'

'They?'

'Some real nice guys that didn't want Mr Alvarez to go travelling. Could be friends of Mr Pancho Valdez. They was laying for us, but we give 'em the slip. We give 'em some lead too.'

'You got some in exchange.'

Gregg put a hand to the side of his face where the dark smear showed. Some of the smear came away on his fingers. He looked down at them.

'Creased.'

'Is it bad?'

'No, not bad. Took some skin off my cheek, that's all. Like I'd cut myself shaving.'

'You're lucky.'

'Sure I'm lucky. An inch to the left and it'd have been curtains for this kid. Well, you got to have luck. Don't get far without it.'

'So long as the luck holds out....'

Pete was saying nothing; his hand was on the tiller and all his attention was absorbed in the task of bringing the ketch out of its hidden anchorage into the open sea. There were mud banks on either side waiting for the keel to slide into them, and the light was bad; but Pete seemed not to be worrying. Perhaps there was no need to worry. Landon hoped so.

He felt the keel scrape lightly over some obstruction, a root perhaps or a half-submerged log. He spoke again to Pete. 'You're still sure?'

Again there was the white flash of teeth. 'Sure I'm sure. That was nothing. We get out all right.'

Gregg said: 'We need to be out of sight of the coast by daylight.'

'That's a tall order,' Landon said. 'It's getting light now.'

'That's so. Well, we gotta do what we can.'

The trees seemed to drift away from them like a dark curtain drawn back to let in the light. The masts were outlined against the sky. The stars had gone. A breeze rippled the surface of the channel as it widened to the sea. The odour of mud and of rotting vegetation was blown away by the clean, fresh smell of the ocean, and the land became a flat silhouette astern.

'You see any boat back there?' Gregg asked. 'You see anything on our tail?'

Gregg had fetched binoculars from the cabin. Landon put them to his eyes and scanned the long line of the shore.

'Nothing.'

Alvarez had come out of the cabin and was looking back also. He had taken off the hat and was revealed as a tall, thin man, with iron-grey hair and slightly stooping shoulders. Landon judged him to be about six feet two inches in height and possibly fifty years old. His face was so deeply lined that it might have been the work of an engraver operating in bronze, and the nose was a beak, sharp-ridged and jutting. There was no need to ask why he had been called The Eagle; he had the very look of the king of birds, lordly and fearless. Under the nose the mouth was thin-lipped, the chin sharp, clean-shaven. His eyes were black; it was as though two drops of tar had been caught in the sockets of his head.

'You're on your way, Mr Alvarez,' Gregg said. 'You should be pleased. We got you away all right.'

Alvarez brought his gaze slowly from the distance of the land and allowed it to rest on the short, tubby American. He looked at Gregg without love, without visible emotion of any kind. He was wearing a white silk shirt, dark-grey trousers, and a zip-fronted gabardine jacket. He looked tired; he looked like a man who had been tired for a long time. He also looked like a man with a mission. He could have been a martyr or an inquisitor.

'There is some distance yet to go, Mr Gregg,' he said, and his voice was dry and metallic, like a voice heard over the telephone.

His English had a slight American flavour; he had probably learnt it in the United States.

'True enough,' Gregg said. He gazed out beyond the bows of the ketch to the wide and empty expanse of sea ahead. 'A long, long way. And I ain't going home. Maybe never no more; maybe never no more.'

4

ENCOUNTER

THE SUN WAS high and hot. The sky was a blue page dusted with the white chalk of lofty cirrus. The wind was light and variable. They had cut the engine and shaken out the sails and were heading south-south-west, moving down towards the Tropic of Cancer and the Yucatan Channel that cuts between the Peninsula of Yucatan and the fiery island of Cuba.

The seagoing launch came up from the north-east, moving fast over a calm sea. They could hear the beat of its engine while it was still some distance off. There was an indication of power in that sound – power, and to spare.

Gregg looked back, chewing on the stub of a cigar. 'I don't like the sound of that baby. I don't like his looks neither. Maybe we better start the engine.'

'It wouldn't help,' Landon said. 'If we're being chased we'll be caught anyway. We haven't the speed to get away from that.'

Alvarez put a hand up to shade his eyes. 'You think it is – our friends?'

Gregg spat over the side. 'No friends to you – or to me. No friends to any of us. Maybe it's them, maybe it ain't. We'll know soon enough.'

He went down into the cabin and came out again with the two tommy-guns. He put them down in the cockpit and went to fetch the Colts. He loaded the Colts and put full drums of ammunition on the two sub-machine-guns.

'Ready for trouble?' Landon said.

Gregg said hoarsely: 'I'm always ready for trouble. I been in trouble all my life. That way I never get rich; I just got nasty.'

Pete muttered softly in his lilting voice: 'You sure got nasty, Mr Gregg. You're right there.'

Gregg swung round on him. 'Who asked you to talk? You speak when you're spoken to. See?'

'I speak when I damn please,' Pete said, and his voice had hardened.

'You trying to get above yourself, black boy?'

Pete made one swift, flowing movement and Gregg was lying on his back in the cockpit.

'Don't call me that.'

Gregg got up raving, one of the Colts in his right hand. He was breathing fast and his eyes were deadly.

'Why, you damned son-of-a-bitch—'

Alvarez knocked Gregg's hand up. His voice had a cutting edge like steel. 'That's enough. What are you trying to do?'

'I'll kill him. I'll kill the bastard, so I will.'

Alvarez said coldly: 'There are other matters to attend to. Don't be a fool.'

Gregg let the gun drop slowly to his side. He gave Pete a cold, hard stare and turned away to watch the launch. Pete shrugged his shoulders, contemptuous of Gregg. He was a tough, strong boy and looked as though he could have dealt very thoroughly with Gregg if neither man had had a gun.

The wind was so light that the sails of the ketch scarcely caused the masts to creak. The motor-launch overhauled them rapidly, as though they had not been moving. They could see the twin white spouts of water churning up from the sharp bows and glittering in the sunlight.

'Could be coastguards,' Gregg said musingly. 'We could have trouble with them too.'

Landon said: 'That isn't a coastguard launch.'

Alvarez took the binoculars from Landon and focused them on the launch. 'They are Valdez's men,' he said.

'We fight, huh?' Gregg said.

'Naturally.' Alvarez turned to Landon. 'And you?'

Landon smiled bleakly. 'It was to be a nice easy job. I knew it wouldn't turn out that way. I'm like Gregg – always in trouble.'

'But you will fight?'

'I'm being paid,' Landon said.

'Ah, yes,' Alvarez said drily. 'You are a soldier of fortune.'

'Or misfortune.'

Pete chuckled and reached for one of the tommy-guns. Nobody had asked him whether he would fight. He just picked up the tommy-gun and chuckled. Nobody needed to ask him.

Gregg said: 'We got no choice really. We got to fight. We just don't have no choice.'

He pulled a short, fat cigar out of his pocket, bit off the end, and lit it. The cigar smoke wreathed the four men in an aromatic cloud.

The launch came nearer. Landon could see men's heads. The beat of the engine was louder, menacing. Gregg suddenly crouched down at the stern of the ketch and began to fire the tommy-gun that Pete had left. The gun stuttered. Bullets lashed the water ahead of the launch, climbed up the bows, smashed glass in the cabin-top.

The launch heeled over to port and went away in a wide curve, not liking the sting in the ketch's tail.

Gregg laughed. 'They'll have something to think about now. What you think they'll do next?'

'Shoot at us,' Landon said. It needed no great powers of deduction to work that one out.

The launch had put a respectable distance between itself and the ketch. The engine beat died away and the bow waves vanished. The launch lay on the blue surface of the sea, rocking gently, and the hot sun shone down upon the two craft alone in the centre of a wide circle of water, remote from the man-made laws of civilization.

'It's a situation,' Gregg said. 'You might say an interesting situation.'

'But not amusing.'

They heard the sudden crack of a gun and the whine of a bullet ricocheting from the surface of the water.

'You were right about the shooting, Mac.'

The launch was on the starboard quarter, perhaps a hundred yards distant, perhaps more – at too great a range for effective tommy-gun fire. Landon, Alvarez, and Pete crouched down in the cockpit while the bullets from the launch bounced off the water, whining, or thudded into the timbers.

Gregg had dived into the cabin. He came up again with the rifle, a .30 calibre Ross. He pressed two clips of cartridges into it and worked the bolt, driving one round up the breech.

'I played with one of these in the Army, that time we had a war on our hands.'

'I thought you'd have been too smart to get hooked for army service,' Landon said. 'Couldn't Cranefield pull the strings for you?'

'I never knew Cranefield in them days. I was a lone wolf.'

The spasmodic firing from the launch had ceased for the moment. Landon peered over the gunwale. He could see a man standing up with a megaphone in one hand. The sound of his voice floated across the gap between the two craft.

'We have come for Alvarez. Give us Alvarez and we let the others go.'

Gregg kneeled down, the butt of the rifle pressed against his shoulder. He squinted down the long barrel and squeezed the trigger. The rifle coughed once. The man with the megaphone jerked like a puppet whose strings have been savagely tugged. He dropped the megaphone and fell forward over the side of the launch. Landon could see the splash he made as he struck the water.

Gregg snapped back the rifle bolt and the empty cartridge case rang as it fell into the cockpit. He slammed another round into the breech and smacked the wooden butt complacently, grinning.

'One less. I ain't lost my touch.'

Nobody else said anything. They watched the launch, waiting for the hunters to make the next move. They would be in a killing mood now; that was certain.

One man was leaning over the side of the launch, apparently searching for the other who had been shot. Gregg fired again, missed, and swore fiercely. The man jumped back and dived for cover.

'They won't fish that joker out,' Gregg said. 'He'll be food for the sharks.' He chewed on the end of his cigar, which had become a soggy mess. 'They'll know we mean business this time.'

They heard the sudden restarting of the engine of the launch, shattering the brief silence. A flock of seabirds moved overhead, their white wings flashing in the sun. The wind lay in the sails of the ketch as lightly as a child sleeping in a hammock. The ketch moved southward with a gentle, peaceful motion, the shadow of its masts and rigging heaving in the bright mirror of the sea. And a dead man went drifting down into the sunless depths where the slime and wreckage of the centuries lay undisturbed.

The launch came round in a wide sweep and the men in the ketch watched it, thinking ahead to the next move in the pattern of the contest.

'They'll be angry,' Pete said. He fondled the tommy-gun that was as black as his own hands. He was wearing a gay check shirt and blue jeans, canvas shoes with rope soles. His head was bare, the hair packed in tight curls. He was a handsome man, young and strong and virile. The idea that the men in the launch would be angry seemed to be amusing to him, to raise his spirits. He stroked the tommy-gun as though he loved it. 'I think we have a fight on our hands now, sure enough.'

'You must be a psychic,' Gregg said.

The launch had come about and its bows were pointed at the starboard side of the ketch. The thunder of its engine rose as it came in towards the sailing craft. It came fast, and the bow wave was a white trough of foam, curling over at the top and tumbling away on either side of the hull.

Gregg fired one round from the rifle, then threw it down and picked up the tommy-gun that he had used before. He sprayed the bows of the launch with bullets.

Alvarez said coldly: 'A waste of ammunition, Mr Gregg. Better to save it.'

Gregg did not hear him. Pete waited, his gun ready. He waited for the launch to come round broadside on to the ketch, presenting a target. He could see no men to fire at; they were hidden by the cabin top.

But the launch did not come round. It continued on its course, heading straight for the starboard side of the ketch and travelling at full speed. The gap between the two boats shrank.

Gregg shouted suddenly: 'By God, they mean to ram us!'

The ketch was moving only slowly under the pressure of its sails. There could be no doubt that the launch would slam into its hull if both craft remained on their present courses; and there could be little doubt either that the men in the launch intended to do just that.

Gregg was shouting excitedly. 'They'll sink us. That's what they're after. They'll cut us in two.' He swung round on Landon who had his hand on the tiller. 'What you going to do? You gotta do something, for Chrissake. Do something.'

Landon said sharply: 'Pipe down, fat man.'

Gregg looked unbelieving. He seemed to doubt whether he had heard correctly. He opened his mouth to make some retort, looked at Landon's face, and said nothing.

Landon was not paying any further attention to Gregg. He was gazing at the launch, at the sharp bows which could slice into the ketch like a ploughshare. He had to get his timing right; a move too early might be as bad as a move too late. And there was so little wind.

Alvarez glanced briefly at Landon, but said nothing. He went into the cabin and came out again with two of the metal canisters that Landon had discovered in the armament drawer. Alvarez waited and Pete waited, licking his lips.

When Landon put the helm hard over there was very little space indeed between the bows of the launch and the ketch's side. The bowsprit came round like a pointing finger, but with agonizing deliberation. Landon prayed for a squall of wind. He got no squall, but the wind came more on the beam, making the ketch heel over slightly to port. It came round slowly, and the launch closed the last few yards that separated the pursuer from the pursued.

Landon had been unable to avoid the collision, but he had reduced its effect. The launch struck the side of the ketch obliquely, so that the bows did not slice but skidded off. The ketch heeled farther over and the launch ground its way along the side, scraping off the paint and gouging deep wounds in the timbers.

Landon left the tiller swinging and made a dive for one of the Colts. Pete's gun was chattering, dinning in his ears. He had a fleeting glimpse of five men in the launch, black-haired, with faces like dull copper. Two of them had carbines in their hands, but they had been thrown off balance by the shock of the collision. One man had a black automatic pistol in his right hand and was firing. A bullet hummed past Landon's head. He heard a scream. A body fell on him, and he crashed down into the bottom of the cockpit.

The sound of the launch's engine receded as it plunged on, away from the ketch. The chatter of Pete's tommy-gun went on. And then there was another sound, clear above the others – the cracking blast of an explosion, followed almost immediately by another. Alvarez had used the canisters.

Landon pushed away the man who had fallen on him and stood up. The man was Gregg. He did not get up; he lay on his back in the well of the ketch, staring up at the sky. There was a dark hole in his forehead, just above the bridge of his nose. It was not a big hole, but it had served its purpose. It was an escape-hatch through which a man's life had leaked away.

He heard Pete's exultant voice. 'We get no more trouble now. Mr Alvarez, that was nice work. You finished them. They gonna burn now.'

The launch was motionless a hundred yards astern of the ketch and there were flames shooting up from it. It was the fuel that had caught fire and was sending its black and crimson flowers up into the air.

Alvarez said without emotion: 'I think they will not put that fire out.'

It was indeed a furnace that only the sea could extinguish. It grew with terrifying speed; it seemed to leap from end to end of the launch in a moment, wrapping everything in the blistering fury of its embrace.

Above the crackling of the fire they could hear the thin sound of a man screaming. They saw him, his hair in flames, drop overboard. They did not see him come to the surface.

A moment later and it was over. It ended in one final thunderous explosion that split the launch into fragments and scattered them over the undulating table of the sea. After that there was no more fire, no more screaming, no more shooting; only a few pieces of floating timber and the sun glaring down upon the remnants; only the ketch with its idly flapping sails and its scarred paint and gouged side.

'That's done for them,' Pete said. He took the magazine off the tommy-gun and sniffed at the breech, savouring the odour of burnt cordite. 'We had our fight,' he said.

*

They sailed southward, the three of them. They left Gregg's body with the wreckage of the launch and continued their voyage, sliding gently over a calm blue sea under a brassy sun and the white feathers of the high clouds. They felt no regrets for the loss of Gregg, for he had been nothing to any of them, nothing but a hired gun, a man of violence who had died by violence.

'He had it coming to him,' Pete said. 'You live just so long and then you get a little bit of lead between the eyes, and you don't see so good, never again. I'm glad it was only him.'

'You didn't like him?' Landon said.

'I didn't say I liked anybody. Maybe so, maybe not. But if it had been you where would we be for a navigator? I can sail a boat, but out of sight of land I'm lost. We need you, Mr Landon. We can do without that Gregg.'

Pete's skin glistened; his neck was like a pillar of ebony. His shirt was unbuttoned to the waist and his chest was visible, deep and powerful. The muscles rippled in his left arm when he shifted the tiller. A tough boy, no doubt about that.

'You're a Jamaican, aren't you, Pete?'

'What makes you say that?'

'Something in the way you talk. It just struck me. Am I right?'

Pete nodded slowly. 'I was born in Jamaica, brung up there, too. I went to Cuba, then to the States, long time ago. Now I got away from the States – maybe for good. Too many men there like that Gregg. I don't go for that talk.'

Landon left Pete at the helm and joined Alvarez in the cabin. Alvarez was smoking a thin cigar and studying some charts spread out on the table. He was calm; he seemed to have banished from his mind all memory of the recent encounter.

On the table, as well as the charts, was a bundle of paper money in a rubber band. When Landon came into the cabin Alvarez looked up.

He said: 'You have not yet been paid, Mr Landon. There is the money. Five hundred dollars. You may count it if you wish, but I assure you it is correct.'

'Not correct,' Landon said.

'How do you mean? Not correct?'

'It's too much. The agreement was for me to receive two hundred and fifty at the start of the voyage and another two-fifty when we get to the other end. That was what Cranefield said.'

'Mr Cranefield is a suspicious man. He would not trust you to carry out your side of the bargain if you were paid in advance. That is not the way I do business. If I do not trust a man I do not use him.'

'But you trust me?'

Alvarez lowered his long, thin body on to the settee, drew on his cigar and stared at Landon. The skin of his cheeks seemed to be drawn in; they were concave; his jaw was strong, sharply chiselled. Two of the upper teeth on the left side of his mouth were missing; there were gold fillings in some of the others. When he smiled, which was rarely, the gold was uncovered, contrasting with the gap on the left.

'Mr Landon,' he said, 'it may surprise you to learn that I know quite a lot about you. I am aware of your record. Otherwise I would not have consented to employ you.'

Landon nodded slightly, watching Alvarez.

'I know that you served Diego Vargas, who is now unfortunately dead. I know others whom you have served. I know that you have no political allegiance, that you work for monetary reward rather than from revolutionary zeal. That is understandable. But I know also that you have never betrayed the trust of those for whom you have worked, even though your life might be in danger. Is that not so?'

'I don't take any credit for that,' Landon said gruffly. 'A man must earn his pay.' He did not want compliments from Alvarez. He knew his own limitations, his own faults. True, he had served different masters; true, he had dabbled in Latin-American politics without any moral feelings one way or another; true again, he had kept faith. But perhaps that too was only from the motive of self-interest. If you went around betraying people who trusted you what did you get out of it? A reputation for treachery and maybe a bullet in the head. You might get the bullet anyway, but it would be for a different reason.

Alvarez said: 'Credit or no credit, it is a point that commends itself to a man like myself. Please take up your money.'

Landon shrugged his shoulders. 'If that's the way you want it.' He picked up the bundle of notes, threw them into a drawer where he had packed his clothes, and pushed the drawer shut with his foot.

'You think they are safe there?' Alvarez asked, and his thin lips twitched, as though he were on the brink of smiling.

'I'm not expecting burglars,' Landon said. 'They're as safe there as anywhere until we reach land.'

Alvarez got up and leaned over the table again. 'When we reach land. That is a matter I think it is time to discuss with you. I have already indicated the exact point on the coast of Anagua at which it is necessary that I should be set ashore.' He stabbed a finger at one of the charts. 'As I told you, it must be done at night. It has been arranged that the – er – reception committee, shall we call it, shall be waiting for me. But an error of judgment on your part would be disastrous. I have no wish to be welcomed back to my native land by the jackals of Sergeant Valdez.' He stabbed again at the chart. 'To the north, here, it is useless. To the south, also useless. You understand?'

'I understand. You don't have to worry on that point.'

'You can guarantee to make your landfall at the right place?'

'No man can guarantee a thing of that sort; there is always the possibility of occurrences that are beyond man's control. But we have an auxiliary engine, and that could help us. As far as it is humanly possible to do so I guarantee that you will be put ashore at the correct spot.'

'Good.' Alvarez dropped back on to the settee and drew again at his thin cigar, watching Landon. 'There is another point. What precisely do you intend to do?'

'I intend to land you as arranged. After that I take the ketch to Santa Marta where your agent will take it. After that I am free. That was the agreement as I remember it.'

'Yes, certainly that was the agreement. But I am going to be generous; I am going to make you a further offer. When you have put me ashore the boat is yours to do with as you wish.'

Landon stared at him in amazement. 'Mine? But why? Why should you make me a gift like that?'

'Perhaps,' Alvarez said, 'in memory of my friend Don Diego and as some compensation to you for loss of five thousand dollars.'

Landon was amazed. This was generosity indeed. He could not

have asked for more. With the ketch he could sail anywhere; there would be nothing to stop him. He wondered whether the gesture had been altogether prompted by liberality or whether there was another motive. It might be that Alvarez imagined that the extra reward would be an added incentive, an assurance that he would carry out his task to the best of his ability. But perhaps that was misjudging Alvarez; men such as he were difficult to fathom. Best to accept the offer with thankfulness and not inquire into the motive.

Alvarez was watching him narrowly.

'There is an alternative, of course. There is almost always an alternative.'

'And that is?'

'I could use a man like you, a man with experience. Pete could take the ketch to Santa Marta; it would simply be a question of following the coast. And if you throw in your lot with me I promise you that you will not lose by doing so. You will have a greater reward as soon as we have overthrown the Valdez tyranny.'

'Are you sure it will be overthrown?'

'There is no doubt whatever. The people are weary of Valdez. My forces already hold many parts of the interior. It is only my coming that is now awaited. I tell you that the days of Sergeant Valdez are numbered.'

'And you think that is a good thing?'

Alvarez leaned forward; his eyes glittered. 'Listen to me. Do you know what Valdez has done to Anagua? Do you know how many people he has slaughtered? Do you know how many lie in his filthy gaols without trial? Valdez is a wild beast. He seized power by force of arms. It is by force of arms that he will be unseated.'

Landon said musingly: 'Before Valdez it was Ramirez; before Ramirez, Gonzago; before Gonzago, Perez. Each one in his turn was a self-styled liberator. Who did they liberate? Not the people of Anagua. So after Valdez it will be Alvarez. But no change, no change really.'

Alvarez gripped Landon's arm, the long, bony fingers digging into the flesh like claws. He said fiercely: 'You should not link my name with those. They were all adventurers, interested only in making their own fortunes. One after another they have oppressed the people and bled the country. I am not a man of that kind. I do not wish to serve myself. I wish only to serve my country and the people of that country. Now do you understand?'

The fingers relaxed. Alvarez leaned back and drew smoke from the cigar, his cheeks scooped out under the prominent bones.

'And Cranefield?' Landon said. 'Where does he come in? Don't tell me he cares two hoots about the people of Anagua.'

Alvarez shrugged, lifting his shoulders up towards his ears. 'One cannot always choose one's tools.'

'Cranefield did not strike me as being a tool. What does he get out of the deal?'

'He will have a financial interest in Anagua as soon as I have taken power – naturally. He works for pay – as you do.'

'I heard something about uranium deposits. That couldn't be what he's so interested in, could it?'

Alvarez smiled fleetingly. 'You use your ears, don't you, Mr Landon? There are no uranium mines in Anagua.'

'But there could be. And that could be what interests our good friend, Cranefield. Well, it's nothing for me to worry about. I am, as you so rightly said, a soldier of fortune.'

'And what do you say to my offer?'

'I'll consider it,' Landon said. 'I didn't do too well out of the last revolution I was concerned with. They hanged Vargas.'

'This time it will not be the revolutionaries who are hanged. You can be sure of that.'

'I hope not,' Landon said. 'For your sake, señor, I hope not.'

5

EDGE OF THE STORM

LANDON TOOK OVER the helm from Pete at midnight and saw the white glimmer of Pete's grin.

'Nothing to report, Mr Landon, sir. All quiet, all very nice and quiet.'

'Thanks, Pete. Go and catch up on your sleep.'

There was scarcely enough wind to keep steerage way on the ketch. The sea looked black.

Pete said: 'I been thinking, Mr Landon.'

Landon, settling down for a long watch, asked: 'What have you been thinking about? Anything important?'

'Important to me,' Pete said. 'I been thinking about my future.'

'Well, that's an important subject to anybody. Come to any conclusions?'

'I came to the conclusion that I ain't getting no place. Not the way I been going.'

'So how do you alter things? Have you worked that one out?'

'Yes, sir, I have. I guess I'd like to come alonga you.'

Landon stared at the dark outline of Pete's head, the stars forming a kind of halo round it.

'You want to come with me?'

'That's right.'

'Where do you think I'm going?'

Pete drew air into his lungs and let it out again in a long, sighing expiration of breath.

'When Mr Alverez leave us you take the boat, go some place. You need a crew then. I'd like to be that crew. Don't matter where you go, Mr Landon; any place suits you, suits me too.'

'I may not take the boat anywhere, Pete. Mr Alvarez wants me to go ashore with him, to work for the revolution. I may do that.'

'Why?'

'When Alvarez is boss of Anagua there could be some rich pickings.'

'You won't do that, Mr Landon,' Pete said softly. 'You rather take the boat. You free then. Nobody tell you, do this, do that. You do just what you damn please and to hell with everybody. You take the boat; ain't that so?'

Landon said: 'I think you may be right, Pete. I don't want any part in Anagua. I've had all the Latin-American politics I ever want. They never made me rich yet.'

'Then you take me for crew, Mr Landon? Cook too. You never taste my flapjacks. They's really something. You take me?'

'I'll think about it,' Landon said.

'You think about it good, Mr Landon, sir. You never get a better man than me. And no strings.'

'No strings to me either – only a record.'

'That record don't mean a thing to me. Maybe my slate ain't so clean neither. Maybe we start again, huh? You and me – start all over again.'

'Get yourself below,' Landon said. 'I'll think about it.'

Without a sound Pete disappeared. He had the gift of moving silently. Landon stayed at the tiller, musing, feeling the soft breeze on his cheek and listening to the faint liquid murmur of water sliding past the hull.

No strings! True enough. Perhaps once he had had some – many years ago; but they had been cut and the ends lost. Now he was a man on his own, responsible to no one but himself. If he were to die this moment no one would feel the loss; it would be just one mouth that the overburdened earth no longer had to feed. No strings.

Make a fresh start, eh? The way Pete had said it, it sounded easy. Wipe the slate clean and start again from scratch. The trouble was you could never do that; you were always affected by the past and always would be; you took it with you like a burden that could never be dropped.

Well, what difference did it make whether he, Harvey Landon, threw in his lot with Ramon Arturo Alvarez, The Eagle, The

Liberator, or sailed away in a two-masted ketch with a black man for his crew? Either way the heavens would not fall, the sun would not cease to rise, nor the moon to glow. Nothing would be altered; nothing but his life and Pete's, and perhaps in a small way Alvarez's also.

Very well, then, he would take the ketch. He would take Pete and to hell with the revolution.

They moved gently over the blue waters of the Gulf of Mexico. The day came and the night, and again the day; and they altered course a few degrees and came down through the Yucatan Channel, keeping to the middle, as far away from the land as possible, for they wanted no contact with other men. They saw no land, for the land was fifty miles away. They saw sea-birds and dolphins and flying fish that flashed like quicksilver in the sunlight; and sometimes they saw a ship, but the ships were away on the horizon and they made no signals.

They came down to the west of Grand Cayman and the east of Ascension Bay, sailing south-eastward with a wide gap of water between them and the mainland of Central America. And somewhere, away to the east beyond Jamaica and south of Puerto Rica a hurricane was building up and beginning to move on a curving, erratic path; and its movement was being observed by anxious men in Cuba and Florida and in all the states of the eastern seaboard of North America.

The ketch was six hundred miles from the centre of the hurricane, but the effect of it was becoming apparent in the sea. It was as though something sinister were moving below the surface of the water. There was a long, oily swell, and the ketch rose and fell with a slow, sickening motion. The air was hot and sultry, with scarcely any wind. The clouds were high – wisps of cirro-stratus that seemed to be hurrying across the face of the sky like fugitives. The sun wore a misty halo, peering down upon the boat with a baleful, menacing eye.

Alvarez came out of the cabin, looked at the sky, and spoke to Landon.

'Do you think we shall be in position tonight?'

Landon said: 'We should be.' He also looked up at the sky. 'But I don't much care for the omens.'

'What do you mean?'

Landon took a handkerchief from his pocket and wiped sweat from his neck and face. The air was like a warm blanket pressing down upon them; it was too thick for easy breathing; it seemed to clog the lungs.

'There's weather coming – bad weather. You can feel it.'

'It is hot,' Alvarez admitted. 'But it is often hot. That means nothing.'

He seemed to be quite unaffected by the heat. His skin was dry. He looked like a man who had been desiccated long ago, so that there was no more moisture in him, nothing to squeeze out of his parched frame.

'I do not think we have anything to worry about from the weather,' he said.

'Look at the sun,' Landon said. 'It's a hurricane sun. I've seen these signs before.'

'But there is no wind.'

'No wind here. Too much wind not far away. The sea feels it.' He made a sweeping gesture with his hand to indicate the long, moving ridges and hollows, smoothed out like sculpted stone. 'And I feel it too – in my bones. I don't like it.'

The Caribbean Sea lay under the haloed sun and the high white clouds, and the ridges and valleys moved across its surface like undulations in a sheet of steel. The sails hung slack and lifeless; there was no ripple at the bows. The shadow of the masts grew and shrank upon the water as the ketch rocked.

Pete came out of the cabin, his face shining with sweat. 'Dinner all ready. Canned beef and fried potatoes. You folks hungry?'

'Where would a man get an appetite in this heat?' Landon asked.

'Sure is hot, Mr Landon, sure is.' He looked at the sun and the sea as the other two had done. 'Hurricane weather. I know hurricanes.' He pointed to the east. 'Some ways over there. That's what make this sea heave.'

Landon nodded. 'Just what I've been telling Mr Alvarez.'

'We ought to get to hell out of here,' Pete said. 'Them hurricanes – you don't know which way they'll go.'

'True enough,' Landon said. 'Let's eat that grub, then we'll start the engine. Mr Alvarez wants to be ashore tonight.'

Pete looked at the sky again. 'Maybe we all better be ashore. Maybe we had at that.'

Night came like the shutter of a dark-lantern sliding across the source of light. For an hour there had been a black wedge of cloud standing on the eastern rim of the sea. When night came they could no longer see the cloud, but they knew that the stars were being blotted out, one after another, and that the wind had come.

The ketch was driving due west with bare masts, heading under engine power for the coast of Anagua where Alvarez was to be put ashore in a rubber dinghy. But already Landon was certain in his own mind that this was not the night for such an operation; there was too much sea running. Even on the fringe of the hurricane, many miles from the eye, the turbulence was making itself felt. The ketch bucked and shuddered; spray came lashing over the gunwale. It began to rain, a few drops at first, big drops splashing on the roof of the cabin; then coming thicker and faster, until it seemed no longer like rain but like a cascade of water tumbling out of the sooty darkness of the night.

Landon, in an oilskin coat and sou'wester, was at the helm. He heard Alvarez's voice and felt rather than saw the man.

'You think you can make it, Mr Landon?'

'Not a hope,' Landon shouted. 'It's no good tonight. Impossible. We must keep off shore. I'm going to bring her round.'

He felt that he had already left it too late. He ought to have turned the ketch about and headed for the open sea earlier than this. In such weather you had to have sea room; land was the danger.

'Where do you intend to go?'

'Out to sea.'

'But that's towards the hurricane.'

'Safer that way than close to land. This is a wrecking sea.'

'You know best, Mr Landon,' Alvarez said reluctantly. 'I must leave these nautical questions to you. But I was hoping to be on dry land tonight.'

'There isn't any dry land.'

He brought the ketch round carefully. The engine spluttered, coughed, then picked up again.

'We don't want any trouble from you,' Landon muttered. 'You'd better keep going.'

The wind struck them on the beam as they came about, and the ketch heeled over, dipping her starboard gunwale. Landon was wearing canvas shoes and he could feel the water washing round his feet. He yelled to Pete.

'Get that pump working, Pete.'

He heard Pete's voice above the piping of the wind and the smack of the waves against the sides of the ketch.

'Yessir, Mr Landon. Right away.'

Landon said to Alvarez: 'You'd better go below. There's nothing you can do out here.'

Alvarez went at once. Landon was in authority here and he did not question that authority. In another situation, on land, it could be different, but here the sea left no room for argument. Landon was glad not to have to point out the fact.

He heard Pete working the pump, singing as he moved the handle back and forth. He seemed to be unworried. Perhaps he had faith in his captain.

The engine coughed again, choked, and died. Landon cursed it for a treacherous piece of machinery and yelled for Pete to leave his pumping and try to kick life into the motor.

The wind hit the ketch like a ram, driving the rain and the sea before it, shrieking through the rigging with the fury of a man possessed by devils. The ketch, its driving-power having failed it, wallowed helplessly. Landon could hear Pete wrestling with the engine. The engine stayed dead.

He heard Pete's voice suddenly close to his ear. 'No gas, I reckon. All out of fuel.'

Landon shouted back at him: 'Get the spare can. Jump to it!'

Pete jumped. He knew the danger of a drifting boat in this kind of sea as well as Landon.

Landon lashed the tiller and went down into the cabin to fetch a torch. There was an oil-lamp in the cabin swinging in gimbals. By its light he saw Alvarez. The man looked ill; there was a yellow tinge about his face, perhaps accentuated by the lamplight. He was half-sitting, half-lying on one of the settees with his feet wedged against the table. He turned his stricken face to Landon.

'What is happening?'

Landon answered savagely: 'The damned engine has cut. Run out of juice. We've got to fill it – quick.'

'You think—?'

'Don't ask me what I think. I don't think anything.'

He grabbed the torch and went out of the cabin, while the lamp flickered, swinging erratically in its gimbals. As he went through the doorway he yelled back over his shoulder: 'You'd better get one of those life-jackets on. You may need it.'

Pete had found the petrol can and a funnel. The engine was in a kind of box with an apex lid. Landon raised the lid and played his torch on the engine. He unscrewed the tank cap and Pete pushed the funnel home. He had scarcely done so when a great wave of sea water came over the side and crashed down upon the engine. It flooded the funnel and ran gurgling into the fuel tank, putting the motor out of action as effectively as a sledge-hammer would have done.

The engine was useless. They could forget about that kind of propulsion now. They would have to heave to and wait for the storm to blow itself out. There might not be much hope that way, but any other way there would be less, perhaps none at all. Landon cursed himself for having allowed the ketch to get into a position where there was so little sea room. He had relied on the engine, and the engine had let him down. But it was his fault.

He yelled at Pete. 'Throw that bloody can away. We'll have to get out a sea-anchor and rig the storm-sail.'

He was thankful to have Pete with him; you only had to tell Pete once; and he was strong and active.

Together they hoisted the storm-sail on the mizzen mast and made it fast in a fore and aft position. Then they crawled for'ard with the sea-anchor, crouching down between the cabin top and the wire rail that was raised on stanchions above the gunwale. The sea-anchor, an iron ring with a canvas bag attached to it and cork floats, had a length of good, stout manilla rope as a cable. They let the anchor go over the bows and paid out about a hundred and fifty yards of rope before securing it to the bitts. Then they whipped it with canvas to prevent chafing where it went over the bows, and the job was done.

The ketch felt the pull of the sea-anchor and came round head-on to the seas and began to ride more easily. Landon went aft again and relashed the tiller. Then he and Pete took turns at the pump until it sucked dry.

'Better now,' Pete said.

For the moment there was nothing more they could do. Either the ketch would ride out the storm or it wouldn't. Landon thought it would, for, though old, it was stoutly built and in good trim. It was not the sea that he was afraid of; it was the land. With the sea-anchor out they would drift before the wind, maybe a mile an hour, maybe more. And the land was not far away.

He made sure that the navigation lamps were burning properly and went into the cabin. Alvarez did not look quite so sick, but he was wearing a blue kapok-padded life-jacket. Pete came in too, drops of water gleaming on the cropped wool of his head. He grinned at Landon.

'Some blow. I never been in one like this before, not at sea. You think that sea-anchor will hold us?'

'If the warp doesn't chafe through. We'll need to watch that.'

Alvarez looked at them inquiringly. 'Anchor. You cannot mean that we are anchored here.'

'Not to the bottom,' Landon said. 'A sea-anchor just holds your ship's head the way you want it. We're drifting, but we aren't shipping much water. We're snug.'

He took off his oilskin coat. 'Pete, how about some coffee? You think you could manage that?'

'Sure thing,' Pete said. 'Coffee coming up.'

He went to make it.

'This alters the timetable,' Alvarez said.

'You can't account for hurricanes. It'll have to be some other night. The arrangements hold good, I suppose?'

'Of course. They will be watching for the signal. They will watch each night until it is given.'

'That's all right then. Just as long as you can trust them to do that.'

'I can trust them,' Alvarez said with the very faintest emphasis on the last word. 'They need me.'

'Let's hope they get you,' Landon said acidly.

'Do you think there is any doubt?'

'With hurricanes there must be a doubt.'

'I rely on you.'

'I'm not a magician,' Landon said. 'I'm just a poor damn bastard of a sailor.'

Pete produced coffee and some corned beef sandwiches. He and Landon ate ravenously, but Alvarez merely sipped the coffee and ate nothing. The oil-lamp moved in its gimbals, but no longer so violently. The ketch rose and fell, riding up on the backs of the advancing seas and slipping down into the troughs that followed them with a sickening see-saw motion. But Landon and Pete were unaffected by it.

They finished the brief meal, and Landon lit a cigarette.

'You'd better get some sleep, Mr Alvarez.'

Alvarez smiled wanly. 'It is not a night for sleep.'

'You'd better try all the same.'

He spoke to Pete. 'I'll take watch till midnight.'

'Okay, Mr Landon, sir,' Pete said.

It was about three hours after midnight when they struck. The shock of the keel grinding on hard bottom woke Landon immediately. He heard the crash of a wave flinging itself against the port side. The ketch heeled over to starboard and stayed heeled over.

Alvarez was rolled off the settee on which he had been lying and fell under the table. Landon could hear him struggling to get up. The lamp, still alight, had swung over in sympathy with the listing of the ketch and now was no longer in line with the sides of the cabin. The yellow flame jumped and flickered.

As Landon swung his feet on to the floor Pete came down into the cabin like a train, water streaming from him.

'She hit something. She's stuck fast now. You better come, Mr Landon. You better come quick.'

'I'm coming,' Landon said.

Balancing himself on the tilted deck, he followed Pete out of the cabin and up the steps of the companion. The ketch was shuddering as if some fever had got into its bones. Grinding noises came up through the boards; it was like an enormous rat gnawing away at them.

Outside the blackness of the night was relieved by the pale glimmer of foam where the seas were breaking. There seemed to be foam all round them. The ketch, lying over on its starboard side, was exposed to the full fury of the wind and wave, and the mizzen sail was not helping matters. Spray lashed Landon's face as he came out of the shelter of the cabin, and the wind dragged at him like a hand.

Pete was yelling: 'It's a reef. Some damn reef. We break up quick now. No help for it. What you going to do?'

Landon knew that Pete was right. The ketch had come to the end of its voyaging. As likely as not the keel was half ripped away. They were well and truly on the reef and there was no way of getting off it. They might be washed off by the sea, but that would be no way out of the disaster. If the ketch slid off the reef it would probably sink in the deeper water; if it remained where it was the waves that were even now beating upon it would break it up as surely as if it had been made of matchboard.

There was no doubt about it; the time had come to abandon ship.

'We shall have to take the dinghy,' he shouted.

There was not a lot of hope in the dinghy either, but it was the only chance. He had no knowledge of where the shore might be, how close they were to land after a night of drifting nor did he know what part of the coast this was. It was all a game of chance now; the hurricane had seen to that. They had caught only the edge of the storm, but it had been enough to sink all their plans fathoms deep in the turbulent waters of the Gulf.

Alvarez struggled out of the cabin. A rush of sea-water struck him, knocking him back. He grabbed a handhold and waited for the flood to pass. It went by, chuckling and gurgling, into the cabin.

'We're taking the dinghy,' Landon shouted. 'The ketch is finished.'

He thought he heard Alvarez answer: 'We are all finished.' But there was so much noise from the wind and the breakers that he could not be sure.

He went to the locker under the starboard gunwale where the rubber dinghy was stored, hauled it out, and opened it up. He worked the gas cylinder and the dinghy began to inflate, swelling up like a balloon. Landon called Pete to give a hand, and together they lifted the dinghy over the leeward side. It danced and bounded on the water like something endowed with life and vitality and an insane desire to be on its way. Only the painter joining it to the wrecked ketch restrained it.

Landon looked round for Alvarez and could not see him. He spoke to Pete.

'Where's Alvarez?'

'I think he went back to the cabin,' Pete said.

A wave pounded the port side and thundered over the ketch. It was as though the whole sea had emptied upon them, and they had to cling on desperately to avoid being swept away. The dinghy tugged fiercely at its painter, and the ketch stirred and groaned like a man tortured upon the rack.

'I'll get him,' Landon shouted.

He staggered down into the cabin and was knee-deep in water. The lamp still burned, but with a low and smoky flame. The glass was blackened and the light was baleful. Alvarez was lying across the table, not moving. There was some blood on his forehead.

Landon cursed luridly and briefly. It was the hell of a time to go getting yourself knocked out.

He gripped Alvarez under the armpits and dragged him off the table. The ketch shivered under the impact of another sea, and it seemed a more urgent shiver, a warning that there was not much time left.

Landon stumbled out of the cabin backwards, hauling the dead weight of Alvarez. The man was heavier than he would have supposed, but perhaps that was because of the drag of the water; the water was trying to hold him back, not willing to lose its victim.

Pete came to lend a hand.

'What's wrong with him, Mr Landon?'

Landon answered savagely: 'Got a knock on the head. God knows how. Just what we wanted. Grab his legs.'

Between them they lifted Alvarez over the gunwale and into the leaping dinghy. It was tricky work. Landon heard the unmistakable sound of timber cracking. Something was breaking up. He felt a sudden blow at the back of his knees that almost brought him down, but with an effort he managed to retain his footing. The ketch leaned farther over to starboard until now the gunwale was completely under water. The sea was up to Landon's waist, and he felt the boards on which he was standing shift with a quick, furtive movement as of a rug being pulled violently from under one's feet. He staggered and fell against the solid bulk of Pete.

Pete put an arm round Landon, supporting him. 'Careful, sir. We better go now. You first?'

'Get into the dinghy,' Landon said. 'Quickly!'

There was a momentary lull, a moment when the dinghy became less demented. In that moment Pete was in beside Alvarez.

'Now you, sir. I hold her steady.'

He reached out a hand to grip the submerged gunwale. The dinghy tilted. Landon groped for the side of the ketch, found something solid under his feet and stood for a moment precariously balanced above the dinghy. At that moment a surge of water swept across the ketch and struck him. He fell forward, missed the dinghy, and went under.

He was engulfed suddenly in a darkness more impenetrable even than the darkness of the night and the storm. Something hard and sharp and jagged scraped the back of his right hand, and he knew that he must have touched some part of the reef which had torn the life out of the ketch. He thrust hard with his feet on the solid rock and came up to the surface within a yard of the dinghy.

He felt Pete's hand grab his hair. Then there was another hand under his arm, and he was lying half in and half out of the dinghy; and even in that moment of peril the thought passed through his mind that in an emergency such as this an inflatable rubber boat was better than any other. It could be swamped, but it would not sink; it was resilient and unbreakable.

He gave a convulsive wriggle, Pete hauled, and he was over the side and into the dinghy.

'Let her go,' he shouted.

It was surely time to be away. They were being threatened by the masts and rigging as the ketch was rolled over on to its beam ends by the wind and the sea. Pete pulled a long knife out of the sheath hanging from his belt and slashed at the painter. The strands parted and the dinghy leaped away from the ketch on the back of a swirling, foaming torrent. The wreck vanished, swallowed up by the darkness, and the three men were borne away upon a buoyant island of trapped air with the white glimmer of broken water all around them, the rain beating down, and the wind flailing.

Landon peered back to the point where the ketch should have been and could see nothing of it. It was to have been his own and now it would be no man's, would be nothing but jetsam and a few pieces of driftwood cast up on some beach. He had lost everything except the clothes he wore; even the dollars had gone; in the excitement of the moment he had forgotten the money, and soon it would be simply a mass of sodden paper, gradually disintegrating. Five hundred dollars – wasted.

A lump of salt foam whipped off the tops of the waves and struck him in the face. He wiped it away and turned his back on the wreck and the reef; there were other matters to engage his attention now.

Alvarez had come to his senses. He gazed about him, bewildered. He put a hand to his forehead and felt the cut.

'You got knocked out,' Landon said. 'In the cabin. We had to dump you in the dinghy.'

'Yes, I remember now. I fell. Where is the ketch?'

'God only knows. We were lucky to get away.'

'Away to what?'

'Who knows?'

The dinghy was sweeping on with all the sickening motion of a scenic railway car, sometimes stationary upon its axis, sometimes spinning violently like a potter's wheel.

Alvarez leaned over the side and was sick, and the wind caught his vomit and flung it away. The light was becoming a little stronger, and Landon could see Alvarez's ravaged face streaming with sea-water and rain. He looked like some grim phantom roused from the dead, and beside him was the dark head of Pete.

'You lost your berth, Pete,' Landon said.

Pete laughed. 'That's how it goes, Mr Landon. You don't know your luck, not from one day to the next. Maybe we get another boat some time.'

'You think we're going to need one?'

'I know we are. We got a lot of life ahead of us. Ain't the finish yet.'

'I hope you're right,' Landon said. 'You should have more life to come than me anyway. You haven't used so much.'

Pete was young and tough and eager. Landon himself had been

like that once. Now he was not young any more, neither young nor eager. Tough perhaps, but with a different kind of toughness from Pete's; the toughness of endurance, the toughness of a body that had been torn and beaten and patched up again, a body that was just bone and sinew and gristle, and no fat, a body pared down to an economical machine that could be driven to the limit of pain and weariness and still come back for more action, more punishment. It was a body forty years old and more, and the iron was in it. The iron was in his soul too, in his mind, in his spirit.

Alvarez said bitterly: 'Where do we go ashore now? Where do we pinpoint our landing?'

'Lucky to get ashore anywhere,' Landon said. 'I'd settle just for land, never mind where.'

Alvarez spat some of the vomit out of his mouth. He might have been trying to spit out the sour taste of failure.

'For me any place but the right one is worse than useless.'

'We can't command fortune. This is how it is. We must make the best of it.'

'Best!' He spat again over the side, and Landon saw in profile the lean eagle's face, angry now under the impact of this disaster that had upset all the carefully laid plans.

But Alvarez's anger passed quickly. He took control of himself, accepting the situation fatalistically.

'It is as God wills. Who are we to complain?'

Beyond the crouching figure of Alvarez Landon saw a flash of lightning zigzag down the sky. And in the lightning's glare was the black silhouette of the mountains of Anagua. Into his mind then came the old Spanish name for Anagua – *Tierra del Trueno* – the Land of Thunder. It seemed peculiarly appropriate to come to it on such a night.

The sea and the wind swept them onward. They were powerless to control the movement of the dinghy and could only wait for it to carry them where it would. It was useless to attempt to paddle. No one could paddle against such a tide even if they had wished to do so. Therefore, they crouched in the dinghy and waited.

The white line of surf came suddenly into sight, and they could hear the thunder of breakers beating upon the shore. Pete yelled: 'There! There! The beach!'

'Or rocks,' Landon said.

They came skimming in fast on the last part of the wave, as though they were riding on a surf-board. There was no doubt about the thunder of the breakers now; it drowned even the sound of the wind; it was a continuous roar that rose and fell, rose and fell. It seemed to threaten them, daring them to venture through.

Landon was trying to prevent the dinghy from spinning with the aid of a paddle, but suddenly they were in a cauldron of foaming, bubbling water and the paddle was wrenched from his hand. The dinghy swung round and seemed to trip on some underwater obstruction. A wave came in behind it and tilted it up and toppled it over, and the men were spewed out like logs of wood being thrown out of an overturned wagon.

Landon lost contact with the others immediately. In the darkness and the swirling water it was each man for himself. He went under and could not feel the bottom. He came up spitting brine, and struggled vainly against the current that was carrying him away.

He knew that he must be close in to the shore; yet he could see nothing but the lashed foam that surrounded him. The wind flicked the spray into his eyes, blinding him. He tried to swim, but was hampered by his clothing. He wished that he had worn a life-jacket as Alvarez had done, but it was too late to think about that now. He went under again and tasted the bitter salt.

He had almost given up hope when at last he felt the solid ground under his feet. He stood up and was immediately flung violently down by a wave. Shingle scarified his face and the breath was hammered out of his body by the weight of the breaker falling upon him. Half-stunned, he yet retained enough of his senses to dig his hands and feet into the shingle and thus prevent himself from being dragged back by the undertow.

When the wave receded he got up and staggered forward, fell, and was caught again, again thrown down with his face grinding into the sand and rock. Once more he struggled to his feet and went up the sloping shore, and when the next wave came it fell behind him and only the spray touched him. He knew then that he had beaten the sea and that he was not to drown.

He felt a surge of triumph, and as he climbed higher up the beach he shouted taunts at the sea, but his voice was engulfed by the wailing and the thunder of the storm. It cracked and died away into a sob, into silence. But still he struggled on, fearing that if he rested now the sea might yet reach out and seize him, drag him back into its watery prison.

He had no means of telling how far he had gone when the black mass reared up in front of him. It was an impenetrable darkness with no break in it. It was as though the night had finally closed in upon him like a steel box, shutting him off from all the rest of the world. He stood there for a moment swaying drunkenly, unable to bring his exhausted mind to bear upon this problem. And as he stood there the wind struck him and flung him savagely against the wall of darkness and it was the steel box sure enough, hard and unyielding.

Fires of pain seared through his head, bright, leaping fires that burst into glittering sparks and then a dull crimson, all-engulfing flame that was the last thing of which he was conscious.

6

LAND OF THUNDER

THE SUN WARMED him where he lay under the shelter of the rock. Steam rose thinly from his gabardine jacket and his soaked trousers. He lay with his eyes closed and his face turned towards the rock, and the sunlight roused him gradually from the sleep of exhaustion.

The wind had died away and the sea had calmed; it muttered softly in the background like an old man mumbling to himself of past glories, of departed strength.

Landon opened his eyes and stared at the rock and the sunlight striking it. He tried to remember what had happened, how he came to be lying there with the sand under him, with his wet clothes and the rock. The murmur of the sea recalled him to a recollection of the recent past. He rolled over and felt the pain and stiffness in his limbs. His face was stiff too; the skin felt brittle, like old paper. His head ached.

The sun flashed in his eyes. He closed them against that dazzling brightness and lay for a while slowly gathering the resolution to get up, to walk, to take on the responsibilities of returning life. There was much for him to do: he had to find Alvarez and Pete; he had to make certain whether they were still alive or whether the sea had claimed them for its own; he had to get food, something to drink. There were a hundred things for him to do.

And he lay there with his eyes closed, still refusing to bring himself face to face with reality.

It was a sound that roused him for the second time, the light scuffling of shingle. He opened his eyes slowly and saw a foot – two feet – bare, brown feet with a little damp sand clinging to them, caught between the small toes. The feet themselves were small and slender, not a man's feet. A boy's perhaps.

Landon turned his head carefully so that he could look at what was above the feet. The movement sent spasms of pain shooting up from his neck, but he accepted the pain.

There were brown ankles, the lower portions of brown legs disappearing into faded blue jeans rolled to the calf. Landon's gaze travelled higher; he saw a blue cotton shirt tucked into the jeans, a slim brown neck, a head of jet-black hair swept back from the face and tied with thin ribbon. The shirt revealed the outline of small, firm breasts and proved conclusively that the owner of the feet was not a boy.

Landon tried to say something, some words of greeting perhaps, but his mouth and throat were so dry and salted that what he managed was no more than a croak, quite meaningless.

The girl dropped on one knee beside him. She touched his face with her fingertips, very gently, and spoke in Spanish. Her voice was as gentle as her fingers.

'You are hurt.'

Landon managed to get some moisture into his mouth and throat.

He said: 'Not badly. I am alive.'

'The others are alive also.'

'The others?'

'Pete and El Aguila.'

He stared at her. She looked very young, her face browned by the sun, her eyes black as her hair and with some of the same glistening quality, as though they had been burnished.

'El Aguila! You know him?'

'Who in Anagua does not know The Liberator?'

Landon pulled himself up into a sitting posture. The movement seemed to crack something in his spine, but you had to move your bones some time. He tried to moisten his lips with the leather strap that had once been a tongue.

'Where are they now?' he asked.

'In my father's house. It is a poor shelter, but—' she made a little deprecatory gesture with her hand, the hand fluttering like a butterfly.

'How did you find them?'

'We saw the light. We knew that some vessel must have been wrecked. My father and I went down to the beach. Pete was supporting El Aguila. With our help they were able to get ashore. El Aguila was exhausted, but Pete insisted on searching for a third man. We searched for a long time, but it was very dark. We thought at last that he must have been drowned.'

'But he wasn't.'

'I am glad,' the girl said simply.

'What is your name?' Landon asked.

'I am Anita Romero. What must I call you, señor?'

'My name is Landon – Harvey Landon.'

He began to struggle to his feet, and more bones seemed to crack in the effort. The joints all appeared to have locked, as though the oil had run out of them and rust had got into the bearings. The girl stood up too, watching him anxiously.

'You don't have to worry,' Landon said. 'I'm in one piece. We'd better go and find the others.'

They came round the rock and on to a stretch of beach. The shore curved away to the right, disappearing round a rocky headland. Drawn up out of reach of the sea was a boat.

'My father's boat,' the girl said. 'He is a fisherman. But the boat is useless. Somebody used an axe on the hull. They made big holes in it.'

'Who?'

'We did not see. It was done at night. But we think it was the police.'

'Why should they do a thing like that?'

'Who knows why the police do anything?'

Landon looked at the sea. The sun glittered on the water. A line of foam marked the position of the reef, but there was no sign of the ketch; the storm had done its work thoroughly.

'The sea took my boat.'

'I am sorry,' the girl said.

From the beach the ground sloped steeply upward. The girl led the way, glancing back now and then to make sure that Landon was following. His limbs were beginning to move more freely now, but his body was bruised and the stiffness penetrated all through it. He was lucky though; nothing had been broken.

They went up a kind of gulley between upthrust shoulders of rocky ground. Rain had washed channels in the soil, and the sun was drawing moisture out of it in steam. There were trees inland and green vegetation, vividly green. In the distance the mountains looked hazy and unreal.

The house was scarcely better than a hovel. Leaning against the wall was a boat's mast with a patched sail wrapped about it and lashed with rope. The roof looked to be in need of repair; there was only one storey; some of the timber was rotting; and indeed there was an impression of poverty about the place, an impression that here was the dwelling of people who were on the very border-line of want.

'I told you it was not a fine house,' the girl said. 'My father is poor. He is, as I said, a fisherman – when he is allowed to fish.'

'Where does he sell his catch?'

'There is a village not far away. But the people there are poor also. There are many poor people in Anagua.'

The house was in a hollow. There was a ridge of higher ground between it and the beach, and behind it a line of hills, thickly covered with vegetation.

'We will go inside,' the girl said. 'The others will be glad to see you.'

The doorway was low; it led straight into the main room of the house. The floor was of pounded earth. The furniture was sparse – the rough wooden chairs, a table, a fireplace at one end.

Alvarez was sitting on one of the chairs, his elbows resting on the table. He was facing the door. On the other chair was a man with abnormally broad shoulders and untidy grey hair. His face was a network of wrinkles, and these with the grey hair made him look old. Yet he might have been little past middle age; a hard life and want can make a man look old before his time.

Pete was leaning against the wall, relaxed but watchful. He grinned suddenly and joyously when he saw Landon.

'By God, the sea didn't get you then. By God, I'm happy – just happy, sir.'

The emotion looked genuine, and the realization that Pete had been really worried about him touched an answering chord in Landon. He was glad to feel that he meant something to Pete.

Alvarez propped his chin on his clasped hands and looked up at Landon.

'I too am glad to see you. We feared that you were lost. Now, perhaps, after all, you would care to take that employment I offered you. Now that it is impossible for you to sail away.'

The grey-haired man had got up. He held his chair for Landon. 'Please sit down, señor.'

'Thank you,' Landon said. He was glad to be seated. His limbs ached.

'Romero tells me that we have not landed in the best of places,' Alvarez said. 'Not the best for our purpose.'

Romero shook his head. 'No, not the best.' He looked at Landon's face, saw the scratches and the dried blood. He turned to his daughter. 'Anita, my dear, bring some water for the señor, to wash his wounds.'

'Yes, Father.'

She went out of the house with a kind of gliding walk, her feet silent on the earth floor. Within a minute she was back again, carrying a tin bowl of water and a cloth. She put the bowl on the table, dipped the cloth in the water, and began to bathe Landon's face.

'I could do this for myself,' he said, but he made no attempt to stop her. The cuts on his face stung sharply under the cool water; the blood and the salt and the sand came away, leaving the torn skin and the cut flesh beneath.

The girl fetched a towel; it was worn and thin, but it was clean. She dried Landon's face, and blood stained the towel as the wounds began to bleed afresh.

Alvarez pushed back his chair and picked up a small piece of wood from the floor.

'Romero has explained to me just where we are. I will show you.'

He began to draw a rough map on the earth floor with the stick. There was a coastline broken by the wide estuary of a river.

'The Rio Chico.'

He marked with a cross a point on the coast to the south of the river.

'That is where we should have landed. That is where I am hourly expected.'

He marked another cross to the north of the river.

'That is where we have in fact come ashore.' He looked up at Landon, his face grave. 'You see what it means? The Rio Chico lies between us and those who were to receive me and to accompany me inland. To cross the Chico would be quite impossible anywhere near the coast. And there are other obstacles. There are Valdez's men.'

'What do you propose to do?'

Alvarez made more marks on the map on the floor. He pointed with the stick. 'At this point there is a revolutionary stronghold. It is in the interior, high up in the mountains. I shall attempt to reach it. It is Oxaca, a strange city. From there it would be possible to reach San Quinton, which was to have been my destination. Oxaca is one hundred and fifty miles away. It is difficult country, and there are police and soldiers.'

He stared at Landon. 'You do not have to come.'

'Is that an invitation?'

'I proposed once that you should throw in your lot with me. I make that proposal again now. But I will not disguise from you the difficulties that lie ahead – nor the danger. You know what will happen if we should fall into the hands of Valdez's men.'

Landon glanced at Romero. Alvarez interpreted the look. He said quickly: 'I can trust this man. The common people are with me.'

'That is so,' Romero said. 'We are sick of dictators. This Sergeant Valdez is a pig, fit only to be hanged.' He appeared about to spit, but restrained himself in deference to the company. The expression on his wrinkled face showed clearly what he thought of Valdez.

Landon said: 'What have I to lose now? Yes, I will come with you.'

Pete shifted his weight from one foot to the other. 'You want another man, Mr Alvarez? I ain't got no other engagement pressing heavy on me right now.'

Alvarez looked at him speculatively. He seemed to be weighing in his mind the possible value of Pete.

'You'd better take him too,' Landon said. 'He was going to be my man.'

Alvarez nodded, coming to a decision. 'Very well.'

Romero looked at the map scratched on the floor. 'You will need a guide. I can get a man from the village who will go with you. I would go myself, but there is Anita.' He gave a jerk of his head, indicating the girl. 'She has no one else. It would not be possible to leave her.'

'I could go also,' the girl said.

The man shook his head. 'No, it is not for a girl.'

Alvarez also looked at her, and his stern face softened a little. 'Your father is right. This journey will not be easy. And there may be other – unpleasantness. You must stay here.'

She appeared about to speak again, perhaps to argue, but Romero gave a sign with his hand and she was silent.

'You can trust the people of the village?' Alvarez asked.

'I know the ones who cannot be trusted,' Romero answered. 'It would not, of course, be safe for you to show yourself there. They have a police house. Four police. It is a small village, but there are four police. That is the kind of country this is – under Valdez.'

Again he seemed to wish to spit, and again he restrained the impulse.

Pete took his knife from its sheath and began to clean the rust off the blade with some earth damped with spittle. He was singing gently to himself.

The girl looked at the knife and then looked at Landon. Landon glanced at the knife too. They said nothing. Pete went on with his cleaning.

Romero snapped his fingers suddenly in exasperation. 'But I was forgetting. You have not yet eaten. Anita, these gentlemen are our guests and they are hungry.'

'Yes, Father,' the girl said. 'I will see to it at once.'

There was a noonday glare outside the house and the heat drifted in. The three survivors dozed. Now and then the girl came in and looked at them, then went out again.

Romero had gone down to the beach. It had been arranged that he should go to the village after dark to find a guide, and that the party should set out on their journey well before daybreak. Romero had hinted that it was not safe to stay in the house longer than was absolutely necessary. The sooner they were away, the better it would be – for all of them.

It was the girl who saw Romero returning. He appeared first in the gap in the ridge that stood between the house and the sea. He came quickly, running down the slope. She could see the sweat glistening on his face.

She stood in the doorway waiting for him and as he came nearer she could hear his hard, panting breath.

'They are on the beach,' he said. 'Two of them – already. Alvarez must leave at once. It is not safe.'

He went past the girl into the house and the three men woke instantly, as men used to danger. Sweat dripped from Romero's face; it gathered on his chin and fell in oily drops on to his bare chest with its mat of grey hair. He moved his arms rapidly in his excitement.

'You must leave immediately. You must hide. They are on the beach. In a moment they may come here. They must not find you.'

Alvarez stood up. He laid a hand on Romero's shoulder and asked in his cold, incisive voice: 'Who are on the beach?'

'The police. Two policemen. Two sons of dogs.' This time he did spit; it was enough to make any man forget his manners. 'They heard that a light was seen offshore last night and so they came to investigate. They have sharp noses, those swine. There was some wreckage on the beach. They found it. It interested them very much. There was a bundle of paper also – very wet.'

'What kind of paper?' Alvarez asked.

'American dollars.'

Alvarez swore. 'Who would have imagined that the money would have been washed up? Did these men speak to you?'

'They asked me whether I had seen anyone come ashore – or any dead bodies. I said no, I had seen nothing, but I do not think they believed. They believe nothing that is not proved to them. They are vermin with small, suspicious minds. They should be—'

'Yes, yes,' Alvarez broke in impatiently. 'One knows all that. But do you think they will come here?'

'I am certain of it. When I slipped away they were looking at some footprints in the sand. They were interested in those also. Señor, you must go without delay. It is for your own sake, not for mine. These men are armed.'

The girl was standing by the door and looking out towards the gap in the ridge. She said quietly: 'It is too late. They are coming.'

Pete laid a hand on the hilt of his knife, but Landon said: 'That will not help us. You heard – the men are armed. Your knife would be useless against a gun.'

'If only we had the tommy-gun,' Pete sighed.

The girl said urgently: 'They must hide in my room. Quickly, before the police get here.'

'It is the only chance,' Romero admitted.

There was a rough dividing wall with a door in it leading to the only other room in the house. Romero opened the door.

'In here, please.'

Alvarez hesitated a moment, then went past Romero into the other room. Landon and Pete followed quickly.

Romero warned them: 'Do not make a noise.' He closed the door.

It was a very small room with a small iron bed. There was a wooden packing-case that served as wardrobe and dressing-table, a stool, a scratched looking-glass, and little else. Landon felt uneasily that they were intruding on the girl's privacy, her poverty, peering into her secrets. Alvarez appeared to have no such qualms; he glanced once at the room with a kind of stern disdain and then took no more note of it.

There was a tiny window, high up in one wall. It was no way out. There was one way only – through the outer room.

They heard the sound of feet outside. Pete put his hand on his knife again. He was breathing very loudly. The air in the room was hot and stifling. Landon felt the sweat beginning to trickle down the back of his neck. Pete's face glistened like wet ebony.

They heard a mumble of indecipherable speech; then Romero's voice, rather too loud. 'I tell you there is no one here. No one except my daughter and myself.'

A man's voice answered. 'That is what you say. We wish for proof. We will search the house. You have no objection?' The tone was sneering, as though it was only too obvious that objections would make little difference.

Romero's voice rose higher; he was losing control of himself. 'I have every objection. You have no right.'

The other voice was suddenly harsh. 'Move aside, old man. We have no time to waste.'

The listeners in the bedroom heard the scrape of boots, and then the voices were clearer, coming through the wooden door that separated the two rooms of the house.

'You see,' Romero said. 'There is no one here.' He was breathing heavily, as if he had been taking some violent exercise. 'No one at all.'

The other voice said harshly: 'What is through that door?'

'It is my daughter's room. There is nothing in there.'

'That we shall see. Get out of the way.'

'No. You shall not go in there.'

The door creaked, as though Romero had backed against it, barring the way. Pete moved softly to the wall on one side of the doorway, the opposite side from the hinges. The knife came silently out of its sheath and rested in his hand.

They heard the policeman's voice, angry now: 'Get out of the way, old man. Move aside.'

'No.'

'Very well.'

There was a brief sound of struggling, a yell of pain and anger; then, startlingly loud, three pistol shots fired in quick succession. The girl screamed once, and then there was a choking, gurgling noise, as though a man were being throttled; finally the soft thud of a heavy body falling to the ground.

A savage kick burst open the bedroom door. It swung inward and a short, thick-set man in an olive-green uniform came through the doorway. He had a dark, heavy face and a neat black moustache. There were black hairs on the back of his right hand, and in the hand was a long-barrelled revolver.

He saw Alvarez and it seemed to surprise him. There was a moment when recognition was evident in his face, a moment in which he hesitated, and that moment was fatal to him.

Pete did a very smooth job with the knife. One could imagine that he had had much practice. The policeman did not even cry out. His mouth sagged open, but no sound came from it except a slight hissing. As he fell Alvarez stepped forward and snatched the revolver.

The other policeman was little more than a boy. He had a thin, coppery face and his moustache was wispy. He seemed bewildered and frightened by the swift movement of events. He already had his gun in his hand when Alvarez stepped through the doorway, but the hand was unsteady and his eyes were scared.

Alvarez's hand did not waver. His voice was sharp and authoritative.

'Drop it.'

The young policeman's grip on the gun relaxed. The revolver dropped to the floor and kicked up a little spurt of dust.

Romero lay where he had fallen just to one side of the bedroom door. He was gasping for breath and blood was spreading a dark stain where the shirt met his trousers. The girl was on her knees beside him. She had her arm under his head, pillowing it. The anguish in her face made Landon's heart sick.

Romero put a hand to his stomach, exploring the pain. He drew the hand up to his face and stared at it. He held it very close to his eyes, as though he had suddenly become short-sighted. The blood on his hand seemed to be a source of wonder to him; he seemed unable to understand, unable to grasp the significance of what had happened to him.

The hand fell, drawing a dark smear across his cheek and chin. He smiled at the girl once.

The sound of the girl's weeping was all that broke the hot and dusty silence of the room.

7

START OF A JOURNEY

THE YOUNG POLICEMAN sat with his arms and legs bound to a chair. He was bare-headed, and his black curly hair shone with oil. His face and forehead were gleaming with sweat; his eyes were bright with fear, and his mouth quivered.

Alvarez was pacing up and down the room, and he was angry. Landon sat on the table, swinging one leg and looking at Alvarez. Pete lolled against the wall, glancing first at Landon and then at Alvarez, sometimes at the policeman.

The girl was in her room. Landon believed that she was praying for the soul of her dead father who had gone to meet his Maker unshriven. Landon did not believe that praying would affect Romero one way or the other now, but if the girl wished to pray that was her concern.

Alvarez stopped pacing. He rested his fingertips on the table and scowled at Landon. His words were simply the continuation of an argument that had been going on for some time.

'I tell you that we must kill him. It is essential to our safety. We cannot afford to leave him alive.'

'It would be murder,' Landon said.

Alvarez exclaimed impatiently: 'Murder! That is your term. I should prefer to call it an execution.'

'What would you be executing him for? This man did not kill Romero. He has simply carried out orders. I tell you that if you shoot him it will be cold-blooded murder, and I will have none of it.'

'I do not ask for you to do it. If you are so squeamish I will take him away and blow his brains out where you cannot see them.'

The policeman's gaze switched from one to the other. He stared at Alvarez with fear, at Landon with hope. He understood what they were saying, for ever since they had come ashore they had spoken in Spanish, as though it were only natural to use the language of the country. Pete understood Spanish also, having learnt it in Cuba, but he spoke it imperfectly.

'It would be murder even so,' Landon said. 'Out of sight or not, it would be murder, and I cannot agree to it.'

'You cannot agree! Do I have to ask your permission for what I do?' Alvarez said. He picked up one of the two revolvers that were lying on the table, cocked it, and levelled it at the head of the terrified policeman. Rivulets of sweat coursed down the boy's face. His voice trembled.

'Do not shoot me, I beg. I beseech you not to shoot. You heard what the señor said: I have done nothing, nothing. You would not shoot an innocent man—'

Alvarez ignored him. He spoke to Landon. 'What is to prevent my killing him now? I have the right.'

'You will not do it,' Landon said.

Alvarez pressed the trigger and the policeman jerked back in his chair. The revolver gave a metallic click and Alvarez dropped it on to the table. He laughed harshly.

'So much for an empty gun.'

'You knew that it was empty,' Landon said evenly. 'You saw me take out the rounds when I cleaned it.'

'Certainly I knew. Do you suppose I should really have killed him here? Anita is in the other room. I should not wish to cause her further pain.'

He seemed to have regained his composure. It was as though all his anger had spent itself in the squeezing of the trigger of an empty gun. He was cool now. He moved away from the table, went to the door, and looked out. The sun was lower than it had been when the policemen had arrived at the house. The shadows were lengthening.

He spoke over his shoulder, carelessly. 'And suppose we do not kill him. How do we dispose of him? Do we set him free to go and spread the alarm, to bring his friends upon us?'

'We can leave him here as he is.'

'To starve to death? Is that your kindness?'

'He will be found.'

'As you say, he will be found, and we shall be followed.'

'Do you suppose we shall not be followed if we kill him? The police are not utter fools. They will not imagine that Romero killed two armed men and then shot himself in the stomach – three times.'

Alvarez pursed his lips. 'My friend, the power of the imagination has no limits. But let it be as you will. We must leave as soon as it is dark.'

The girl came out of the inner room and closed the door behind her. Her eyes showed the traces of weeping; but there were no tears now. The time for tears was past.

She looked at Alvarez and said: 'I must be your guide now. There is no time to get a man from the village, even if it were safe.'

Alvarez stared at her. 'You! Do you know the way?'

'The first part. I can show you how to get clear of the coast. You do not wish to stumble into the police, do you?'

'We do not. There has been enough trouble of that sort already. But you cannot come with us. It is out of the question.'

She glanced at the policeman meaningly. 'I cannot stay here.'

'She is right,' Landon said. 'It wouldn't be safe for her here. Not after what has happened. The police would take her at once.'

He could imagine the questions they would put to this girl and the way they would handle her. Valdez's men had no reputation for gentleness.

'She will be a liability,' Alvarez said impatiently. 'In a venture of this kind there is no room for women.'

'I don't think that's true. She looks strong enough. Who knows? She might outlast all of us.' He smiled at the girl. 'What do you think, Anita?'

She answered his smile with another that passed fleetingly across her face and was gone. Landon was glad to see that she could smile at all. She was taking the death of her father well. She was very much alone in the world now – and young. But youth is resilient.

She said: 'There is no need for you to worry about me. I am not a weakling. I have had to work.'

Landon turned to Alvarez. 'You see?'

'It was not her physical endurance that I was questioning,' Alvarez replied.

'What was troubling you, then?'

Alvarez stirred the dust of the floor with his foot, erasing the map that he had drawn there. He seemed to come to a decision. 'Very well, then; let her come. And now we had better prepare for the journey. There is not much time.'

Pete pushed himself away from the wall with a loose, flowing movement. His hands rested lightly on his belt. The more Landon saw of this man the more he respected him as a companion in tight corners. He was useful with any weapon – or with no weapon at all.

Pete said: 'You're right there, Mr Alvarez. We wanta get out while the going's good. We don't want no more police snooping around.' He looked at the revolvers lying on the table and added as an afterthought: 'Not that we couldn't maybe handle some more.'

They left the house soon after darkness had fallen. They took the two revolvers and the ammunition that the policemen had carried. They took rolled blankets and some cornmeal that was in the house, a little coffee, and other provisions that were there also. It did not amount to a great deal, but it was something. They took two filled water-bottles, two tin drinking-mugs, and a small frying-pan. It was not a well-equipped expedition, but Alvarez had one possession that might be useful – a thick wad of Anaguan pesos that had been in a waterproof money-belt and had survived the wreck of the ketch. With money you could do much, even in a country as sparsely populated as the interior of Anagua.

Anita had pulled a woollen jacket over her shirt. She still wore the blue jeans and a pair of moccasins on her feet. She went with the three men into an unknown future, taking with her nothing but a small wooden cross and a faith in the righteousness of Alvarez's cause.

They left behind them one man tied to a chair and two bodies buried in shallow graves. The girl left everything but the clothes she wore, the tiny cross, and the memory.

They went uphill, away from the sea, with the girl leading. It was a steep path that they followed, and sometimes they stumbled, stones loosening under their feet.

When they had gone a short distance they stopped and looked back, but there was no sign of the house; it had been swallowed up in the darkness. They could hear the faint murmur of the sea, and then suddenly something else, something that was far more threatening – the sound of men's voices, shouting. They saw a light appear below them, and the light moved; it was a white beam that might have come from an electric torch held in a man's hand.

'Let us go on,' Alvarez said. 'It seems that we were only just in time. We should have killed that man as I wished to do.'

'The man knows nothing except that we have gone,' Landon said. 'He doesn't know where we are going. He can tell them little.'

'But they may come quickly. We have no time to spare. We must hurry.'

They climbed with a sense of deeper urgency, and the girl did not hold them back. It was, in fact, she who sometimes had to wait for them. She seemed as sure-footed as a gazelle, and untiring.

They did not pause again until they had reached the crest of the hill. Below them and to the left lights were visible.

'It is the village,' the girl said.

They looked back the way they had come, and there was only darkness. There was no evidence of pursuit.

'They will talk,' Alvarez said. 'Perhaps they will talk a long time before they decide what to do. These policemen have small brains. They know much about torture, but little about other things. They will talk and argue and curse one another, but it may be morning before they decide to follow us. We must be well on our way by then.'

He spoke to the girl. 'If you are ready we will go on.'

'I am ready,' she said.

They went downhill now, but away from the lights of the village. They passed through belts of trees and across cultivated ground, always with the girl leading, never at a loss, as though she knew the country so well that she had no need of a light to help her find the path.

Somewhere a dog barked. It went on barking for a long time, until the sound faded with distance. The path, if it was a path, went uphill and down like a switchback. They sweated under the weight of their loads, but no one was willing to show the first sign of weakness. Alvarez followed the girl, then came Pete, and finally

Landon. Landon could hear Pete's breath whistling through his nose; he was a big, heavy man and perhaps he found the going harder than did either Landon or Alvarez, who were both sparely built. The girl had no load to carry; that made it easier for her.

Landon glanced at the luminous dial of his wrist-watch. It was waterproof and had survived the immersion in sea-water. He saw that they had been travelling for nearly three hours. They had come into more open country, the sky was clear, and he could tell by the stars that they were moving in a westerly direction, away from the coast. The idea would be to penetrate into the heart of the country before anyone could get on to their trail, then strike out for Oxaca. So far there had been no hint of pursuit.

'We will rest now,' Alvarez said suddenly.

Pete dropped his load to the ground with a sigh of relief. 'I don't say no to that.'

He took off his shoes and massaged his feet.

'Any blisters?' Landon asked.

'No blisters. I got tough feet.'

'You'll need them. One hundred and fifty miles is a long walk.'

'I can do it. I done longer.'

They drank a little water, moistening their parched mouths. They were a shadowy quartet in the starlight, and a strange quartet at that, Landon thought, thrown together by circumstance and setting out on a hazardous project.

The girl sat a little apart from the others, silent. Landon felt compassion for her. Three strangers had been cast up by the sea on to her doorstep, and they had brought with them violence and suffering. Now she had nothing to look forward to but more violence, more suffering, and little reward. For him it did not matter; he could take what came, as he had always done. Pete also was an adventurer, and Alvarez was a man with a mission; no one need pity him. But the girl was different, a child who was alone in the world now that her father was dead; alone and an outlaw.

He moved nearer to her and said softly: 'It will be all right. We shall get through.'

He wished to comfort her, but he sensed the foolishness of the statement. There was not even the ring of truth in it. How could he tell that it would be all right? How could anyone tell?

Her face was pale in the starlight when she looked at him. 'I know,' she said. 'El Aguila must get through. My country needs him. He is the only man who can help us.'

Landon had not been thinking of that side of the question. The success or failure of the revolution meant nothing to him except in so far as it affected his own fortunes. If Alvarez won he would get his reward, if not he might find a hangman's noose about his neck or a bullet in his heart. But he had no moral feelings about the matter. He was cynical enough to believe that Alvarez might be little different from Valdez if he ever came to power. They all lined their own pockets.

The girl looked at things from another angle. Anagua was her country and she believed passionately in the revolution. To her Alvarez was indeed The Liberator.

'You are not tired?' Landon asked.

'A little,' she admitted. 'But it is nothing. I can go on.'

Alvarez was sitting with his knees drawn up almost to his chin. He moved his feet and they made a harsh, scraping noise on the ground.

'You know,' he said, 'that we must head for the mountains. How long do you think it will take us to reach them?'

'A day. Perhaps two days,' the girl said. 'It is hard to tell.'

'We need a mule,' Landon said. 'Something to carry the packs.'

'We may be able to find one. I agree that an animal would help. There is some bad country ahead.'

The girl said: 'I have never been farther than the mountains. I do not know the way beyond.'

'We shall find the way,' Alvarez said.

They were fortunate in finding a hide-out in which to rest during the day. It was not so much a cave as a slit in a hillside, with a rough tangle of growth that had formed a roof over the top. There was a bush and creepers growing close against the entrance, and they might have passed it by if Pete's sharp eyes had not detected the line of the fault.

It was becoming light and the country was too open for it to be safe for them to travel farther; therefore, they were thankful to find the refuge, and to creep into it and sleep.

'When we reach the mountains we will travel by day,' Alvarez said. 'For the present it is safer to move only at night.'

'That's true enough,' Landon said. 'This part is too open. A man on a horse could ride you down and you wouldn't stand a chance.'

'Nobody is going to ride us down,' Alvarez said.

The three men divided the day between them into watches. There was always to be one awake, so that they should not be taken by surprise. They exempted the girl. She protested that she was able to share the watches, but she was overruled.

'There are enough of us,' Alvarez said. 'It is not necessary for you to keep awake. Go to sleep, my child, while you may.'

It was in Pete's watch that the aircraft came. The noise of its engine woke them all.

The sun was high now, for it was a little past noon, and golden fingers of sunlight probed down through the tangle of roots and creepers above their heads. In the narrow slit it was hot and airless.

Landon opened his eyes and raised his head. He saw Pete squatting on his haunches near the opening, his head tilted to one side. He was listening to the note of the aircraft engine. Landon listened to it. Alvarez and the girl listened also.

The sound grew in volume, reached its maximum, and faded slowly.

Pete's pent-up breath came out in a long sighing exhalation. 'He's gone.'

But the sound grew louder again. It was obvious that the plane had turned and was coming back. This time it passed closer to where they lay hidden. From the amount of noise it was making they judged it to be flying very low.

'It don't have to be looking for us,' Pete said.

'No,' Landon said. 'It could be four other people.'

The third time it approached the plane threw a shadow across the roof of the hide-out, so that momentarily the golden pencils of light were cut off, only to appear again as the plane flew away.

'He's giving the place a real looking over,' Pete said. 'Good thing nobody left his boots outside the door.'

'He will not be able to see us,' Alvarez said. 'There is no danger of that. If we had been in the open it would have been different. It is well that we should travel only at night while there are vultures like that looking for us.'

The sound of the engine died away for the last time and they did not hear it again. But half-way through the afternoon, Landon, peering through the screen of growth across the entrance, noticed two horsemen riding slowly towards the hill. He looked back over his shoulder and saw that the girl was awake. He told her to waken Alvarez and Pete. She did so. The others woke swiftly and silently.

'Two horsemen,' Landon said. 'Heading this way.'

Alvarez crawled to the entrance and looked out. One of the horsemen dismounted and bent down to examine the ground. After a few moments he straightened up and handed the reins of his horse to the other man. He took a carbine from a saddle-holster and began to climb the side of the hill, moving slowly and warily.

Alvarez spoke quietly to Pete without turning: 'Bring the guns.'

Pete slithered forward with the revolvers. Alvarez took one and Landon the other. They waited.

The man with the carbine came nearer. He was wearing an olive-green shirt and breeches, and leather riding-boots. He had a bandolier over his shoulder and a leather belt round his waist with a holstered pistol. On his head he wore a peaked cap with a chin-strap and a badge of some kind that glittered when the sunlight caught it.

'Another policeman,' Alvarez muttered. 'The country is crawling with them.'

The man held the carbine ready in the crook of his arm. He had a heavy, dark face, and his stomach bulged. They could see the sweat glistening on his skin, and there were dark, sweaty patches on the shirt. When he was about ten yards away from the hide-out he paused.

Landon held the revolver in his right hand and supported it with his left forearm. He squinted along the barrel through the small opening in the bushes and aimed at the policeman's chest. The air felt hot and still and humid. He could feel the sweat running down between his shoulder-blades; his shirt clung to him underneath the armpits.

The policeman's gaze rested upon the entrance to the hideout. He was so plainly in view to the watchers inside that they were convinced that he must be able to see them also. The man was very close to death at that moment. But the moment passed, and the policeman who was holding the horses shouted something that Landon failed to catch. He sounded impatient.

The man with the carbine turned away and went back down the hillside. They saw him put the carbine back in the saddle-holster and get on to his horse. Then the two men rode away.

8

TO THE MOUNTAINS

THEY CAME TO the house early in the morning. It was perhaps flattery to call it a house; it was a dilapidated wooden structure, low-roofed and rotting. There were a few sheds scattered about in no conceivable order, and there were two donkeys grazing. They were tethered to stakes driven into the ground, and round each stake was a circle of bitten-down grass.

The man was unshaven. He had ragged, baggy trousers and bare feet. He had an old straw hat on his head and his black, greasy hair was visible under the brim. The hat looked as though rats had been gnawing at it. The hair looked like that also. The man himself might well have been gnawed by rats; he was ragged enough.

He watched them as they approached – Alvarez, Landon, Pete, and the girl. He gave no sign of liking what he saw.

They said nothing as they went towards the man. They had travelled a long way in the night and they were tired and hungry. They were dirty too, but it was the weariness and the hunger that affected them most.

The man did not move as they approached him. He seemed to be chewing something; his jaws moved rhythmically. A jet of brown juice suddenly spurted from his mouth and fell to the ground. His jaws continued champing.

The four travellers halted within a few yards of the man.

'Buenos dias, amigo,' Alvarez said.

The man grunted. He did not look like a friend. He seemed to resent their presence. His eyes were watchful and suspicious. The hair on his chin had not been shaved for a week; there was a brown stain where the tobacco juice had dribbled on to it. His neck was thin and stringy, his skin darker than saddle leather.

'What do you want?' he asked.

'Food,' Alvarez said. 'Perhaps other things. Food first of all.'

'There's little food here.' The man's voice was harsh, ill-tempered.

'We can pay for what we have.'

The man's expression became a shade less unfriendly. The promise of payment undoubtedly made a difference.

Alvarez looked at the tethered animals. 'If you would be willing to sell one of those donkeys we might be able to come to an arrangement.'

'I need my donkeys.'

Alvarez shrugged. 'Perhaps we will discuss it later. For the moment food is the more important subject.'

The man did not move. 'There was something said about payment.'

Alvarez felt in his pocket and pulled out a roll of paper money. The man's eyes glittered when he saw it. Alvarez took one of the notes and handed it to the man, who looked at it, held it up to the light, and stowed it away in the pocket of his trousers.

'Come,' he said. He turned and led the way towards the house. The others followed.

There was a woman in the house. They supposed she must be the man's wife. She was a shapeless and bulging piece of flesh wrapped up in black cloth. She could not have been much more than four feet tall and she had a gross, stupid face in which the eyes seemed to be almost lost behind rolls of fat. She had long, unkempt black hair, and every crease in her skin had become so deeply ingrained with dirt that she presented to the world a veritable network of black lines that might have been the representation of some intricate system of railways.

The man snarled orders at her. She made no answer, but waddled off through a doorway at the back of the earth-floored room, and after a while they could smell the good, rich odour of coffee and something else that might have been stew.

There was a rough bench that did service for a table, its surface stained and greasy from the innumerable meals that had passed across it. There was a wooden form and one armchair that had once been upholstered with American cloth stuffed with horse-hair. The cloth had worn away to shreds and the horse-hair was coming out in thick wads. Landon wondered where the chair had come from; with its ornately carved legs and arms it looked like an intruder from some other world.

The man began to smoke a black pipe, puffing fumes into the room. He squinted at Alvarez. Alvarez was the one who interested him. He ignored the others.

'You've come far?' he asked.

Alvarez did not answer. He sat on the end of the wooden form and made patterns on the floor with the toe of his shoe. The man had perhaps not expected an answer. He sucked again at his pipe.

'You go to Limas perhaps?' he suggested.

'Perhaps,' Alvarez said. 'Perhaps we go to Limas, perhaps not. It is not of interest to you, my friend.'

'No, that is true. Of no interest to me.' Again he squinted at Alvarez through the haze of tobacco smoke. 'It is a strange thing. It seems to me that I have seen you before – somewhere – some time. Could that be so?'

'It is not impossible. And again it might have been some one who looked like me.'

'True, true. And yet I think it was you, señor.'

'Very well. You think so. It is of no importance.'

'No – of no importance – as you say.'

The woman came back with a saucepan of stew. Landon supposed it must have been a stock-pot which she had heated up. She brought plates and some coarse bread, and served the food. She went away again and came back with coffee.

They began to eat hungrily, not questioning what was in the stew; perhaps it was better not to ask questions of that sort. The stew was dark, almost black, and very thick; the lumps in it were quite unidentifiable; they might have been anything from goat to alligator, for they had sunk their individuality in the general mess. The travellers did not care; they were hungry and would have eaten worse concoctions without hesitation.

While they were eating the man kept looking at Alvarez, as though he were imprinting Alvarez's features on his memory. He sat on the horse-hair chair and puffed at his black pipe, and the smell of the tobacco mingled with the smell of the stew and the coffee and the damp odour of rottenness that seemed to come from the walls of the house and up through the earthen floor.

When they had finished Alvarez returned to the question of the donkey.

'You can surely spare us one.'

'I have need of my animals,' the man said.

Alvarez took the wad of money out of his pocket and riffled it with his long, thin fingers. The man's eyes glittered hungrily.

'If we were pushed to it,' Alvarez said, 'we could perhaps take what we require by force. We are the stronger party. Would it not be wise of you to accept payment?'

Pete chuckled. As though absentmindedly, he drew his knife from its sheath and spat on the blade. He began to clean it with a handful of earth from the floor.

For the first time the host seemed to acknowledge the fact that there were others in the room besides himself and Alvarez. He looked at the knife and at Pete speculatively. Pete grinned at him, but it was not the kind of grin to give any man confidence in his own safety.

The girl looked from Pete to the man sitting in the dilapidated armchair. She seemed tense and nervous.

Landon was relaxed, enjoying the situation. It amused him.

'Better to sell property than to have it taken away by force,' Alvarez said gently.

The man took the pipe out of his mouth. 'How much will you give for a good donkey?'

The sun was becoming hot when they left the farmstead. There was a leer on the man's face as he watched them go. There was a little hatred also; it showed in his eyes.

The donkey carried the load now. They had bought some provisions off the man and a five-gallon can of water. They were better equipped for the journey now than they had been, but they badly needed sleep. Ahead the way lay upward. There was no discernible road.

The farmstead was becoming small in the distance when Landon glanced back. He put up a hand to shade his eyes and called to the others.

'See there!'

They all stopped and stared back at the farm. Beyond the house a man was riding away in the opposite direction, raising a little cloud of dust.

For a few moments they were all silent; then Pete said: 'That looks like a horse. I didn't see no horse down there.'

'Could have been in one of the sheds,' Landon said. 'That man seems to be in a hurry.'

'Too much hurry.'

'He could have business,' Alvarez said.

'True enough; he could have business.' Landon allowed his hand to drop. 'And it might be bad business – for us. He said he'd seen you before.'

Alvarez nodded.

'I think he recognized you,' the girl said. 'He looked a bad man. He was not a man you could trust.'

'I agree,' Alvarez said. 'I think it would be advisable that we do not rest today. We must put a distance between this place and ourselves.' He looked questioningly at the girl. 'You are not too tired?'

'I am not tired,' the girl said quickly.

They turned and went on, prodding the donkey into motion. The air was hot and humid, like a Turkish bath.

Landon's stomach was troubling him. He was not sure whether it was the recurring pain of the old wound or the effect of the stew that he had eaten, perhaps too heartily. The pains stabbed at him as he walked and the sweat ran down his face. He wondered whether the others felt any pain. They had said nothing. Pete looked the sort of man who could eat anything; he probably had a stomach like a goat's, one that was able to digest old army boots as easily as boiled fish. But the girl and Alvarez seemed to be feeling no qualms either, so perhaps after all it was simply the old wound grumbling.

Alvarez was leading now, and the girl followed him. Even in the faded blue jeans and cotton shirt she managed to appear neat and graceful; every movement she made seemed to give evidence of her youth and vitality. Watching her, Landon felt a sudden stab of pain that had nothing to do with the old wound but might have been the result of looking back on forty-one years of life.

Pete was holding the halter of the donkey and following the girl. He walked with the loose-jointed movement of his race, and as he walked he crooned softly to himself in time with the rhythm of his tramping feet.

The way became steeper. They were moving into the foothills of the mountainous region that stood like a hump in the central part of Anagua. Landon wondered how a man could have any love for such a country, as Alvarez must have if he were not interested solely in grasping power for his own ends. There was that possibility, of course; though what was power in a land such as Anagua? Here was a country of fewer than a million inhabitants; a poor, backward country, where roads were little more than mule tracks and railways scarcely existed; a country of thick rain forests, of lakes and swamps and volcanoes; a country of poverty and wretchedness and passion, of cruelty and injustice and fear. As far as he, Landon, was concerned, you could keep it. He regretted the loss of the ketch in which he could have sailed away from it all. But then he looked up and saw the slim figure of the girl and wondered whether he regretted so much after all.

They travelled on all day and saw no other human being. Once they heard the heavy beat of aeroplane engines and they took cover; but the plane did not come low; it went straight on, not deviating from its course.

'The mail plane,' Alvarez said.

Landon said: 'You think so?'

'It could be. Not every one is looking for us. We must not develop a persecution mania.'

'You don't have to develop it here. It comes in the ready-to-use packet.'

In the evening it began to rain. They found an overhang of rock and made camp beneath its meagre shelter. It rained heavily all night and water poured down on the rock, making a cascade that splashed them where they lay huddled in the blankets. The donkey stood patiently, taking it with stoicism. It was not a good night, but they were worn out and slept despite the rain.

By daylight the storm had spent itself. Soon the sun came up, hot and fiery, and when they continued their journey everything was steaming in the heat – the earth, the donkey, the blankets. It was the Turkish bath again, and the air was filled with the scent of rottenness and decay.

Landon's face itched under the scabs that had covered the scratches. It felt stiff, as though the skin had been dried out and baked. He rubbed the scabs, trying to allay the itching.

'If you do that,' the girl said, 'they will bleed again. You could get blood-poisoning. You should leave them alone and they will heal quickly.'

'They irritate me.'

'You should think about something else.'

'Very well. I will think about you.'

'I am not worth thinking about,' she said. It was a simple statement of fact made without coquetry.

'I'll think about you just the same.'

He thought she seemed half embarrassed. She looked into his eyes and looked away again, as though she had seen something that affected her, something that she had not noticed until this moment. He saw with some surprise that a tinge of deeper colour had crept into her cheeks.

'Let us be on our way,' Alvarez said harshly.

Pete looked up at the sky and stretched his long limbs. 'I hope it's the right way.'

'Do you doubt my leadership?' Alvarez asked.

'I don't doubt your leadership. I just hope, that's all.'

Alvarez grunted, only partly satisfied with this answer. They started the donkey and went on.

It was afternoon when they saw the horsemen. There were four of them, and they were perhaps half a mile away, possibly more. They seemed to be following the trail that the men and the girl had made. The metal of stirrups and bridles glittered in the sunlight.

'Our friend did his work,' Alvarez said. 'The bloodhounds are on our tracks.'

'Some friend,' Pete grunted. 'I bet he likes to be paid twice for everything.'

'It is not an uncommon desire.'

The way was not steep enough to prevent the horsemen from riding. It was a long, narrow ravine climbing and twisting between steep sides like walls. There was no way out except by going on or going back. Behind were the horsemen, ahead was the unknown. In a short while it was certain that the horsemen would overtake them.

'We shall have to fight,' Alvarez said.

Landon said: 'We have two revolvers. I imagine each of those men has a carbine. We're in a bad position for fighting.'

Alvarez nodded. 'So we must find a better one.'

He looked up at the cliffs on either side, searching with his eyes for a position in which they would be able to defend themselves. There were rocks, boulders, a little sparse vegetation clinging to the crevices.

Landon pointed at the right-hand wall some fifty yards ahead. 'There, perhaps.'

It was a kind of horizontal cleft that might have been three hundred feet above the floor of the ravine. It looked as though a gigantic axe had sliced into the rock face, paring some of it away and leaving a narrow platform with a protecting rampart some four or five feet in height.

'I don't like it,' Alvarez said. 'But we have no time to search for anything better. We shall have to try it.'

They went up the steep slope with difficulty, for it was not an easy climb. In many places the rocks were loose and went rolling away from them, bounding and crashing downward. The donkey showed some unwillingness to go higher, but Pete dragged on the halter and the donkey followed, its small hoofs slipping on the treacherous surface.

The cleft was wider than it had appeared to be from below. Between the inner and outer walls there was a shelf ten feet wide. At one end a great boulder blocked the entrance; the other end was open, but a shoulder of rock jutting out from the cliff face shielded it from cross-fire except at very close range, and a man would have to come near indeed to threaten them at that point. It was as good a defensive position as they could have hoped to find.

'It will do,' Alvarez said.

They unloaded the donkey and tethered it, and each of them drank a little water. They examined the revolvers and put them within easy reach and waited for the horsemen.

'If they ride past,' Landon said, 'we shall know they're not chasing us.'

'They will not ride past,' Alvarez said.

'In any case it was well to take precautions.'

The girl was sitting down with her back to the outer wall, her knees drawn up towards her chin. She looked tired. Perhaps she had not slept well the previous night.

Landon looked down at her. 'Are you afraid, Anita?'

She answered him frankly: 'Yes, I am afraid. But it does not matter. It makes no difference whether I am afraid or not.'

It was almost on his tongue to tell her that there was no cause to be afraid, but he stopped himself. He knew that there was very good cause, and he knew that the girl knew also.

He touched her head lightly with his hand and said: 'I think we can beat them.'

Her smile was uncertain, a quivering of the lips. 'I am sure we can beat them too, but it doesn't stop me from being afraid.'

Pete announced suddenly: 'They've stopped.'

He was lying on the ground at the open end of the cleft and peering round the corner of the rock. Landon also had a look, keeping his head low.

The horsemen were motionless in a little group, and it was possible now to make out the familiar olive-green uniform and the saddle-holsters with the butts of the rifles sticking out of them. The men were looking up the hillside and talking to one another with an occasional gesture of the hands.

'They won't be able to ride up that slope,' Landon said. 'They'll have to dismount. That's a sure thing.'

As if they had heard his words, the men at that moment got off their horses and tethered them to some scrub. They pulled the carbines out of the saddle-holsters and looked up the hillside again, the guns ready in their hands.

'If we had a rifle,' Pete said regretfully, 'They'd all be dead men. That damn donkey-seller must have told them we didn't have no rifle. I wonder just what he gets out of the deal.'

'Honour,' Landon suggested ironically.

Pete laughed shortly. 'That's one feller that wouldn't give two cents for a whole barge-load of honour. He got paid.'

He shifted his position, staring down the slope. 'What are those boys up to now?'

One of the men had put down his carbine and seemed to be tying a rag of cloth to a stick. After a few moments he began to advance up the hillside, waving the stick from side to side. The piece of cloth was white; it looked like a handkerchief.

'They want to parley,' Landon said. He spoke over his shoulder to Alvarez. 'Maybe I'd better talk to him. Might be best if you kept out of sight. This could be a trick.'

Alvarez said coldly: 'Do you think I am afraid?'

'I don't think anything of the sort,' Landon said. 'But I think it would be best if I did the talking just now.'

Alvarez bit his lip, but did not argue. He sat down under cover of the rock.

Landon allowed the man with the stick to climb to within thirty feet of the shelf. Then he said sharply: 'Stay where you are.'

The man could see Landon's head. He could also see the revolver in Landon's hand. He did not seem to be impressed by either. But he stopped nevertheless. He rested the end of the stick on the ground and leaned on it. He stood there, insolently at ease, the sweat stains showing darkly through his green shirt.

'What do you want?' Landon asked.

The man was tall and bony. He had a thin black moustache and a nose that had once been broken and then had been set badly; there was a kink in the middle. His chin was long and pointed and his eyes were restless.

'To talk,' he said. His voice was thin too; it sounded under-nourished.

'To talk about what?'

The man shifted his weight from one foot to the other. One side of his face seemed to slide upwards while the other side went down. Landon supposed it must be some form of a grin. It was most certainly the crookedest grin he had ever seen.

'About El Aguila, for example.'

Landon lowered the revolver; it was making his arm ache. The man looked capable of any treachery, but Landon did not think that treachery was in his mind at that moment.

'Who is El Aguila?'

The man put a hand over the rag on the stick; he twisted it into a tight roll and released it again. He seemed to be contemptuous of the flag of truce. It was expendable.

'Do not pretend ignorance,' he said. 'We all know that Ramon Arturo Alvarez is behind that rock.' He spoke the name with disdain and spat when he had finished, as though to clear the taste of it from his mouth.

Landon waited.

'We want Alvarez,' the man said.

Landon said nothing.

The silence was like a heavy weight pressing down on the afternoon. At the foot of the slope the three other men were standing together, smoking. Landon could see the tobacco smoke rising above them in a thin cloud like steam. They were in no hurry. They had time. They had all the time in the world.

'We can take Alvarez if it should be necessary,' the man said. 'But it would be simpler if you gave him up to us. There would be less unpleasantness – for all.'

One had the impression that, either way, it did not greatly concern him. Either way, Alvarez was there for the taking.

'If you had Alvarez what would you do with him?'

'We have orders to take him for trial. For myself, I would hang him from the nearest tree – so.' He put his fingers round his throat and gave a vivid and gruesome impression of a man strangling. 'But we have our orders.'

'And the rest of us – if we give Alvarez up?'

'We are not interested in any others, only Alvarez. The others can go where they please.'

Landon did not believe it. Giving Alvarez up would be no easy way out. They had helped the revolutionary leader, and that made them revolutionaries also. The offer was simply a trick. But the answer would have been the same even if he had not seen through the trick.

'Start moving,' Landon said.

The man looked surprised, not understanding. 'What did you say?'

Landon raised the revolver again and pointed it at the policeman's chest.

'I said to start moving. Go back to your friends and tell them it didn't work.'

'You refuse our offer?'

'You heard what I said. We don't do that sort of business. Get away from here while you can still walk. Go before I lose my patience.'

'You are a fool,' the man said. He turned and went back down the hill, without haste, contemptuously. On his way he tore the rag from the stick and thrust it into his pocket. He threw the stick away. The time for that sort of thing was over.

'Kill him,' Pete said urgently. 'Shoot him now while you have the chance.'

'No,' Landon said.

'Give me the gun. I will shoot him.'

'No.'

Pete sighed. 'Have it your own way, Mr Landon. But it would have shortened the odds.' He sounded regretful that this opportunity should have been allowed to pass. 'It's them for the next move now.'

The man with the broken nose had rejoined his companions. Landon saw him light a cigarette. None of them seemed to be in any hurry to get on with the affair. One man did lie down, put his carbine to his shoulder, and fire a shot, but it was no more than a warning, not expected to accomplish anything. The bullet struck the rock guarding the ledge and ricocheted with a venomous whining noise.

After that there was a long period of inaction. The men kindled a fire and appeared to be preparing a meal. They ate and drank and smoked again. The afternoon dragged on its way and the shadow of the cliff laid its canopy over the ledge where the four waited for the other four to show their hand.

'Perhaps we should have gone on,' Alvarez said. 'They will wait for darkness and attack us then.'

'If we had gone on,' Landon said, 'we should have had no chance at all. We did what we had to do.'

'They are in no hurry.'

'They do not have to be. Time is with them.'

'I think they will wait for darkness.'

'They are coming now,' Pete said.

They spread out like a fan and came up the slope carefully and slowly. When they were about half-way to the ledge they lay down and began to fire their carbines. The bullets ricocheted off the rocks and went sobbing and whining into oblivion.

Landon tried one answering shot with the revolver, but the range was too great and the target difficult. It was a waste of ammunition, and they might have need of every round.

'They will have to make a rush if they want to get us,' Alvarez said. 'And they won't find it easy.'

Landon looked at the girl. She was sitting down under the shelter of the rock with her hands clasped tightly together. Her lips were trembling slightly, but she was controlling her fear well enough.

It was not possible to keep watch on all the attackers without the risk of a bullet in the head, but none of them could approach too closely without being seen. In the end, however, it was from above that the danger came and not from below. For while three of the policemen kept up their harassing fire, the fourth man moved away to the right and climbed with some difficulty to a point above the ledge, one hundred feet higher up the cliff.

It was the girl who saw him first. Above the defenders the cliff rose almost sheer for that first hundred feet, then swept back in a steep slope on which there was a hazardous footing for a brave and agile man. It was on this slope that the fourth policeman was now perched. He was in fact lying across the slope with one hand grasping a ragged bush that grew out of a crevice and his revolver in the other. He had left the carbine behind him, apparently realizing that the climb would be difficult enough without that added handicap.

Alvarez, Landon, and Pete had been keeping watch for a sudden attack from below, but not one of them had thought to look upward to the cliff above, for the sheer face of the rock had seemed to assure that they were safe from that direction. Moreover, the persistent carbine fire had drawn their attention, as it was probably calculated to do. But the girl, sitting with her back to the outer rock, had glanced up and seen the man above with the revolver in his hand.

Her shout of warning coincided with the crack of the revolver. The bullet struck the rock a yard to the left of the girl, ricocheted, and clipped the donkey's tail. The donkey began to lash out furiously with its hoofs, tugging at the rope which tethered it.

Alvarez swung round and fired three shots in rapid succession at the man above. One of the shots chipped the cliff and scattered splinters of rock into the man's face, blinding him. He screamed with pain, put his hands to his bloody face, and released his hold on the bush and the revolver.

The revolver clattered down, bounced once, and fell at the feet of Pete. He stooped and picked it up.

The man was still screaming. Suddenly he began to slide; a few stones and a little earth preceded him, dropping on the ledge with the sound of hail falling. The man himself seemed to hover for a moment at the edge where the slope dipped to the sheer face. He took his hands away from his eyes and his fingers scrabbled wildly in a last desperate effort to save himself. Then he fell. He turned over once as he fell and landed with his head doubled under him, so that his neck took the full force of the shock. The snapping of the bones sounded startlingly loud.

Landon saw that it was the man who had come to parley earlier in the day, the man with the bent nose. There was more than the nose bent now.

Pete said with no show of emotion: 'You should have shot him when I said. It would have saved him the climb.'

Alvarez was calming the donkey. The girl was crouched down by the rock, trying not to look at the dead and mangled body, and finding it impossible not to do so.

There was no sound of carbine fire. Landon said sharply to Pete: 'What are the other boys doing? Have a look, Pete.'

Pete peered cautiously round the side of the rock. 'Ain't doing nothing,' he said. 'I bet they was leaving it all to this one. He seems to have been the sweat rag.'

Landon took a blanket and spread it over the dead man. He put his hand gently on the girl's shoulders.

'It was a quick death,' he said. 'Don't let it trouble you. Don't think about it any more.'

He felt her shuddering under his hand.

'They're going away,' Pete said.

He lifted the revolver that the policeman had dropped and took careful aim at the retreating men. He squeezed the trigger and nothing happened.

'Son of a bitch,' he grumbled. 'That fall did for the gun too. Just when I thought I'd got me a rod.'

He frowned with disgust at the bent mechanism of the revolver and threw it down on to the ground.

'They've got away now,' he said. 'Them three.'

The men stopped at the foot of the slope, sat down, and began to smoke.

Landon said: 'We'll get rid of this joker now. We don't want him lying here, getting in our way.'

He pulled the blanket away from the dead man and unfastened the cartridge belt. In the pockets of the uniform were some cigarettes and a little money and a clasp knife. Alvarez, Landon and Pete shared the cigarettes between them. The girl did not smoke. She turned her head away when they dragged the body out.

The men at the foot of the slope looked up and saw Landon and Pete hauling the body. One of them reached for his carbine, took aim, and fired. The bullet kicked up a spurt of dust, but it was not close. A second shot was no better. The man was not an expert marksman.

They dropped the body and hurried back under the shelter of the rock. There was no more carbine fire, and an uneasy silence settled over the afternoon. It became cooler. Shadows crept down the side of the ravine and the sweat dried on Landon's shirt.

The three men at the foot of the slope got up, mounted their horses, and rode off in the direction from which they had come. The others watched them until they disappeared round a bend in the trail.

'They gave up easy,' Pete said. 'Looks like they don't like to fight.'

Landon looked inquiringly at Alvarez, the leader. 'Do we go now?'

Alvarez shook his head. 'We will wait for darkness. I do not trust those men. It could be a trap.'

'No trap,' Pete said confidently. 'They just got tired of the game.'

'Nevertheless, I think we will wait.'

Pete shrugged his broad shoulders. 'If you like it that way. I don't argue. But I think we get no more trouble from those bright boys. They had all they wanted.'

Landon took one of the cigarettes out of his pocket, broke it in two, and lit one of the halves.

'You don't understand how important El Aguila is to these people. They won't let him get away as easily as that.'

'No,' Alvarez said. 'Not as easily as that.'

'I still say they went for keeps,' Pete said.

Night came quickly. They left the dead man and went down the steep slope to the floor of the ravine and continued on their way. The moon came up and the land was black and silver, and their shadows moved on beside them, leaping over boulders and hiding in gullies. The clicking of the donkey's hoofs was a small and lonely sound in an empty world. The men spoke little and the girl was silent, busy with her own thoughts.

The horsemen came rapidly up the ravine – the three who had gone away, but who had not gone far. Alvarez had been right and Landon had been right, and Pete wrong.

The horsemen did not use their carbines; there was no need. The gap between the two groups shrank away and vanished almost before the fugitives had had time to realize what was happening. Landon heard the thunder of the horses' hoofs, the jingle of snaffles, and the crack and whine of pistol fire. He ran forward, seized the girl's arm, dragged her away to one side of the trail, and flung her down behind the shelter of a rock.

He got the revolver into his hand, cocked it, and fired. He saw Alvarez also fire once, then drop his gun, and fall sideways to the ground. He did not get up.

One of the horsemen rode at Landon, kicking spurs into his horse's sides. Landon slipped under the animal's head, grabbed the bridle in his left hand, and rammed the muzzle of the revolver into the rider's belly. He fired once and the man went over the side of the horse. The horse took fright and galloped away down the ravine. The man's right foot was caught in the stirrup. The horse dragged him, his head beating on the rough ground.

It was a swift, brief, deadly struggle with no words spoken. The pistol shots, groans, yells of anger or of pain, the neighing of the horses, the jingle of metal and the clatter of hoofs: these were the sounds of the combat. It had begun suddenly and as suddenly it was ended.

Pete had slashed one of the policemen in the arm with his knife, and the odds now in a moment seemed bad to the attackers. First the man with the slashed arm wheeled his horse and galloped off; then the other, finding himself alone, lost courage also and turned away. Landon fired three times at the retreating figures before they were lost to sight in the shadows. The sound of their hoofbeats gradually became fainter and fainter until they too faded away into the night.

Alvarez was still lying where he had fallen with his face to the ground. Landon went to him and kneeled down. There was a dark stain visible in the moonlight on the left side of Alvarez's head just above the ear. It stretched across his temple and from it drops of blood dripped on to the earth. The top half of the ear had been mangled by a bullet; it was impossible to see what other damage had been done. But Alvarez was breathing.

Landon shouted to Pete. 'Where's that donkey?'

'That damn' animal,' Pete said. 'He ran away.'

'Catch him. I want some water and a bandage.'

'He went away up the ravine.'

'Go after him. You can run.'

'Sure, I can run,' Pete said. He went off in pursuit of the donkey which had taken fright at the noise of the encounter and had kicked up its heels to better effect than ever it had done before.

The girl came and kneeled beside Landon. Her face looked very pale in the moonlight.

'He is not – dead?'

'No, he's not dead. Help me turn him over. Be careful with his head. His ear looks bad, but that's nothing to worry about.'

They turned Alvarez gently over on to his back, and the girl pillowed his head in her lap, holding it off the rough ground. Alvarez breathed heavily but did not wake.

They heard Pete coming back with the donkey. It had not gone far with its load, and he had found it less than a hundred yards away, standing perfectly motionless, as though waiting for someone to claim it.

'Give me the water,' Landon said.

Pete took the water-can off the donkey and handed it to Landon, who soaked a handkerchief and began to wash Alvarez's wound.

After a while he said: 'El Aguila is a lucky man. They clipped the skin and knocked him out, but the ear is the only real damage.'

They were bandaging the wound with a strip of cloth when Alvarez opened his eyes.

9

THE CITY OF THE VALLEY

THEY HAD TRAVELLED a long way, and it had been hard going. Days had passed and they had left the vegetation of the lower ground far behind them. Now they were in a lofty world of barren rock, of sharply rearing peaks and scattered boulders, of rough, stony ways, of precipices and chasms and harsh, biting grit that the wind blew into their faces to erode and ravage the skin. By day the unshaded sun glared down upon them and at night they huddled together in an almost Arctic cold.

But Alvarez was not depressed. He seemed to believe that the worst was already behind them. After their encounter with the four riders there had been no further sign of pursuit. Since then they had seen no other man.

'We have done well,' Alvarez said. 'When we reach Oxaca we shall be safe – for the present. And we shall reach Oxaca soon now, very soon.'

He still had the rough bandage round his head, but he said that he was feeling no ill effects from the wound.

'Probably those men have spread the tale that I have been killed,' he said. The idea seemed to provide him with a certain grim amusement, for his lips twitched slightly.

'An inch more and the tale would have been correct,' Landon said. 'How long do you think it will take us to reach Oxaca?'

'Two more days, perhaps.'

'How can you be certain that the city is still in revolutionary hands?'

'Nothing is certain,' Alvarez replied. 'But you must realize that much of Anagua has for a long time been out of Valdez's hands.

There is San Quinton City for example, where we have a garrison. Valdez controls both the Pacific and the Caribbean coasts but he lacks the necessary strength to carry out a large campaign and capture our strongholds in the interior. You cannot use tanks in the mountains and the jungle. Even aircraft are at a disadvantage, and Valdez has not many war-planes at his disposal anyway. I think there can be little doubt that we shall be welcomed in Oxaca.'

'I hope so. A diet of beans and cornmeal becomes monotonous.'

Alvarez laughed. 'In Oxaca there will be a greater variety. You will have meat and fruit.'

'I can't wait for it,' Landon said.

As usual Alvarez was leading the way. Landon dropped back to speak to the girl.

'Are you all right, Anita?'

'I am very well, thank you.'

She showed no sign of excessive weariness; she seemed to have as much stamina as Alvarez striding on ahead, as the big black man leading the donkey, as Landon himself. She looked slight and delicate, but there was a fibre of toughness in her that was mental as well as physical.

Landon wondered what she intended to do after this journey was over. She had nothing in the world; there were no relatives or friends to whom she could go for help; that she had told him. She was alone.

He felt pity for her, and perhaps more than pity, perhaps a deeper emotion. He wished to protect her, and he had no means of doing so; he was a soldier of fortune without the fortune, dependent on what Alvarez might throw him if ever Alvarez should find himself in a position to throw anything to anyone. There was no certainty about that, no certainty about anything.

The girl looked at him, giving a shy, sidelong glance as they walked beside each other. 'Your face is healing.'

Landon put a hand to his cheek and felt the rough bristle that had grown there. Perhaps in Oxaca it would be possible to shave. He hoped so. He felt dirty and ragged, and he would have wished that the girl did not have to see him like that.

'The scratches were nothing,' he said. 'I've had worse than those in my time.'

Again she glanced at him, at the lean, bony face with its growth of beard. This time she did not look away again at once, as though she had grown more confident.

'You have done much fighting perhaps?'

'There was a war,' he admitted. 'And other things.'

He wondered whether he were trying to impress her, trying to make a hero of himself. When the thought came to him he scowled. He did not think of himself as a hero; he did not especially wish to be a hero; there was no money in medals. So why try to swagger before the girl?

'I did as little as I could,' he said.

'I do not believe that is true,' the girl said. 'It is something you say, but it is not quite true.'

'Perhaps not. Perhaps it is something we say.'

'And now,' she said, 'I think you are tired of fighting. You would like to give it up. You would like to do something else. Isn't that so?'

She was right, he thought. He was sick of this kind of life. He ought to go back to England and get a job, settle into a groove, lead an ordinary, humdrum, hard-working existence. It sounded easy; it sounded the right thing to do; but the trouble was he just could not imagine himself doing it. He was forty-one, he was penniless, and he supposed he would just go on working for people like Cranefield and Vargas and Alvarez until somebody put a bullet through his skull or he grew too old and decrepit to be of any more use to such employers. It was not the kind of prospect to bring forth yelps of delight.

'There's nothing else for a man like me to do,' he said.

'If you were to marry—'

He laughed harshly. 'Women don't marry rolling stones. They want security. I've got no security to offer. Nobody would want to marry me.'

'I think that somebody might,' the girl said.

Landon glanced at her quickly and saw that she was staring straight ahead. From the expression on her face he could not tell what she was thinking.

'It will never come to that,' he said coldly.

She did not look at him.

Alvarez suddenly came to a halt and waited for the others to come up to him. He pointed into the distance ahead.

'There. Do you see it? Over there.'

They all looked in the direction indicated by his pointing finger. There was a long vista of boulder-strewn plateau with rocks standing up here and there as high as cathedrals, eroded into grotesque and fantastic shapes, as if a mad sculptor had been at work on them. A wind moved across the plateau, raising little spurts of dust. The dust was scarifying; it acted on the skin like sandpaper, roughening it and opening sores.

Landon put up a hand to shade his eyes. He could see something shimmering in the distance; it might have been a trick of the light, a kind of mirage.

'Lake Zacapa,' Alvarez said. 'Beyond the lake is Oxaca. It is the lake that waters the town. Without Zacapa there would be no Oxaca. You will see later what I mean.'

'How far to Oxaca now?' Landon asked.

'We shall not be there today,' Alvarez replied. 'We have done better than I expected but it is still a long way off.'

He pointed a little to the right where a conical peak rose from the plateau. 'That is Monte del Fuego – the Mountain of Fire.'

'A volcano?'

'Yes.'

'Is it active?'

'There have been minor eruptions during the past hundred years, but nothing serious.'

'It could threaten the town.'

'It could. But the people of Oxaca have become used to living under worse threats than that. They are inured to danger.'

'I don't think I should care to live under the shadow of a volcano.'

Alvarez laughed. 'And yet you have not always sought the safest path, have you, my friend? You have walked in much danger.'

'That's different,' Landon said.

'A different kind of danger, certainly. Perhaps you prefer it. Each man to his taste. Let us move on. We have a long way to go.'

They went on slowly across the plateau, and the distance was so great that they seemed scarcely to be moving. But the shimmer of the lake became gradually clearer, so that it no longer appeared to be a mirage, and the outline of the volcano became harder also.

The sun moved down the sky and it became colder and the wind probed them. Pete shivered; he rubbed his hands on his trousers to put warmth into them, and he sang to himself very softly. There was a melancholy character to the singing; it was a kind of sigh that matched the sighing of the wind among the barren rocks. The donkey's ears twitched and its little hoofs picked their way daintily over the rough ground, like the feet of a fastidious dancer in a deserted ballroom.

They reached the edge of the lake just before darkness fell. The water lay in a rocky bowl. It had a steely look, cold and uninviting, and on the farther shore, perhaps a mile distant, the cone of the volcano reared itself towards the sky. The wind came across the lake, rippling the surface; at the edge the water made a faint lapping sound as it fell upon the hard ground. Nowhere was there any sign of life.

'A pleasant spot,' Landon said. 'Seaside resort.'

Pete chuckled softly. 'You can have it, Mr Landon, sir, you can have it. For me, I could think of nicer places to spend a vacation.'

They camped without fire, since there was no fuel. They ate cold food and drank cold water. They fed the donkey and spent the night huddled in the shelter of a rock.

In the morning they set out early and moved southward along the shore of the lake. The sun warmed them and they forgot the bitter cold of the night. The sunlight glittered on the water and gilded the slopes of the volcano. From the summit of the cone a thin column of smoke rose into the air.

Landon pointed it out to Alvarez. 'Is that usual?'

'I have seen it before,' Alvarez said. 'When it is like that they say in Oxaca that the old man is smoking his pipe. Sometimes there are noises; quite often the ground shakes. That is when the old man's stomach is rumbling.'

'I'm glad they can make a joke of it.'

Alvarez gave Landon a keen glance. 'It is necessary to make a joke of these things. You can live with a joke.'

'Depends on the joke,' Landon said. He watched the old man smoking his pipe. It was not the kind of joke he much appreciated.

At the southern end of the lake the ground sloped steeply upward into a massive wall of rock. In the centre of the wall was a V-shaped depression like a cleft chopped out with two strokes of an axe. It would have had to be a mighty axe. Landon could see that the lake water flowed out through this narrow gap, but he could not tell where it went since his view was blocked by the great wall of rock.

He asked Alvarez, but received only as answer the non-committal statement: 'You shall see.'

They climbed up a gulley with the donkey dragging on the halter and dislodging small pebbles with its hoofs. The pebbles went bounding and skidding down the gulley like hail rolling down the slope of a roof.

'Come up, now,' Pete said persuasively. 'Don't make it look so hard, my boyo.'

He hauled on the rope and the donkey went up after him, its neck stretched out and the pack swaying.

The ridge was about fifty yards wide at the crest, but it narrowed towards the centre where the lake flowed out through the cleft, diminishing to little more than thirty. Where the water rushed through it the cleft was some fifteen feet across, and they could hear the roaring and gurgling of the torrent as it was forced into this narrow gap by the pressure from behind.

'Take care where you step,' Alvarez warned them.

He walked to the farther edge of the ridge and the others followed him. And suddenly the full wonder of it burst upon them: one moment they were in an empty, uninhabited world, a rocky, barren plateau open to the sky, the next moment they were gazing down upon the evidence of civilization. Like a map spread out at their feet, like a child's toys, were houses, streets, squares – a city.

Alvarez gave a sweep of the arm, like a man exhibiting proudly some valuable possession. There was the smallest hint of triumph in his voice, for had he not successfully led them through the wilderness to this land of promise?

'Oxaca!'

Below them the ridge fell away almost sheer for perhaps a hundred feet, then gradually the slope became less and less steep until finally it levelled out into the valley where Oxaca lay. To their right the torrent burst from the cleft in a great spout of glittering water, curving out from the cliff face and falling unimpeded for almost two hundred feet before striking the solid rock. From this source a stream flowed down through the wide valley, past the town, and on into the distance, where there were green plantations and cornfields and every evidence of a profitable agriculture.

Alvarez had said that it was the lake that had made the city, and the truth of this statement was now evident. The water from Zacapa flowed out through the narrow gap in the rock wall and irrigated the valley below. Zacapa was a huge natural reservoir for Oxaca, and the supply was regulated by the narrowness of the cleft which formed the only outlet for the lake.

'You see now?' Alvarez asked.

Landon nodded. 'So that is Oxaca. Who would have expected to find civilization in the midst of this wasteland?'

'It was founded by two Jesuit fathers many years ago. The people are still very devout. That is one reason why they would never accept the godless yoke of Valdez.'

'Could he not force them?'

'It is not easy to reach Oxaca with an attacking army, and the city is self-supporting. Valdez has left it to its own devices.'

Landon pointed to the precipice with its fearsome drop that even a skilled mountaineer might have hesitated to tackle.

'How do we get down without parachutes?'

'There is a way down. It is difficult but not impossible. It is over there.' He pointed to the left away from the waterfall. 'Come, we had better be on our way. We are not so close to our journey's end as you might suppose, and I should like to arrive before nightfall.'

'Me too,' Pete said.

The girl was staring down at Oxaca as though fascinated by the sight, unable to draw her gaze away. Landon touched her lightly on the shoulder and she looked up, startled by the touch.

'Looks good. Don't you think so?'

'It looks very good,' she said.

'We are going down.'

She turned away from the precipice. 'I am ready.'

Alvarez was right about the descent. It was not so simple as a funicular railway from the crest of the ridge would have been; by such means the journey would have been short. As it was, they had to make a long detour before reaching a part of the ridge down which it was possible to take themselves and the donkey. When they reached level ground they found themselves some miles below the city in the cultivated land where the valley widened out into a green expanse of trees and crops, grassy meadows and irrigation trenches.

A patrol of armed and mounted men came from the north and intercepted them. It was obvious that their approach had not been unobserved.

'They are watchful,' Alvarez explained. 'They do not expect Valdez to come, but they are on the watch for spies.'

The leader of the patrol was a grave, handsome man, in whose face youth and experience seemed to be at odds. He was wearing a wide-brimmed hat and baggy trousers stuffed into short leather riding-boots. He had a coppery skin and high cheekbones, but he didn't look pure Indian. Landon judged him to be of mixed blood, as most Anaguans were – part Spanish, part Indian, part black.

There were ten men in the patrol. At a sign from the leader they halted and sat, motionless and expressionless, on their horses, waiting.

The leader said: 'Who are you? Where do you come from?'

Alvarez answered: 'We come from the coast. I am Ramon Arturo Alvarez – El Aguila.'

The horseman stared at him, and there was a little stir among the others.

'El Aguila?'

Alvarez nodded. He had been washed up by the sea, he had not shaved for many days, his clothes were ragged, and there was a bloodstained bandage encircling his head. It was not easy to believe that such a man was indeed he who was to direct the revolution, who was to push Valdez from his perch and liberate the people.

'You have proof of this?'

Alvarez answered coldly: 'I am the proof.'

In spite of his rags and his unshaven face there was something in his voice and his bearing that commanded, if not belief, at least respect. The horseman inclined his head slightly.

'We will go to Colonel Cainas.'

People in the streets of Oxaca stared at them curiously as they went past, people with grave, unsmiling faces, dark-skinned people with prominent noses and black hair. The houses were of shaped stone; they looked solid enough to withstand the wear of centuries, four-square and indestructible.

A constant sound as of distant thunder puzzled Landon at first. One might have supposed it to have been caused by the wind, had there been any wind, but the air was still. And then the source of it became apparent to him. It was the waterfall. He looked up and saw, towering above the city, the rocky wall on which they had so recently stood. And out of the wall the torrent spouted in a foaming, glittering arc, the spray gilded by the sunlight. It had been impressive from above; from below it seemed even more majestic; it was beautiful yet terrifying – the servant of the city that could perhaps become its master.

'Some fall,' Pete said.

They came to a paved square and went across it in their compact group with the horsemen hemming them in, and in front of them rose a tall grey building, a flag hanging from a flag-pole on the roof. There was a wide flight of stone steps and a massive doorway at the top. On each side of the doorway stood a soldier in a drab uniform armed with a rifle.

The horsemen, at a sign from their leader, dismounted. The leader handed the reins of his horse to another man and said to Alvarez: 'You will please follow me.'

'And the others of my party?'

'They also. Come.'

He went up the steps and the four followed him, leaving the donkey with the patrol. The sentries at the doorway saluted, and the horseman in the baggy trousers returned their salute perfunctorily. They went inside.

Colonel Cainas was a small man with silver hair and a smooth, youthful face on which the troubles and worries of sixty-two years had left scarcely a trace. Unlike most Anaguans, his skin was pale, as though he had lived all his life protected from the direct rays of the sun. He was sitting behind a big, heavy desk of polished wood in a room so austerely furnished that it could have been mistaken for nothing else but what it was – a military office. Pushed away against the walls at some distance from Cainas were two uniformed clerks busily writing. On one wall was pinned a large-scale map of Anagua with coloured pins stuck in it, presumably to indicate the disposition of government and insurgent forces. A faint odour of disinfectant impregnated the air.

Alvarez looked at Cainas and said: 'Well, Armando. I imagine that you, at least, will recognize me, disgusting as I must at this moment appear.'

Cainas pushed his chair back and stood up quickly, almost shouting in surprise and excitement. 'Ramon, my dear friend. But this is amazing, truly amazing.'

He came round the end of the desk and gripped Alvarez's hand. He stood in front of Alvarez and looked into his eyes. 'How in God's name do you come here?' He stood back and stared at Alvarez's ragged clothing, at the bandage round his head, dark with dried blood. 'And in such condition. You have been wounded. Badly?'

'Not badly. For the rest, it is a long story. You shall hear it all later. Plans went wrong. I have had great difficulty in getting here. I must go on rapidly to San Quinton. There is much to do and little time to waste.'

'Of course, of course. But we must have a doctor look to that wound.' He pointed at the dirty rag that served as a bandage. 'That dressing looks scarcely hygienic.'

'It was the best available,' Alvarez said.

For the first time Cainas appeared to notice that Alvarez was not alone. His gaze flickered from Landon to Pete to the girl.

'And these others. Who are they?'

'Friends,' Alvarez replied. 'Very good friends in adversity. If it had not been for them I should not be here now. I should not even be alive.'

Cainas turned to them, spreading wide his arms, hands cupped in a gesture of welcome.

'To have saved the life of El Aguila is to have earned the gratitude of every patriotic Anaguan. I thank you. From the bottom of my heart, I thank you.'

Landon shifted his feet impatiently. Colonel Cainas was altogether too demonstrative for his taste. He was afraid that any moment the colonel might start to embrace him – or at least to embrace the girl; she had no dirty growth of beard on her face.

'We were saving our own lives also.'

'Modesty,' Cainas said. 'But I admire modesty. It is my opinion that—

He stopped speaking. There was a rumbling noise, rather like the sound of many steam-rollers going down a cobbled street. Landon could feel the floor shaking. A pen rolled off Cainas's desk. Some pieces of plaster fell from the ceiling. The map on the wall trembled a little, as though a wind had blown upon it; but there was no wind.

The clerks stopped writing and looked at Cainas. He stood with his head slightly on one side, listening. Then the noise died away, the room ceased to vibrate, and the clerks applied themselves again to their work as though nothing had happened.

Cainas smiled. 'The old man's stomach,' he said. 'He has been eating unwisely.'

Landon could feel the sweat damp on his forehead. 'Is that all it was? I thought it was an earthquake.'

Cainas said calmly: 'An earth tremor. It is quite usual here. Luckily the houses are strongly built. They do not collapse easily.'

'Very lucky,' Landon said. He could feel his nerves still jangling. Perhaps when you had lived with this sort of thing for years, for a lifetime, you became used to it. He hoped he would not be staying in Oxaca long enough to acquire immunity to such shocks – even though the houses were stoutly built. It was well enough at sea to have the deck shifting under your feet, but when you were on dry land you expected something rather more solid.

'How often does this happen?' he asked.

Cainas shrugged. 'The frequency varies. It seems to go in cycles. We have had as many as six in one day. That is exceptional. Sometimes there are months when we scarcely know that the old man is there. He seems to go to sleep.'

'I hope he goes to sleep now,' Landon said.

Cainas shook his head. 'That is not likely, when the old man is smoking his pipe he does not sleep.'

10

THE GALLOWS-TREE

LANDON CAME INTO the room with a towel slung over his shoulder. He felt fine. He had slept well, he was shaved, and he had had his hair trimmed.

The sun shone in through the bedroom window and he felt younger, exhilarated. He threw the towel on the bed he had slept in and stood, bare-chested, in front of the open window, breathing in deeply. There was something rejuvenating about the fresh morning air and the sunshine; today he felt no more than thirty years old, perhaps no more than twenty-five. Here he was, Harvey Landon, a new man, ready to start all over again.

He lifted himself up on his toes and stretched his arms above his head; he swayed rhythmically, first to the left and then to the right. His body felt supple, tough and strong and agile. It was good to be alive.

Pete woke suddenly. He propped himself up on one elbow and stared at Landon.

'You feeling mighty active, Mr Landon?'

Landon bent forward, touching his toes and straightening again. 'Looks like it, Pete. Time you were out of that lousy bed. Unless you don't want breakfast.'

'You bet I want some breakfast. Jus' lead me to it.'

He pushed back the sheet and swung his feet to the floor. He sat up, yawning and stretching himself. Suddenly he stared at Landon's stomach where the old scar tissued showed, rucked and pallid, like a badly welded joint.

'Lord, sir, you got scar there. I never saw that before. What they try to do? Slice you in halves mebbe?'

'Something like that,' Landon said. He had forgotten about the scar. There was no pain in his belly now; the iron was lying low. Some time it might wake up again, but for the present it was leaving him in peace. He began to pull on his shirt. 'I can smell the breakfast, Pete. You'd better get a move on.'

Pete smelt it too. He needed no urging.

They had breakfast in a cool, whitewashed room with a bare stone floor. The table and chairs were plain and solid, built, as everything in Oxaca appeared to be, on a stout-hearted plan to outlast the centuries.

The girl and a plump, black-haired woman who looked all Indian brought in coffee and fried ham and eggs. The girl was in a cotton dress, and it was the first time Landon had seen her not wearing the jeans. Somehow, it made her look more mature; she was a woman now, and there was nothing of the boy left.

She noticed that he was looking at her and coloured. 'I borrowed the dress. It is a little too big.' Her fingers touched the white belt that held the dress in at the middle, confining it to the slender contours of her waist. 'You think it looks silly perhaps.'

'It looks fine,' Landon said. 'I never saw you in a dress before. I like it.'

The girl's colour deepened. She did not look at him. 'I am glad you like it,' she said.

When they had put the food on the table the woman went away and the girl was about to follow her.

Landon said: 'Hey there! Have you had breakfast?'

She paused in the doorway. 'I will eat mine with Mrs Gomez in the kitchen.'

'You will not,' Landon said. 'You ate with us before. You still eat with us. Aren't we good enough for you?'

'Of course, señor. It is I—'

'Then fetch yourself a plate and cup.'

'It is not right—'

'It is right. Do as I tell you.'

She hesitated a moment, then gave in to his wishes. He got up and moved a chair for her.

'Where's Mr Alvarez?' Pete asked.

'Busy,' Landon said. 'He's got a lot of things to work out with Colonel Cainas. You know he means to move on to San Quinton?'

'How far is that?'

'Hundred and twenty miles – as the crow flies.'

'Any road?'

'No road. That's so, isn't it, Anita?'

'Mrs Gomez says it is jungle between here and San Quinton,' the girl answered. 'They will have to cut a way through.'

'Why does Mr Alvarez have to go to San Quinton?' Pete asked. 'What's wrong with staying here? It's comfortable.'

Landon drank coffee. It was good coffee. Mrs Gomez was a good cook. 'El Aguila is not interested in personal comfort. He is interested in revolution. San Quinton is the starting-point. If we had landed him at the correct place the reception committee would have met him and taken him to San Quinton. That was the plan. San Quinton is the real heart of the revolution.' He turned again to the girl for confirmation. 'Isn't that so, Anita?'

'Yes, señor. San Quinton is a big city – bigger than Oxaca. El Aguila's men hold it. It is there they are waiting for him.'

'They aren't waiting for me,' Pete said. 'I think I stay here.'

'I shall go to San Quinton with Alvarez,' Landon said.

Pete looked at him for a few moments, then shook his head and sighed. 'That makes two of us. San Quinton it is.'

The girl said nothing.

Landon and Pete sat on the step outside the house smoking cigarettes made from strong local tobacco. The sun was shining; it was warm, but not too hot for comfort; they were well fed, and in Oxaca everything seemed to be at peace.

They watched people going past in the street, wagons drawn by mules or oxen, one or two horsemen, a woman in a hard black hat driving a pig, some other women with baskets. In the background was the sound of the waterfall, never ceasing.

'Nice place,' Pete said. 'Peaceful.'

There was no motor traffic of any kind, no exhaust fumes polluting the air. Here it was as though one had moved back into the past, into an earlier civilization. It was, as Pete said, peaceful. Landon wondered whether it were too peaceful to be true.

Then he saw the prisoners coming up the street. There were four of them and they were roped together, their hands tied behind their backs. They walked like men who are in the last stages of exhaustion, as though only partly conscious of their surroundings. Six armed horsemen rode with them. When one of the prisoners stumbled and fell a horseman leaned down from the saddle and lashed him about the head and shoulders with a leather whip. The prisoner struggled to his feet and the little group moved on, heading towards the main square, the Plaza Diego Rozas, and the headquarters of Colonel Cainas.

A woman suddenly ran in among the horsemen and spat on the prisoners until she was pushed aside; but for the most part the citizens of Oxaca showed little interest in these captives.

Landon and Pete watched them in silence until they were out of sight.

'What do you think that was?' Pete asked.

'I think it was a posse of horsemen and four prisoners,' Landon answered. 'Have you got any other ideas?'

Pete grinned. 'That's what I think it was too. No business of ours, hey? Just internal trouble.'

'Like the old man's bad stomach.'

'Sure, sure. Like that,' Pete said. 'Nothing to worry you and me.'

Alvarez was sitting at a desk writing. He had had a room cleared for him at Colonel Cainas's headquarters which was to be at his disposal so long as he should stay in Oxaca. Alvarez was in khaki drill trousers and a khaki shirt with a black tie. The dirty bandage had disappeared from his head and had been replaced by strips of sticking-plaster. His damaged ear had been repaired with stitches, but it would never be quite the same again; some of it was lost for ever. He still looked a little drawn and tired, but his eyes were bright and restless. Again it occurred to Landon how well the name of Eagle suited him.

Alvarez put down his pen and looked at Landon.

'It is arranged. We leave for San Quinton on Thursday – in two days' time. It will be a small party – picked men. In that way we shall travel faster, and time is valuable.'

'Only two days? Not much rest.'

119

'There is no time for rest. The hours are precious. I don't think you quite understand even yet what I have to do.'

'You haven't told me.'

Alvarez played with his pen. 'It doesn't matter. I cannot explain to you the whole of our plans. But I can tell this much – it is essential that I should reach San Quinton without further delay. Valdez knows I am in the country; that is a misfortune we could not have foreseen. It forces our hand. Have you decided what you will do? Will you come to San Quinton?'

'I've come so far,' Landon said. 'I may as well see it through to the end. Another thing, I don't like it here. The ground shakes too often and the old man smokes his pipe too much.'

Alvarez smiled faintly. 'I understand that if you live here long enough you become used to such disturbances.'

'I don't want to live here as long as that.'

'Good. So you will come. And Pete?'

'He'll come too.'

'That completes the party. You will be prepared to set out on Thursday.'

Alvarez picked up his pen and pulled some papers towards him. It was the signal for dismissal. He was a busy man these days.

Landon said: 'And Anita? She goes with us too?'

Alvarez answered coldly: 'We cannot take the girl. That is out of the question.'

'She has come with us so far. Why shouldn't she go on for the rest of the way?'

'Because I say it is not possible.'

'If it had not been for her we should probably not have been here now. She wishes to go with us; she has told me so. I think you owe it to her to let her go.'

Alvarez looked at Landon keenly. 'Tell me, what is your interest in this girl? Surely you are not becoming foolish concerning her.'

Landon's jaws tightened. 'What is so foolish in asking that her wishes should be considered? We ought to be sufficiently grateful to her for that. She has lost everything because of us.'

'She is not the only one who has lost everything for a cause. But she is unimportant. She is only a peasant.'

'I thought you were working for the good of what you call –

peasants. Is that how you really regard the people of Anagua – as dirt?'

Alvarez's face was bleak; he spoke stonily. 'We will not discuss the matter further. I have said that the girl shall not go. That is enough.'

Landon stood up. 'Then I shall not go either.'

'As you wish,' Alvarez said.

Above the town, shadowing the afternoon sun, was the smoke from Monte del Fuego. There was no wind to stir it; it was a black column, spreading out as it climbed higher. The sun was a red glow, like blood splashed upon the sky; and the torrent, falling from its lofty perch, was reddened also, as though there too blood had been added to the water.

In the Plaza Diego Rozas men were putting the finishing touches to a raised wooden platform. Above the platform stood four gallows-trees, gaunt, grim, forbidding.

Landon and Pete leaned against the wall of a house on one side of the square, smoking cigarettes and watching.

'Nice-looking piece of work,' Pete said. 'Pretty.'

Landon grunted. 'Not so pretty if you're climbing the scaffold with your hands tied behind your back.'

Pete shifted his weight from one shoulder to the other. The cigarette waggled in his mouth as he talked.

'One thing – they can work fast in this town when they feel like it. They bring prisoners in in the morning. By afternoon they have the gallows up for them. That's not wasting any time.'

'Charged, tried, sentenced, and executed, all in one short day.'

'I don't think they go a lot on trials,' Pete said.

'Maybe they don't go a lot on justice either.'

'Maybe.'

They saw a man leading a donkey and cart across the square. The wheels of the cart clattered on the paving-stones and came to a halt under the shadow of the scaffold and its grove of leafless trees. From the cart the man lifted four coils of rope.

'Everything laid on,' Pete said. 'There's efficiency for you.'

The Plaza Diego Rozas was beginning to fill with people. It was a calm, silent crowd, and its very lack of emotion seemed to make it all the more menacing. The faces of the men and women were stern and sad; it was as though living under the constant threat of the volcano had taken away from them the gift of laughter, had made them cruel, pitiless, hardened to the idea of death.

When the four prisoners appeared there was a low murmur of voices, a slight stirring among the crowd. Half a dozen soldiers armed with rifles cleared a way through and the people moved back obediently. The doomed men walked between the rows of watchers to the scaffold.

Landon and Pete left the wall and began to force their way through the crowd also. Men and women looked at them with curiosity, recognizing them as the two who had come with El Aguila, The Liberator. It was this fact perhaps that commanded respect; men drew aside politely to let them through, as though they had been officials, so that in a short while they were at the foot of the scaffold.

Already the prisoners were on the raised platforms and the nooses were being slipped over their heads and tightened about their throats. Landon looked up at them and saw that they were all young men, one no more than a boy. The boy was shaking; he seemed unable to control his limbs. The other three were impassive, as though the events that were taking place were of no concern to them. They had dark, leathery faces and prominent noses; their black hair shone with grease.

When he felt the rope touch his neck the boy shuddered violently and his head jerked. His lips were moving; he might have been praying. The man on his right said something to him sharply. The boy pressed his lips together, striving to gain control over himself, but the fear was in his eyes. The man on the extreme left stared contemptuously down on the crowd and spat.

Landon caught sight of Alvarez standing with a little group, of whom Colonel Cainas was one. He pressed his way towards them.

Alvarez did not notice Landon until he felt the touch on his arm. He had been staring up at the scaffold, apparently engrossed in his own thoughts.

Landon said hurriedly: 'Why are these men being hanged?'

Alvarez drew his attention away from the scaffold. For a moment or two he simply looked at Landon without answering. Then he said: 'Because they are Valdez's men. Also because they are traitors. Thirdly because they are spies.'

'They have been tried?'

'Tried and sentenced.'

'Quick work. Who was the judge? You?'

Alvarez's eyes were bleak, his voice cold. 'That question does not concern you.'

'I thought justice was the concern of every man.'

'In this case you have no conception of what justice is.'

'So that boy up there has to be hanged. Would it shake the revolution so much if he were to be allowed to live? Would it overthrow all your plans?'

Colonel Cainas had been listening to the exchange of words; he seemed to be faintly amused. He glanced at Landon with a half-mocking smile twisting his lips. Cainas had a sleepy look about him; he had the appearance of being bored by the whole affair.

'You should not let a little business of this kind upset you,' he said. 'It is not important. An example to others, you might say. But of no great importance.'

'Ask the men with ropes round their necks whether they agree with you.'

Alvarez broke in sharply: 'Let us not argue about the matter. I have already said it is no concern of yours.'

Landon stared into Alvarez's eyes. He said softly: 'After Ramirez, Valdez; after Valdez, Alvarez.'

Alvarez's face darkened with anger. 'What did you say?'

'Nothing. Nothing of importance. I was simply thinking aloud.'

'It would be better for you if you thought elsewhere. Do you understand?'

'I understand,' Landon said.

He moved away from Alvarez, away from the scaffold, and the crowd opened to let him pass. When he had gone a dozen yards he heard the boy scream – once – only once.

There was a kind of massed sigh, a sound of pent-up breath being released from a thousand throats.

Landon did not look back.

*

At sundown the four bodies were still swinging from the gibbets.

'They will be cut down tomorrow and buried,' Mrs Gomez explained. 'It is the custom.'

'This happens often?' Landon asked.

'Not often, no. But it happens.'

Mrs Gomez appeared unmoved by the execution, as though it was, as Cainas had said, of no great importance, a small matter that had to be attended to and then forgotten.

When Landon went along to the Plaza Diego Rozas people were going about their normal business, scarcely troubling to turn their heads towards the grim trees with their dead fruit. To them also it appeared to be a matter of no importance.

Landon turned away from the scaffold. He did not understand these people. Were they callous or were they too elemental to pay any homage to the idea of death? Perhaps, living in Oxaca, you had to be like that.

On the way back to the house he met the girl. He thought with what grace she walked; there was something almost regal about her bearing. And yet Alvarez had called her a peasant. It showed how very blind a man like Alvarez could be.

'Well, Anita,' he said. 'What do you think of Oxaca now that you've seen a little of it?'

'It is well enough, señor.'

He took her arm and turned her about so that they were walking side by side.

'Not señor. It's time we abandoned the formality. My name is Harvey, as I told you. You'd better call me that.'

'But señor—'

'Not señor, just Harvey. It's easy enough to say, isn't it?'

He grinned at her, and she smiled back, a little uncertainly, as though she were still shy of him.

'I think so. It is not a difficult name.'

'Say it then.'

'If you wish. Harvey.'

He laughed. 'You see. It can be done. Remember it.'

'I will remember,' she said. 'Always.'

Darkness was coming quickly. The outlines of the houses were becoming blurred and shadowy.

'So you think Oxaca is well enough,' Landon said. 'No more than that?'

'There are things here that I do not like,' the girl said. 'But there are bad things everywhere. Is that not so?'

'Everywhere.'

He did not ask her what in Oxaca she did not like. Perhaps there was no need to ask, since these were the things that he hated also.

He turned to look at her and saw that her hair had taken on a reddish tinge; and then he saw that the redness was on her face also, and on the dress she was wearing and on her hands; on his own hands too.

It was the reflection of a red glow in the sky, a fiery, menacing red. He thought at first that it was the setting sun, but the sun had already gone down and this glow did not come from the west.

'It is the mountain,' the girl said. 'Look! It is the Mountain of Fire.'

It was like a beacon lighting up the sky with its baleful glare. It towered above them, above the waterfall with its everlasting thunder, above every living creature in Oxaca. It was the fire in the sky that was perhaps a warning of things to come.

'I do not like it,' the girl said. 'It frightens me, that mountain.'

She shrank closer to Landon like a child seeking comfort and protection. He put an arm round her shoulders and felt her tremble a little.

'There is nothing to fear,' he said. 'Nothing at all.'

Yet he did not believe his own words, and he did not think that the girl believed them either. He thought that there was indeed much to fear. It might have been imagination, but he seemed to feel the ground tremble underneath his feet.

11

MOUNTAIN OF FIRE

IT WAS THE shaking of the bed that woke Landon. He awoke to darkness and a low rumbling. He heard Pete's voice, tense, urgent.

'You awake, Mr Landon?'

'I'm awake,' he said.

'What you say this is? Damn' earthquake again?'

Something fell to the floor and broke. Then the vibration ceased abruptly and there was a strange, uneasy silence, as though the house, the whole city, were waiting for the next blow to fall.

'I'm getting up,' Landon said. He knew it would be impossible to go to sleep again. He had not yet become sufficiently hardened to earth tremors.

'Me too,' Pete said. 'I don't like this, not one bit, I don't.'

They dressed quickly by the light of a candle and were ready when the next tremor came. It was more violent than the first; the floor seemed to lift, the walls to tremble.

Landon looked up at the ceiling. He saw a crack suddenly open up and zigzag across the plaster. A lump fell down, just missing Pete and throwing up a cloud of dust. The noise was louder; they had to shout to make themselves heard. It was like a continuous roll of thunder, but it seemed to come not from the air but from the ground.

'Time to get out of here,' Landon shouted. 'I'm going to find Anita.'

He took the flickering candle and went out of the room with Pete following. For a second time the rumbling and the shaking died away, but this time the silence was broken by the sound of voices, in the house and outside. There was a note of alarm in the air.

Landon shouted: 'Anita! Are you there?' And almost immediately she was beside him. He could see by the light of the candle that she had put on the shirt and the blue jeans that she had worn on the journey to Oxaca.

She put a hand on his arm. 'You think this is something very bad? You think there is danger?'

'I don't know,' Landon said. 'I haven't had enough experience of these things. But I'd feel safer outside – much safer.'

Mrs Gomez appeared, a strange-looking apparition in the candlelight.

Landon said to her: 'That was a bad shaking. Was it normal? Have you had it like that before?'

'We have had shakings, yes,' Mrs Gomez said. 'But not so much noise. The noise I do not like. But it will be all right. No danger.'

The last words were spoken without any real conviction. It was obvious that even Mrs Gomez, who had lived in Oxaca all her life, was just a little bit alarmed; perhaps more than just a little. She too had a candle in her hand. She put her head on one side, listening.

'You see, it is over now. Nothing more. You can go back to bed.'

'Are you going back to bed?' Landon asked.

She answered hesitantly: 'I? In a little while. Very soon. I am not sleepy.'

'I'm not sleepy either. I think I'll take a walk outside. Are you coming, Anita?'

And then it came a third time, and it was like an explosion. Something heavy crashed to the floor just as they stepped out of the house. Until this moment the air had been still and breathless. Now a sudden gust of wind, so hot that it might have passed over a hearth of glowing coal, swept down the street and extinguished the flame of the candle.

Landon dropped the useless candle, but there was still a light in the city; it came from the volcano, and it was a gloomy, baleful light. The mountain was like a torch; there was a black stem reaching up into the sky, and from this stem branches of fire sprouted out and fell in glittering cascades.

'The mountain is burning,' Mrs Gomez cried. 'It is burning. Oh, Holy Mother of Christ, it is on fire.' Her voice broke and quavered.

Some men went past down the street, running. Landon wondered where they were going. He wondered whether they themselves knew. Perhaps they were just running because they felt a compulsion to do so. Perhaps soon everybody would be running.

Landon, the girl, Mrs Gomez, and Pete did not run; they stood in a little group staring up at the red glow in the sky, at the sprouting tree of flame that had grown like a genie out of the crater of the volcano.

'I never saw a volcano go off pop before,' Pete said musingly. 'It's pretty. But I wouldn't care if I wasn't seeing it. No, sir. I'd like to be a thousand miles away from this place.'

Landon questioned Mrs Gomez again, for hers was the voice of experience. She knew Oxaca and Monte del Fuego, had known them for many years.

'Have you seen it like this before?'

'Never,' Mrs Gomez said, and she shook her head so violently that the circles of fat round her neck seemed to vibrate. 'Some smoke there has often been, but not fire such as this. I have never seen these flames coming out of the mountain.'

More people ran past down the street, the patter of their feet inaudible, so that they might have been ghosts or shadows flitting past.

'I think we oughta go too,' Pete said uneasily.

'Go where?'

Pete shuffled his feet. 'I don't know. Somewhere.'

Landon was about to answer when the fourth tremor occurred. It made him dumb. The subterranean rumbling was a fearful sound. Again the earth shook, and a house not far away suddenly collapsed, hurling great blocks of stone into the street. In the distance they could hear other buildings that had stood for centuries capitulating at last, falling before this latest onslaught.

Landon pulled the girl away from the buildings, out into the middle of the street. It was safer there. At any moment a wall might fall on them.

But again the tremor passed and again there was silence except for the constant rushing of the waterfall and another sound that was like distant and spasmodic gunfire.

'Let's go now,' Pete said urgently. 'Time we got away.'

Landon thought Pete might be right. It might be better to get out of the town, away from the danger of falling masonry. 'Yes,' he said. 'Let's go.'

He clasped the girl's hand and felt it tremble in his own. Some more men and women and a number of scared children hurried past; one of the women was carrying a baby and the baby was crying. Some of the men shouted savagely, revealing their terror. One, running blindly with head lowered, crashed into Landon; Pete put a hand on his shoulders and threw him aside as if he had been a doll.

'We better go, Mr Landon. We better go.'

Landon spoke to Mrs Gomez. 'You will come with us? It isn't safe here.'

Mrs Gomez hesitated. She looked back at her house, which was still standing, the red glare of the fiery mountain illuminating it dully, as if putting the mark of blood upon it. Finally she shook her head.

'No, I will not leave the house. This is my home.'

'You must please yourself,' Landon said. 'We are going now.'

He tugged at the girl's hand and they began to run. Pete ran beside them, moving easily with a long, loping stride. Above them the mountain exploded in sudden gusts of anger, and the sounds of that anger rolled across the city, threatening it with destruction.

There were many people in the streets. They seemed bewildered, not knowing what to do. Some ran one way, some another; many were crying out the names of relations or friends, searching vainly in the red half-darkness of the night. Others merely stood as though petrified, waiting for the next blow to fall.

In many places the streets were partly blocked by fallen stone, and in the dull, baleful light it was necessary to pick one's way carefully. Occasionally the ground trembled, but not so violently as it had done before; and here and there were cracks in the road surface that varied in width from a mere inch or two to a yard and more, their depth impossible to gauge.

Landon kept the girl close to him, and Pete protected her on the other side. Landon was glad to have Pete with him.

'We'll make for the higher ground,' he shouted.

He heard Pete answer briefly: 'Okay,' and they ran on with the volcano above them still sending up its cascades of fire, and the explosions coming in faster and faster succession.

The air was hot and sulphurous; it bit into the throat and breathing became painful. The girl stumbled suddenly and nearly fell. Landon peered at her anxiously.

'Are you all right, Anita? Can you go on?'

She answered at once: 'Yes, I can go on.'

Then the ash began to fall, lightly at first, like thin dust, like a dry, hot rain, silent and choking. As they went on the ash spread a soft carpet under their feet, deadening the sound of their footsteps.

At last they were away from the houses and the air seemed a little clearer, though it was still hot, still ash-laden. They paused for a moment and looked back at the city, but it was no more than a vague, sprawling mass with nothing clearly visible, nothing solidly drawn, so that it was quite impossible to tell how many of the buildings had fallen to the ground and how many were yet standing. At one point a fire was burning, thrusting a flickering column of flame into the sky; but it was a small pale candle compared with the fire that leaped like an angry demon from the crater of the volcano.

Pete said hoarsely: 'Let's be moving on. Don't seem too good hereabouts. Ain't healthy.'

There was a trickle of people coming out of the city. Soon the trickle might grow to a flood. It would be wise not to be caught in that flood of terror-stricken humanity.

But as they started forward again the final devastating shock occurred, the one for which the others seemed to have been mere heralds. The ground seemed to rock and sway with the ferocity of it, and all three of them were flung down as if by a sudden blow. Half-stunned, choked and blinded by the dust, their ears were deafened by the rumbling thunder that came up through the earth's crust, the stable that had become unstable, the solid that was no more solid but a shuddering, cracking skin stretched over a boiling cauldron that was casting up smoke and gas and fire and ash.

So they waited while the earth shook, and as they lay there they heard the last great clap of thunder that was the bursting open of the dam above the town, the great rock wall that held the lake in check. And when the rumbling of the earthquake had died away there was this other sound, fearsome as any of those which had preceded it, as terrible and awe-inspiring. It was the sound of thousands of tons of water rolling down from its lofty perch in a great and rushing wave that was to overwhelm and devour the city.

It was the girl who realized it first. She pointed upward. 'The wall! The wall is broken and the lake is coming down!'

Landon jumped to his feet and saw the glare of the volcano reflected on the water. He had no means of telling how wide the gap was that had been torn in the rocky wall or how much of the lake would be drained. He knew only that a vast and ever-increasing torrent was flowing down into the valley where the city lay with no defence against this rising and encroaching flood.

He gripped the girl's arm and yelled at her: 'Run now! Run for your life!'

They went across the cultivated ground, stumbling, staggering, sometimes falling, but always struggling up again and pressing desperately on towards the safety of the higher ground, where the terraced fields hung on the sides of the valley.

As they ran the ash still fell and the sulphurous air burned their lungs until the fire seemed to be raging within them, devouring all that was inside their bodies, so that soon they would be nothing more than hollow, burnt-out shells, dead, dry cages of skin and bone that would lie in the dust and would themselves at last crumble away into dust also.

Behind them the water came like a tide. Glancing back they could see a line of white where the foam was carried high on the shoulders of the advancing flood. It struck the houses at the edge of the city and was broken by them but not stopped. It came on with irresistible momentum, swirling through the earthquake-ravaged streets and bursting in at windows and doorways.

'Higher,' Landon croaked. 'Higher yet.'

He pulled the girl with him and went on, Pete staying with them, keeping close behind. The way became steeper, a track leading up between the terraces, winding, snake-like.

The sound of the torrent rushing down the valley was like waves tumbling on a rocky shore; it was a monster swallowing up all that stood in its path. One by one the houses were engulfed and the tide spread out over the fields and grassland, reaching from one side of the valley to the other, a great expanse of turbulent, scum-covered water, with bits of flotsam riding upon its surface – uprooted trees, furniture, empty barrels, dead dogs, planks of wood, men. And still more thundered down from the precipice, churning a great cauldron of foam where its fall was broken so many hundreds of feet below.

Landon and Pete and the girl struggled on, but the way became increasingly difficult, for the earthquake had shaken many of the terraced fields away from the valley wall, breaking them loose until they fell in cascades of unstable, shifting earth. In these landslips the three fugitives from destruction became bogged down, their feet sinking into the broken soil and slipping backwards almost as fast as they tried to draw themselves up.

Inexorably the water pursued them, creeping up the sides of the valley, unhindered by landslide or fallen tree or broken rock. Here the water was silent, but for a low gurgling as it sucked at the earth and turned it to mud, loosening it and dragging it down. As in a nightmare, they tried to run and their feet were clogged; it was like treading through a vast tank of glue; they were like flies dragging their sticky feet across an endless expanse of fly-paper.

And at the same time they were being choked by the hot breath of the volcano and the falling ash. It was a fearful, weary journey that seemed to have no end.

The girl was the first to crack. She stumbled, tried to get up, and failed. Landon reached down to help her and felt the water close over his hand. It was an icy touch contrasting violently with the heat of the air. He yelled to Pete to help him, and his voice cracked, as though it had become scorched and shrivelled.

He heard Pete's voice: 'Okay, okay. I'm here.'

One on either side of her, they lifted the girl as the water crept up their legs and the earth turned to slime beneath them. They dragged her a little way, and suddenly the ground seemed to be swallowed up and they were in the water with nothing solid under their feet, with the icy grip of the flood about them, pressing in upon their ribs and forcing the breath out of their bodies.

Landon could feel the pull of the current. He began to tread water, looking for the girl. He saw her head bobbing above the surface, and he swam to her. She did not need his help now. The shock of the water had revived her and she was a good swimmer. Having lived so long on the edge of the sea, she had had plenty of opportunities to practise the art.

Landon shouted: 'Keep close to me.'

He struck out towards the water's edge, but already the flood had risen higher and they were now a good thirty yards from the shore with the current running strongly. Landon felt his whole body freezing in the grip of the ice-cold water and he could no longer see where it ended and the land began.

He was beginning to weaken; his arms and legs were leaden weights scarcely moving in obedience to his will. He wondered vaguely where the girl was; he became worried about her. He could not see her any longer; he could see nothing; he had lost his bearings and could not tell which was the right direction. It did not matter greatly, since he no longer seemed to have any power to swim. His legs dropped and his head went under.

The hazy idea occurred to him that this must be the end of everything for Harvey Landon, the end of the long, long struggle, the long, losing game of life. And he did not care. When it came to it at the last it was easy to let go, to relax one's hold and just slide over the edge into oblivion. There was really nothing to it, nothing at all. It was dead easy.

But then it was not so easy after all, because he came to the surface and his hand touched something hard and unyielding. Instinctively he gripped it and his head cleared and he realized that he still wanted to live, wanted to more than anything else because, whatever its drawbacks, life was still very sweet and preferable to that dark, unknown world beyond the grave.

He saw now that he was clinging to one of the upper branches of a tree, one that had not been uprooted by the earthquake and still had its head above the flood. And soon another fact became apparent to him: the water was no longer rising; the branch to which he was clinging stayed above the surface and was not engulfed.

Suddenly he thought of the girl. He began to shout her name, not realizing that the shout was scarcely more than a whisper.

And then he saw in the red glare of the volcanic torch that

miraculously she was still close to him, had in fact been near all the time. She too was clinging to a branch of the tree. He saw her face turned towards him, and the relief that she felt was evident in her voice.

'Harvey ! I thought you were lost.'

'Two of us thought the same thing,' he said. But he did not think she heard him.

He looked for Pete, but could not see him. He moved along the branch, bringing himself nearer to the girl.

'Do you know where Pete is?'

'No. I did not see him go.'

'Perhaps he got to the shore. He's a strong boy, a good swimmer.'

'The water has stopped rising,' the girl said.

'Yes, I noticed that too.'

He stared across the surface of the water, trying to discover the outline of the shore. He thought he could detect it, maybe forty yards away.

He spoke to the girl. 'We'd better try to reach land. No use hanging on here. Do you think you can do it?'

'I am sure,' the girl said simply. 'You need not be afraid for me.'

It occurred to Landon that perhaps she felt he was the one whose powers were to be doubted. The thought nettled him; it put him on his mettle. He would not be shown up by a girl.

'Let's be on our way,' he said, and let go of the branch.

It was a long forty yards. There was a current flowing and their clothes hampered them, but Landon had recovered much of his strength, and in the end it was the girl who tired and he who had to help her over the last few yards of the swim.

And then he was dragging her up out of the water on to the higher ground, where the ash now lay inches deep, and they no longer had the flood to contend with, only the hot, sulphur-laden air and the falling ash, falling without sound and without cessation.

The girl lay on the ground with her wet clothes clinging tightly to her body, revealing the outline of her small, firm breasts. Landon kneeled down and put an arm about her shoulders and drew her to him and kissed her. As she clung to him he could feel the shuddering that went through her, and he kissed her again and knew that she was weeping. It was the reaction, he thought, just the reaction.

'Don't weep,' he said. 'Don't weep, my dearest.'

12

REFUGE

LANDON HEARD PETE shouting. He stood up and helped the girl to her feet. Pete appeared like a black shade.

'That you, Mr Landon? Lord, am I glad to see you! I thought you was gone, sure did.'

He came up and touched Landon's arm as if to make sure that this was truly flesh and blood, a solid man and no ghost risen from the dead.

'I been looking everywhere. I didn't see where you went when that water come up. You all right?'

'I'm all right,' Landon said. 'Anita is too.'

'I'm glad about that – real glad.'

Some object flashed out of the murky sky and fell into the water with a hissing splash.

'I think we better shift,' Pete said. 'It's rocks now. That mountain don't mean to give us a hell of a lot of rest. No, sir.'

They moved off on a slanting course, climbed away from the gurgling flood water and at the same time heading off to the left to put as much distance as possible between themselves and the volcano which still sprouted its black tree with the fiery branches. Here and there they encountered other men, but not many. Pete tripped over a body, but the body did not move, and they went on.

Landon thought suddenly of the four spies hanging from their scaffold in the Plaza Diego Rozas. No one would cut them down in the morning. Perhaps they had already floated away with the scaffold and the gibbets. Certainly they had not been the only ones to die. Perhaps they were laughing now.

As they went on it seemed to grow darker. The ash fell so thickly that they were scarcely able to breathe. They were menaced too by the falling stones; many of them, still red hot, fell like meteors, whistling down from the sky and striking the ground in sudden showers of sparks.

In the thickening darkness they began to lose all sense of direction; they climbed instinctively, keeping together, fearing to be left alone in such a world of horror. If they were to die they did not wish to die alone, deserted on the ravaged slopes of the valley.

It was a journey that by its very nature must seem interminable. The ash, for ever deepening and shifting under their feet, was a brake on their progress; its bitter sulphurous taste was on their tongues and in their throats; it stung their nostrils and brought tears to their eyes; it seemed to go into them and shrivel the substance of their very lungs. They had been frozen by the flood water, but now they were sweating again in this heated air; the sweat ran down their faces and ash clung to their sweaty skins until Landon and the girl were as dark as Pete. And still they struggled on, even though they had lost all hope, even though it might have been easier to give in, simply to lie down, and smother their burning faces in the dust.

It was Pete who saw the torch first. He grabbed Landon's arm and pointed, as though not trusting his voice, or perhaps having no breath left for the luxury of speech.

The light showed faintly through the gloom. It wavered from side to side like a lamp swinging from a chain; but it did not go out.

Landon croaked one word: 'Come.' And they went towards the light as men have been known to follow a will-o'-the-wisp. But this was no misleading spirit beckoning them to disaster, and it was nearer than they had supposed, the appearance of distance having been the effect of the dust-laden air. In fact it was not a lamp but a flaming torch that a man was waving rhythmically to and fro, a torch to light them a way to safety.

He was standing on a ledge to which some steps roughly hewn out of the rock led upward, and he was wearing a steel helmet to protect his head from falling stones. When he saw Landon and Pete and the girl he shouted to them to come up to the ledge.

'Quickly, quickly! There is no time to lose.'

He pointed with the torch to the rough steps, showing them the way. The girl was exhausted and could not climb. Landon and Pete supported her, one on her left side and one on her right. Together they went up the steps, not quickly as the torch-bearer had urged them to do, but slowly, as men who are calling upon the last dregs of their stamina.

The man with the torch leaned down and helped them up the last two steps.

'Follow me,' he said.

He turned and led the way along the ledge, and the others followed him, Landon and Pete still carrying the girl.

Their guide seemed to lean upon the rocky wall that rose in a dark mass from the ledge, and then a broad beam of light came out from the hillside, and they saw that a massive iron door had swung inward to reveal a cavern hollowed out of the solid rock.

For a moment they hesitated, stunned into immobility by this totally unexpected sight. But the guide shouted impatiently: 'Quickly, quickly! This way!' So they followed him in and he swung the great door shut with a hollow clang.

Immediately it became easier to breathe. The air inside the cavern was cool and dustless. It had a stale, musty odour, but they were past caring about a small defect of that sort. To Landon it tasted as good as any air he had ever breathed, and he sucked it down into his lungs with thankfulness.

Where they were standing the cavern was like a narrow tunnel, the roof no more than eight feet high at the apex. Here and there hung oil-lamps that gave out a soft yellow light. Beyond this light the tunnel curved away into the depths of the mountain; it was like an outsize rabbit hole scraped out of the rock.

Landon turned to look at the guide and saw that he was a short, stocky man with a hard, expressionless face. He was also an impatient man. With a quick jerk of the hand he signed them to follow him and set off down the tunnel at a pace which they, with the girl to support, could not hope to equal.

But there was not far to go. The tunnel bent sharply to the right and then they found themselves in a vast chamber roughly circular in shape with a roof at least twenty feet high from which lamps hung on long chains. Here were gathered men, women, and a few, very few, children.

'My, my!' Pete said.

Landon saw Alvarez almost immediately. He was standing with Colonel Cainas, and the amazing thing was that neither man had any marks on himself or his clothing to indicate that he had been through any such disaster as earthquake or flood or volcanic eruption. There were a few others also who appeared to have escaped completely unscathed, but the rest of the people were in a similar condition to that of Landon and his companions, covered with dirt, drenched with water, ragged, exhausted. Some lay on the floor, others sat with their knees drawn up to their chins just staring in front of them in a dazed, unseeing way. Some of the women were weeping; the children looked bewildered and frightened; they clung to the women for comfort and protection.

Alvarez detached himself from the small group of army officers and walked to meet the newcomers. He seemed shocked by their appearance. It was as though, despite the presence of others in like condition, it had yet required the coming of these three who had accompanied him on the long and difficult journey from the coast to bring home to him the full magnitude of the disaster that had struck Oxaca.

'I feared that you were lost,' he said. 'It is a miracle that you have come through alive. I fear the death-roll will be very heavy.'

He spoke to the man with the torch. 'How is it outside, Alonzo?'

The man answered hoarsely: 'Worse, señor. There is much ash falling; rocks also. It is very bad.'

'Go back to your post. There may be others yet.'

'I will go,' the man said. 'But I do not think there will be others.'

He went away, carrying the flaring torch in his right hand.

Alvarez asked: 'Is the water still rising?'

'No,' Landon said. 'It seems to have reached the limit.'

'That is something to be thankful for.'

'It has done its work,' Landon said. 'There is no need for it to rise higher.'

The girl had recovered in the cool air of the cavern; she was able to stand without help.

'You are all right now?' Landon asked.

'Yes – now. I am sorry I caused you so much trouble.'

'Forget it,' Landon said.

He gazed round him and saw what appeared to be bunks lining the rock walls; it was as though this were a vast dormitory or barrack-room. He wondered why people should be lying on the ground when there were bunks available, and he put this question to Alvarez.

Alvarez gave a strange smile. 'Come with me,' he said. 'We will look at these beds.'

Landon went with him, and when they had approached closer to the wall on one side of the cavern he saw that these supposed bunks were in fact rows and rows of shelves stretching up to the very roof. They would have been suitable for the storage of fruit or vegetables, but this was not the purpose for which they were being used.

'Would you care to sleep on one of these?' Alvarez asked. 'It would perhaps be possible to make room.'

There was not much light shining on the shelves, but there was enough to reveal their gruesome burdens. On each shelf, naked and grinning, lay the skeleton of a human being.

'The dead of Oxaca,' Alvarez said. 'In the old days they were buried here. The custom has died out, but no one disturbs these bones.'

'I see.'

They turned away from the grim bunks whose occupants would never awaken, and Alvarez said: 'You are perhaps wondering how I escaped.'

'I am surprised to see you so unmarked. Your clothes are not even dirty.' He looked down at his own drenched and muddy clothing contrasting so sharply with Alvarez's immaculate appearance. 'It seems you haven't been touched by the flood. You must have got away in good time. Did you guess it was coming?'

'No, I did not guess. No one could have foreseen such a disaster. But I was already here with Cainas and a few others – on business. You see, my friend, this is not only a burial chamber. At the far end, as you can see, there is a door. Beyond that doorway is a storehouse.'

'What kind of a storehouse?'

'In fact, a magazine. Arms and ammunition.'

'I begin to understand.'

'It would be difficult to find a safer place.'

'Even with the volcano erupting?'

Alvarez smiled faintly. 'I must confess that there were moments when I had fears for our safety up here. Fortunately this cavern seems to have been out of the line of the main tremors. We had a little shaking, but nothing serious.'

'What do you intend to do?'

'My plans have not been altered. I shall go to San Quinton as arranged.'

'And Oxaca?'

'Oxaca is finished. It was not in any case of any great strategical importance. It was too isolated.'

'And is that all it means to you? The destruction of a town that had no great strategical importance. Does the tragedy, the loss of life, mean nothing?'

Alvarez spoke coldly. 'Naturally it means something to me. No one could be unmoved by so much suffering. But you must understand, my dear Landon, that I have a greater purpose, and the fate of one small city cannot be weighed against the fate of the whole country. Nor would any number of tears that I might shed be of any help to those who have died. It is to the living that my own life must be dedicated. It is they who cry out under oppression. The dead of Oxaca have no more troubles than these skeletons.' He pointed to the shelves. 'It is no good casting our gaze behind us; we must look forward to the future.'

Landon stared at the lean, hard face of The Liberator, wondering just what it was that drove such men as this. Alvarez had no doubts about the justice of his own cause; he could not afford to have doubts. And each setback that he encountered served only to harden his will, to strengthen his determination. In order to achieve his aims, pity, love, and indeed all human emotions must be subordinated to the one overruling purpose.

'As soon as it is possible to do so,' Alvarez said, 'I must press on to San Quinton. Already far too much time has been lost.'

'What puzzles me,' Landon said, 'is why you ever left the country. Surely the leader's place was here – in Anagua.'

Alvarez answered with his thin-lipped smile: 'Some one had to deal with Cranefield. Successful revolutions are rarely completed without some help from outside. It is necessary to have arms. And men like Cranefield do not deal with subordinates. You understand?'

'I understand. I wonder whether Cranefield is going to burn his fingers.'

'I don't think so. I think Mr Cranefield will do well enough out of the business.'

'We shall see about that,' Landon said.

He watched Alvarez move away to rejoin Colonel Cainas and the small military group who stood aloof from the rest, not mixing with the dirty and bedraggled survivors.

The girl was sitting on the floor, and Landon noticed that she had wiped the grime from her face and had pushed back her hair.

'You're looking better,' he said.

'I feel better, much better. I must thank you for helping me.'

'Nonsense.' He sat down beside her, thankful to rest his legs. 'It looked at one time as if you would have to rescue me. I thought I was going to drown.'

'I am glad you did not,' she said simply.

He laughed. 'Well, if it comes to the point I'm pretty glad about it too.'

She looked down at the ground as though shy of meeting his gaze. Perhaps she was remembering how he had kissed her, and was unsure of herself. Landon watched her, noting her confusion and guessing the cause. He saw that she had a small scratch on her left cheek, but no other apparent harm.

He said: 'I don't think I want to die just yet.'

'You must not speak of dying,' the girl said earnestly. 'You must not die.'

'We all have to some day.'

'But not yet. Not for a long while.'

He spoke lightly, making a joke of it. 'If you say so, Anita. It's an order. No dying for another forty years.'

'You are laughing at me,' she said. 'You should not do that.'

Pete drifted towards them with his loose-limbed, rolling walk. He looked as strong as ever, the long-bladed knife still in the sheath hanging from his belt. Whatever happened, the knife went with him.

'I been looking at the boneyard. Nice place this. Nice class of lodgers.'

'They don't trouble anybody,' Landon said. 'They're quiet.'

Pete chuckled softly. 'Quiet as the grave. They got through troubling other people a long, long time ago. You ask Mr Alvarez what he means to do now?'

'He's going on to San Quinton just as he planned to do. Nothing stops El Aguila. In fact, when you come to think about it that's about the only course open to him now. No point in staying here.'

'No point at all. You going with him?'

'He didn't mention it, but at a rough guess I'd say we'll all be going.'

'Can't be too soon for me. I've known better health resorts than this one.'

The man with the torch came out of the tunnel half-carrying, half-dragging a woman. She was almost completely naked, and her whole body was caked with mud. There was a gaping wound in her left side from which the blood was running, mingling with the dirt. She was practically unconscious from exhaustion, her head lolling forward, her eyes blank.

The girl got up and ran to help. Another woman brought a blanket. Together they did what they could for this poor creature, but all their efforts were to prove in vain. Soon after she had reached sanctuary the woman died.

After that no more men or women came past the iron door to safety. Landon counted the survivors and made the number forty-five. If there were more they had not come this way. For himself, he did not believe that there were any others.

13

PATH THROUGH THE JUNGLE

OXACA WAS DEAD and the mountain was silent. The flood had receded, leaving its scum and its wreckage on the sides of the valley, but much of the city still lay drowned under twenty feet of water.

In the higher parts houses, or the rubble that had once been houses, stood up like rocks thrusting their heads above the surface of the sea. The water swirled and eddied past them, flowing along the once-busy streets, where now only dead men lay waiting to rise again with the buoyancy of putrefaction and float away down-river.

It was a grotesque, appalling scene. Here a corpse hung upside down in the branches of a tree where the flood had tangled it before dropping away; here a cart was half immersed in mud, its shafts thrusting upward to the sky as if in supplication; here a terraced field had collapsed into a long black streak stretching like a horse's flaring tail down the littered hillside; and here the legs of a man were visible sticking out of the sludge as in some grim painting by an artist of the macabre surrealist school.

Over all the land the grey ash of the volcano lay thickly, blurring the outline; and still there was the constant roar of the waterfall as it tumbled from the breached wall of the lake far above the drowned city. For the lake had not been completely emptied, and now that its level had dropped it was flowing out through the narrow part of the breach, so that the torrent had shrunk again to its original size.

Soon the level of the water in the town would drop still lower, and one by one the buildings and other objects that were still submerged would reappear. But there would be no life in Oxaca, no life ever again; for the few who had survived were moving out; they were going with Alvarez. They would leave the dead behind them, the dead city and the dead people, and they would hack a way through the jungle to the new life and the new hope of San Quinton, one hundred and twenty miles away to the south.

It had not been Alvarez's plan. Left to his own choice, he would have taken a handful of picked men and would have pressed on rapidly with that small party. It was Colonel Cainas who stood out against him and insisted that all should go. He stood on the hillside and pointed down at the scene of utter desolation.

'There is nothing here, nothing but bitter memory and putrefaction and disease. There are not enough left to cleanse and rebuild Oxaca even when the floods have gone. Oxaca will never live again. All that is left here is death, and we cannot leave these people to that.'

'Time is precious,' Alvarez objected. 'The women and children will hold us back.'

'There are ten women and only two children still living,' Cainas said. 'It would not be human to leave them. We must all go together.'

Landon, standing beside these two men, saw Alvarez make a gesture of impatience. He was eager to press on without delay, to get to San Quinton, and from San Quinton to go forward to the next point on his march towards the liberation of Anagua. Yet one thing after another seemed to be holding him back: acts of man, acts of God, all combined to impede his progress.

Cainas went on persuasively: 'The larger party may be no slower than the small one. It is, after all, not so very large. At best it will be a difficult journey. At worst – who knows? I think there are some of us who will never reach San Quinton.'

'I shall do so,' Alvarez said.

Cainas gave him a quizzical look. 'I hope so.'

'If I fail, all fails. Therefore, I must not fail. I shall reach San Quinton.'

Cainas nodded. 'So be it.'

Landon went to find the girl. 'We are all going to San Quinton. It has been decided. What we do when we get there remains to be seen.'

'If we get there.'

'We shall do that,' Landon said.

'It will not be easy.'

'Anything is possible to a determined man – or woman.'

The girl shivered suddenly. 'I shall be glad to leave this place. It seems evil.'

There was a shadow lying upon them; it was the black column of smoke rising from the silent mountain; it had come between them and the sun. The cloud rose from the cone of the volcano like an evil spirit. It seemed to gloat over the devastated city.

Landon thought again of the four prisoners who had been hanged in the Plaza Diego Rozas. Perhaps they had laid a curse upon Oxaca. He dismissed the idea as foolishness. Those victims had not affected the issue. Oxaca had been doomed even before they had arrived.

Nevertheless, he too would be thankful to leave this scene of death and desolation.

He said: 'What will you do in San Quinton, Anita?'

She answered frankly: 'I do not know. I suppose there will be something.'

For both of them, Landon thought, for himself and the girl the future was uncertain. They would go with Alvarez to San Quinton; and after that, what? There was the great question-mark lying upon their lives.

He echoed her words. 'There will be something.'

They came down from the high ground to the tropical rain forest where the air was humid and stifling in the shadow of the trees and creepers. They came with what food they had been able to salvage, with a few blankets, and some pitiful bundles of clothing. They carried machetes for cutting their way through dense undergrowth, and the men had small-arms – sub-machineguns or revolvers. But they did not take a great quantity of ammunition, for ammunition is heavy and there were no pack animals to carry the load.

'It is unlikely that we shall encounter any of Valdez's men,' Cainas said. 'Only at the river is it at all probable, but the risk is slight.'

It was the river that worried Alvarez, the Rio Chico, stretching its black and shining body between them and San Quinton, barring the way. Somehow they would have to cross the river, and sometimes Valdez sent motor-launches or gun-boats up the Chico, and sometimes these patrols would massacre a village to show that Valdez was master in his own country. But the patrols did not venture far from the river, being fearful of the dark recesses of the forest and the primitive and hostile people who lived there.

It was the children who died first, the boy and the girl. After that the mother of the boy showed no will to live either. She would have stayed with the five-year-old body of her child, but the others would not allow her to do so. They could not persuade her to come willingly; therefore they had to resort to force – for the woman's own good. But the woman outwitted them, for she slipped away into the jungle during the night, and they did not see her again.

The girl had no mother. Her father mourned for her briefly, but he went on with the rest.

There were others also who died, and some who had to be helped forward – ones who were weak or who had suffered injury in Oxaca. These weaker ones delayed the whole party; the strong and vigorous men who could have forged ahead were kept back by the necessity of holding the group together. Alvarez fumed with impatience, but was helpless; and the survivors pressed forward slowly through the damp, oppressive heat of the forest.

It was hard going. Often they gained only a few yards in an hour; sometimes they were forced to make wide detours round a swamp or flooded ground; and always Alvarez was moving back and forth, urging them to go faster, filled with a feverish energy that never abated.

The food dwindled, the rain came, and the green walls of the forest prisoned them in a tiny, sweating world that had no sky and no horizon, only a deep engulfing shadow and a smell of rottenness and decay.

When he was not taking his turn with a machete Landon stayed close to the girl. After the children and the mother and another woman and two men had died he watched her anxiously, looking for any sign of weakness. But the girl seemed strong and always returned the same answer to his questions about her health.

'I am well, thank you.'

He never ceased to be amazed at the reserves of stamina in her slender body.

*

There were thirty-eight of them left when they came to the Rio Chico, and there was no more food.

There was no clearly defined bank to the river, for the rains had swollen it. The trees grew close in upon it and the water had risen to flood the ground around them. The trees stood knee-deep in water with great roots arched above the surface. And beyond the trees the river ran, dark and silent and turbid, three hundred yards in width, three hundred yards of swiftly flowing, alligator-infested water that had to be crossed if they were to reach San Quinton, if they were not to die here of hunger and privation and disease.

It was a problem calculated to exercise all the undoubted ingenuity of Alvarez and Colonel Cainas, and it was a problem that might well have remained unsolved had it not been for the unwitting intervention of Pancho Valdez, the Generalissimo.

Not Valdez in person, for it was not his habit to penetrate the depths of the Anaguan jungle. That was a task, like all other unpleasant tasks, for subordinates. Valdez intervened only by proxy. And it was ironical that he should have been the one to help his worst enemy in a situation that might well have ended not only in the death of Alvarez but also of any hope of a successful uprising.

It was a small reconnaissance party of which Landon and Pete were members that found the village. It was close to the river and perhaps half a mile west of the point where they had come upon this great barrier. It was a village of such miserable poverty that it was difficult to understand the basic urge that could drive men to go on living in such primitive squalor. And yet men had lived there, had slept in these hovels, had scratched a little area of cleared ground into a semblance of cultivation, had taken fish from the river, and managed somehow to live at the lowest, most impoverished level.

But the village was dead now, and these which had once been houses, miserable ones, certainly, but the homes, the final refuge of desperately poor people, were now no more than a few charred remains, ashes and charcoal piled on the blackened earth.

The villagers were still there, and would remain there, having no power to leave. But they would have no need of the burnt houses, nor the fish from the river, nor the produce of their meagre gardens. For they too were dead. Upside down, they hung from the branches of the surrounding trees, lashed there by the ankles, hanging like grotesque, bloated fruit waiting for the harvester. Men, women, and children, all were there, all naked, all brutally, even obscenely, mutilated. There was nothing to indicate that they had been dead before they had been strung up and much to suggest that they had died slowly and painfully. Some of the bodies were still warm, and the ashes of the ruined houses still smouldered. The massacre had obviously been only recently carried out.

Landon looked at the young officer who was in command of the party.

'Who did this?'

Lieutenant Montojo said briefly: 'Valdez's men. Who else?'

'But why? For what purpose?'

Montojo, a man who had been smart and immaculate at the beginning of the journey, but now was mud-stained and unshaven like all the others, pointed towards the river and a heap of charred wood that had not been a house.

'There is your reason.'

'What is it?'

'Those were canoes.'

'I don't understand,' Landon said.

The lieutenant snapped his fingers impatiently. 'It is so obvious. Valdez knows that Alvarez has landed north of the Rio Chico. He knows also that El Aguila must try to reach San Quinton. Therefore he does his best to make difficulties in crossing the Chico. You understand now?'

'But why this?' Landon indicated the mutilated corpses.

'It is a way they have of amusing themselves – Valdez's men. They have a sense of humour.' Montojo's voice was bitter. 'Also I think they are afraid. In their hearts they are frightened, and that makes them cruel. In this way they try to kill their fear, to prove how brave they are. But fear does not die as easily as a man.'

'I could smoke a cigarette,' Landon said. The air was heavy with the stench of death.

'If there were cigarettes.'

Montojo was holding his sub-machine-gun under his arm, alert, ready for any eventuality. The jungle stood around the village and the clearing, and who could tell what might be hidden behind that green wall?

'This thing was recent,' he said. 'They may not be far away.'

Landon stared at the green wall and saw a movement. He held his own gun ready, holding it in his sweating hands. It was very exposed in the clearing; there was no cover, no protection. He kept watch on the place where the movement had been; he cocked the gun and held it with the muzzle pointed at the place. Montojo brought his gun round also.

'You saw something?'

'Something moved. I don't know what it was. It was low down, near the ground.'

'Nothing moving now.'

'No, nothing. And yet I am sure—'

He stopped speaking. There was the movement again, a leaf stirring – with no wind to stir it.

'There,' he said. 'You see now?'

'I see,' Montojo said.

They waited, watchful and silent. The dead fruit hung on the trees, warning them of the pleasant ways of Valdez's men. They held their guns ready and waited in the hot, still, silent air; and the sweat dripped from their foreheads and ran into the stubble on their cheeks.

They watched the place where the leaf had stirred, and they saw the man come out of the jungle.

'Holy Mother of Christ!' Montojo said.

He came on his belly, sliding like a snake. He had no right to be alive, and yet he lived and moved, and it was a pain to see him. He moved in spasms, as though some puppet-master were jerking the strings that controlled the hacked-off stumps of his arms and legs. He had neither hands nor feet; his limbs ended at the elbows and the knees with bare, raw bone, torn flesh, and wet blood.

'With machetes,' Montojo breathed. 'They have done this thing with machetes. It is more – amusement.' His youthful face seemed to have aged suddenly. He turned to his men and snarled savagely: 'Help him. Bring him here.'

They hesitated a moment, then two of them stepped forward and lifted the mutilated object from the ground. The man had a dark, pock-marked face and a shallow forehead; his black hair was long and greasy and tangled. A sound bubbled out of his throat; it was like the scream of a man who has no more strength to scream.

They brought him and laid him at Montojo's feet, and the lieutenant kneeled down and said: 'Who did this?'

The man gave no sign of understanding. Montojo spoke again in some language that Landon did not know. The man's eyes seemed to betray a glimmer of understanding mingled with his anguish. The flies had gone back to feed upon his wounds and his voice was like the faint rustle of dead leaves. Montojo put an ear close to the quivering mouth.

After a while he stood up and said: 'Take this man away. Do what you can for him.'

As the limbless body was carried away he turned to Landon and said: 'The wretch will die of course. It is a wonder that he should have lived so long.'

'What did he tell you?'

'Little that I could not have guessed. It was Valdez's men. They came suddenly, without warning, from the river. They did their work and went.'

'How long ago?'

'Not long. I think that poor devil was trying to tell me where they went, but it was difficult to understand. Perhaps they are not far.'

'Do we look for them?' Landon asked.

Montojo nodded. 'We look for them.'

They did not have to look far. It was a grey-painted fifty-foot diesel launch with a twin .50 calibre Browning machine-gun mounted in the bows. It was made fast to the end of a rickety wooden jetty that had been built out into the river, probably by the villagers who were now dead.

There was one man on deck, dressed in the brown drill uniform of the Anaguan army. He was squatting on his haunches by the machine-gun, smoking a cigarette. He did not appear to be very alert.

Montojo and the others crouched under cover and watched the launch. From it came the sound of men singing; it had the strident quality of drunkenness. The man on look-out threw the stub of his cigarette into the water and began to roll another.

Landon spoke to Pete. 'Think you could take care of that joker?'

Pete grinned. 'Just watch me.'

He stripped off his clothes and went into the water like a seal, silently, without a splash. Landon, watching for his head to appear above the surface, almost missed it. It came up well away from the bank and it scarcely showed against the dark background of the river. Then it was gone again. Pete certainly knew how to swim; perhaps he had once dived for coins thrown from ships in Kingston harbour.

The next time the black head appeared it was close to the launch, but on the far side. The look-out stretched himself, yawned, and squatted down again, watching the shore, the direction from which any attack might be expected to come. But it was obvious from the sounds of revelry that the crew of the launch were not fearing any attack. The look-out was a gesture to security, nothing more.

Landon saw Pete come up over the side, naked, with the water shining on his ebony skin. He put his arm about the look-out's throat, and the man made no sound. The strong right arm of Pete crushed the voice of fear before it had the chance to escape. There was to be no warning for Valdez's men carousing in the cabin of the launch.

Landon, Montojo, and the other men ran along the jetty with their guns in their hands. The jetty shuddered under their weight and the vibration communicated itself to the launch. A man came out of the cabin, stared in astonishment, and gave a yell of warning. The singing stopped.

A gun flamed from the side window of the cabin and Montojo flung up his arms and fell over the edge of the jetty. Then they were tumbling on board the launch with the sub-machine-guns stammering; and there was blood running down on to the decks and men clutching at chests or stomachs where the bullets had gone in and burned like flame.

Landon, remembering the village and the trees hung with grisly fruit, remembering the man with the chopped-off limbs and the children and women with their mutilations, killed without compunction. He stood in the doorway of the cabin and saw the bottles, and the men bemused with drink, and he fired the gun in short and deadly bursts.

Blood spurted on to the centre table and splashed the glasses and the plates, mingling its scarlet brightness with the food and wine until from the broken bottles and the torn and broken men there flowed a stream of sweet and sticky essence that dripped from the edges of the table and lay in slippery pools upon the cabin floor.

It was brief and bloody and final. From the moment when Pete had come up out of the river to strangle the sleepy look-out to the moment when it was all over, no more than three minutes had elapsed, three short, fierce, brutal minutes during which twenty men had died.

Surprise had made the task easy; it had been done quickly and it had been done thoroughly. Valdez's men were dead, and their bodies lay in strange, unnatural positions in the close and reeking confines of the cabin.

Montojo also was dead and Landon took charge, stepping as if by right into the position of authority.

'Throw these carcases overboard,' he said. 'We need the boat. We don't need them.'

There was no questioning his leadership. He had the air of a man who has had experience of giving orders and of having those orders obeyed. One by one the bloody corpses were dragged out of the cabin and rolled over the side.

Pete came aft, naked, grinning, the muscles rippling under his gleaming skin. Landon thought again as he looked at him: A tough boy, no doubt about it, a most tough boy.

'I got rid of mine already,' Pete said. 'It was easy. You didn't get hurt?'

'No. But they killed Montojo.'

'Too bad. That lieutenant was a good kid.'

The bodies made a great splash as they went into the water, and some things that might have been logs came swiftly from the far bank of the river.

'Alligators,' Landon said.

'Nice bit of food them snappers will have.'

The water became agitated; the foam turned red.

'They could have had a feed earlier,' Landon said. 'You were swimming down there – remember? They could have had a bite out of you.'

Pete grinned, and his teeth were like polished ivory against the ebony background of his face.

'Them alligators don't go for black men.'

'I wouldn't trust them.'

Pete looked down at the bloodstained water and shook his head.

'Nor me, Mr Landon. Nor me.'

14

SAN QUINTON

THE LAUNCH PROVIDED them with the means of crossing the Rio Chico, and there was a stock of food on board that was to sustain them on their journey south. They took what they required from the launch and then destroyed it; and they went on slowly and painfully towards their destination with the great river behind them and no other insuperable barrier to bar their way.

So at last they came again out of the jungle and on to the higher ground where San Quinton lay, and saw the houses of the city standing in a kind of shallow bowl among the hills with the cultivated fields of corn and sugar cane and tobacco stretching away into the distance. And it was a sight that was good to see.

San Quinton was a larger Oxaca without the waterfall and the volcano. It was a city able to provide for itself and the only threat to its existence came not from natural disasters such as those that had annihilated Oxaca but from the dictator of Anagua, Pancho Valdez; and even this ever-present threat did not bear heavily upon the inhabitants, since it was well known that Valdez had no urge to risk his resources in a campaign that would bring little good to him if it were successful and might be disastrous if lost.

In San Quinton Alvarez gathered his forces for the march to the coast. He found himself now at the head of an army of five thousand armed men with such a variety of weapons as even Landon, with all his experience of Central and South American revolutions, had not previously seen. But what might be lacking in arms and armour was more than made good by an almost religious fervour. These men went forth to battle in the spirit of crusaders, not weighing their own weakness against the strength of the enemy. They knew that the common people of Anagua were with them, and they felt that with this support and with El Aguila at their head they could not fail.

Landon and Pete and the girl went with them. They seemed to be caught up in this revolutionary tide that was sweeping to the Pacific; they were creatures without roots and they allowed themselves to be carried along under the momentum of a cause in which only the girl was truly interested. Landon was cynical. 'We're liberators, Pete. We're helping to lift the yoke of the tyrant from the shoulders of the oppressed. It should make you feel good.'

Pete grinned. 'You don't kid me none, Mr Landon. You and me, we don't give two rusty pennies whether it's Valdez or El Aguila that has his hands on the steering-wheel of this country. Money in the pocket and grub in the belly, that's all we care about. Ain't that so?'

'Maybe it is,' Landon said, 'and maybe it isn't. But we've got a stake in El Aguila and we'd better go along with him and see that he delivers.'

The army of the liberators took the trail to Santa Rosa on the coast, and no one stood in its way. Perhaps Valdez thought that Alvarez could not so soon have reached San Quinton; perhaps he imagined that The Eagle had died in the jungle. It was said that Valdez himself was on the other side of the country, in Villanova, on the Caribbean coast. Certainly he made no move to check the swift advance of Alvarez's men, sweeping down to Santa Rosa, the good seaport that was essential to the successful completion of Alvarez's plan of campaign.

Perhaps Valdez had grown fat and lazy; perhaps he had been lulled into a sense of security in the long years of his dictatorial rule. Whatever the reason, the fact was that Alvarez was allowed to approach within a mile of the outskirts of Santa Rosa before a single shot was fired against him.

And even then it was only a half-hearted resistance by troops who lacked firm leadership. For the military commander of the port, Colonel Hernando Costa, was a soft, pliant man who could not make up his mind whether to fight stoutly or give in at once. In the event he did nothing. He waited for things to take their course.

The result was that hundreds of his own men went over to the rebel side and the revolutionary army swept into Santa Rosa like a flood and proclaimed the rule of Alvarez to the accompaniment of kisses and flowers from the delighted populace. Whereupon Costa, ever a man to detect which way the wind was blowing, quickly presented himself as a true believer in the cause of freedom and offered his humble services to the glorious liberator.

Costa was a surprisingly young man to have occupied the position of military commandant of a town as important as Santa Rosa, with its docks and harbour installations. But it was rumoured that he had a sister who had danced her way into the innermost councils of the Generalissimo, and influence at court is a valuable promoter. There was a saying in Santa Rosa: 'Costa runs with his sister's legs'. But it was with his own that he was likely to trip up.

He looked like a man who ate too much and took too little exercise. His flesh seemed to quiver when he moved. He had pock-marked cheeks, a soft, damp mouth, and sleepy eyes. His hands also were soft and damp, and he spoke with the smallest suggestion of a lisp.

Landon did not care for the look of Costa. He said to Pete: 'That man would sell his own mother to save his skin. Alvarez ought to throw him straight into the lock-up.'

But Alvarez felt that he could make use of Costa, and he did not even strip the youthful colonel of his rank. He professed to believe that Costa's conversion to the revolutionary cause was a genuine one. But he watched Costa and he gave orders for other men to watch him also. The ex-commandant might not be a prisoner, but he was not altogether a free man.

In Santa Rosa the liberators worked fast. The port had fallen easily, perhaps too easily, but Alvarez was under no illusions. He knew that Valdez, however deeply he might have fallen into the habit of luxury and pleasure in the playground of Villanova, would react violently to the loss of such a key town as Santa Rosa. Oxaca and San Quinton had never worried him greatly. Rebel strongholds in isolated places in the interior of the country were not of any great concern; his aircraft would bomb them occasionally, but he would not risk sending an army that might be whittled down by guerilla warfare and fail in the end to achieve the purpose for which it had been sent.

But while Oxaca and San Quinton were one thing, Santa Rosa

was quite another; it was a sea-port, and through it arms and ammunition might flow to the rebels in such quantities as to make them a real and imminent threat to the established government. Therefore, Valdez would most probably use every means within his power to recapture Santa Rosa and damp down the fires of insurrection before they had time to spread all along the Pacific coast and thence across the country to the Caribbean and Villanova itself.

Santa Rosa was built round the curving shore of a bay, a natural harbour with a narrow exit to the sea between two arms of land reaching towards each other like the jaws of a gigantic pair of pincers. Piers for the accommodation of ocean-going ships jutted out into the bay, and along the waterfront was a litter of sheds and warehouses. A collection of small craft – yachts, motor-boats, and fishing-vessels – moved about the harbour or lay at their moorings, stirred by the idle lift and fall of the water. It was a peaceful, even idyllic, scene under the brilliant sun, with the air shimmering in a haze of heat; but the threat of Valdez lay upon the town, and there was a sense of feverish expectancy about all that went on in the days immediately following Alvarez's coming.

Landon and Pete were accommodated in the army barracks where Alvarez had set up his headquarters. The girl was given lodgings in the town, and it was understood that work would be found for her in the revolutionary cause, as it was to be found for Landon and Pete. Landon knew guns, and the Army of Liberation was short of instructors. Alvarez suggested that he should become an instructor.

'I am not forcing it on you,' Alvarez said. 'You are free to go if you wish.'

'Where would I go?' Landon said.

'Exactly. Where would you go? Later I shall be in a position to reward you for your services to Anagua.'

'You believe so?'

'Of course. The tide has started to flow. Nothing will stop us now.'

'Tides usually recede again.'

'But not this tide; this one moves only forward. It will sweep Valdez away as if he had never been. You have seen how the people welcomed me.'

'I hope they don't turn against you later.'

'They will not. Be assured of that.'

'We shall need more guns,' Landon said. 'There are not enough here.'

Alvarez smiled. 'The guns will come. You have not forgotten Cranefield?'

Landon's eyes narrowed. 'Of course. I should have remembered – the man who will not burn his fingers.'

'Precisely,' Alvarez said.

The barracks were too small to hold the liberating army. Tents were put up and a canvas town appeared overnight. The camp was situated on the Santa Rosa airfield. There were a few obsolescent fighter aircraft there, but there were no pilots to fly them. Some of Colonel Costa's pilots offered their services in the new cause, but Alvarez did not trust them. Once in the air they might find their old allegiance too strong; they might fly to Zamora, another port farther south, or even across country to Valdez's headquarters at Villanova. The aircraft remained grounded.

On the second day a ship came into the port of Santa Rosa. Landon and Pete were down by the docks and saw it entering the harbour. It looked to Landon to be about seven thousand tons net register, an old vessel of the wartime Liberty type with flush decks and thick, squat masts and samson posts.

Landon spoke to Pete. 'What ensign is that she's flying? Can you see, Pete?'

Pete shook his head. He was not good on ensigns. They did not interest him.

The ensign drooped at the stern, then fluttered out as a breeze caught it. It was quartered in blue and white and yellow and red, with a gold star in the centre. Landon grinned; it amused him to see a ship of Anaguan registration bringing arms to feed the revolution; it was a kind of poetic justice. So that was what happened when you allowed your ensign to be used as a flag of convenience: one day a ship came sailing in under that flag to help a man like Alvarez to overthrow the government.

'That's the Anaguan ensign,' Landon said.

Pete looked puzzled.

'You mean that's one of Valdez's own ships bringing supplies for the revolution?'

Landon shook his head. 'I don't think Valdez has any ships – not of that size anyway. But there are plenty of foreign-owned vessels registered in Anagua, just the same as there are in Panama and Liberia and Costa Rica. It pays. Ask the Greek millionaires.'

'I don't get it.'

'Lower taxes. Slacker regulations. I sailed to Philly in a Panamanian tanker, but it was a Greek who owned it.'

He wondered how Cranefield handled a job like this. He did not believe this was Cranefield's ship; the financier would be too wary to be involved as closely as that. Men like Cranefield covered their tracks. Perhaps this ship also had a Greek owner, and perhaps the Greek was hand in glove with Cranefield. Whatever the set-up, it was no affair of Landon's.

The ship came up slowly to the wooden pier that jutted out into the harbour. One mooring-rope came down over the bows and another over the stern. Dockside workers looped them over bollards; winches pulled the ropes inboard; the ship leaned its weight against the pier, rope fend-offs groaned under the pressure, and the pier creaked. A gangway was rolled into position and made fast. Alvarez himself was the first to step on board.

Landon said: 'I think I'll go and have a look too. Might be interesting.'

'I'll come with you,' Pete said.

Already there was an armed sentry at the foot of the gangway, but he recognized Landon and Pete and made no move to prevent them from going on board. Landon read the name of the ship – *Southern Voyager* – and somehow it felt good to be climbing a gangway again, even if the ship was flying so peculiar an ensign.

Alvarez had disappeared, probably to the captain's stateroom. Dockers were coming on board now, starting to roll back the tarpaulins from the hatches. Landon wondered how well they had been screened. With all the ammunition that this ship must undoubtedly contain, it would have been easy to carry out sabotage. But that was Alvarez's business, and presumably he had assured himself that there was no unavoidable risk.

Winches began to rattle. The hatch boards had been taken off and piled on one side. Steel hatch beams were lifted by the derricks, and men went down into the tween-decks. There was no delay. To the revolutionaries every minute was precious, with Valdez breathing down their necks.

Landon walked across to the coaming of number three hold and looked down. In the tween-decks were light tanks and armoured cars. They might not be of the latest design; they might not all be new; but for a revolutionary army in a small country like Anagua they could be very, very useful. With a shipload like this Alvarez could really get moving.

Landon, who had had experience of these things, could guess at the quantity of warlike equipment a ship of the size of the *Southern Voyager* would hold – tanks, troop carriers, field-guns, mortars, machine-guns, ammunition – thousands of tons of it. There was no doubt about it, Alvarez's journey to see Cranefield had certainly been worth while.

He moved away from the hatch, keeping a watchful eye on swinging hooks that could crack a man's skull and spill his brains out on the deck. He saw a jumbo derrick dropping its heavy-lift pulley into the hold, the wire rope slipping smoothly through the sheaves; very soon the first tank would be coming up, and then another and another, to make a hard steel spearhead for the revolution.

One thing was noticeable – there was no deck cargo. Arms ships usually carried tanks or vehicles on deck; but perhaps that would have made the *Southern Voyager* too conspicuous. She must have been hanging about not far over the horizon, waiting for Alvarez's signal, or perhaps in a port of some other Central American state, one that was sympathetic to Alvarez's cause.

A man in a spotless tropical suit came out of a doorway and cannoned into Landon. He apologized in English. He had an American accent that matched the suit.

'Must think to look where I'm going.'

'It pays to keep your eyes open on board ship. You can walk into real trouble if you don't.'

The man glanced sharply at Landon. He was tall and loosely built, young, with a long, well-shaven jaw, ginger hair, and a dusting of freckles. His was the kind of skin that got burnt off in the tropics; there were scorched flakes of it hanging to his nose.

'Hey, are you English?'

'That's what the passport says – when I have one.'

'Well, what in heck are you doing here?'

'I came with Alvarez. I'm one of the glorious Army of Liberation.'

The American nodded. 'I get it now. Your name's Harvey Landon.'

'Right in one.'

'I heard about you. My name's Anderson. Call me Earl. Tell me, what happened to that feller Gregg? Is he still around?'

'No,' Landon said. 'Gregg won't ever be around any more. We ran into a bit of trouble. Gregg got killed.'

'Too bad,' Anderson said. But he did not sound heart-broken. 'A guy like him, it's likely to happen any time. So you had trouble?'

'That was an understatement.'

Landon was wondering what Anderson's place was in the set-up. He did not look like a ship's officer, and he seemed to be well informed; he had known about Gregg. Perhaps he was one of Cranefield's bright young men. If Cranefield had any. Anderson illuminated the situation himself.

'I'm a prospector – if you're wondering.'

'Prospector?'

'With a geiger-counter.'

'Oh – I see.'

He remembered then that he had heard something about the possibility of uranium deposits in Anagua. So that really was Cranefield's interest. It might be just one of many. Cranefield was the sort of man who would like plenty of irons in the fire. But just how well did Cranefield know Alvarez? Alvarez was the kind of ardent nationalist who might be capable of kicking the ladder away once he had used it to climb the wall. Cranefield might yet burn his fingers. The prospect afforded Landon a certain amount of innocent amusement.

Anderson said: 'I'll be moving along. Plenty to do. Things to pack. They're giving me a hotel room ashore. I'd say it'll be the hell of a room in a dump like this. Maybe I'll be seeing you around.'

'Maybe.'

The prospector walked away, looking clean and tidy and well-ironed in his tropical suit. Landon looked down at his own stained clothes and gave a shrug. Perhaps Anderson would be like that before he got away from Anagua.

Pete said: 'These boys work fast. I never thought they had it in 'em. I thought they was just a lot of *mañana* boys, but they're going at this job like there was a war on somewheres.'

'There is,' Landon said. 'For them.'

He stood under the shadow of the midships superstructure and watched the jumbo fetching up a tank. Wire ropes were hooked to steel lugs at the four corners of the tank, and the massive hook of the pulley gripped them as a man might grip the handles of a tool-bag. The tank came up slowly, twisting about its axis. The dockers hauled on ropes to keep it straight, but twenty tons was a weight that took a deal of holding. A corner of the tank caught under the lip of the hatch and the winch driver was not nearly quick enough in releasing the pressure; he kept the winch hauling just a moment too long. A wire snapped. The tank swung sideways, tilting. Another wire parted into frayed, tangled halves, each broken end like an old, worn-out shaving-brush with the bristles curling back. The winch driver, either inexperienced or too excitable, began to draw in fast instead of paying out slowly. The tank struck the lip of the hatch a second time and the last two wires gave way with a high, angry twanging sound. The tank fell on its side, turned over, and crushed two men in the tween-decks, killing them outright.

Pete rubbed his jaw. 'They don't do it too good, Mr Landon. You could call that a case of more haste, less speed. They're going to lose some time fixing that gear. Alvarez won't be pleased.'

'It'll take longer to fix the men.'

'Plenty of men,' Pete said.

It was that evening when they had the first reaction from Valdez. Five light bombers attacked the port.

Landon had gone to see the girl. He had not spoken to her since their arrival in Santa Rosa, and that seemed a long time to him now. He was missing her. He tried not to admit the fact to himself, but it was so. In the long and bitter journey across the country the girl had somehow become part of his life; she had been there, near to him, always. Now she was no longer near, and he wanted her. He called himself a fool; he told himself that the girl was scarcely half his age; he told himself that after a week away from her she would pass out of his mind like a dream of yesterday. But it was no use. He wanted to see her again, and he wanted to be able to see her always.

She was living in a part of the old town, not far from the waterfront. It was an old brick building, a kind of poor tenement house, children playing in the dust outside and an endless smell of cooking within.

Landon made inquiries and was told that the girl was not there. A woman with matted hair and a moustache, and a fat, sagging bosom gave him information.

'She went out early. She has not been back all day.'

'Do you know where she went?'

'No, I do not know that. She did not tell. She is a child who does not talk much.'

'Thank you,' Landon said. 'I will come again later.'

He walked away from the house. The children scarcely troubled to look at him; they were absorbed in their game.

He was at the corner of the street when he heard the aircraft, and at that same moment saw the girl. It did not occur to him at first that the planes might be attacking the town; he had forgotten that Alvarez had no airmen. He was thinking only about the girl. He quickened his pace as he went towards her.

She saw him coming, and she halted, waiting for him to come to her.

He said: 'Well, Anita!'

She looked into his face, as though she were checking up on a memory. She was wearing the same old blue jeans and cotton shirt that he had come to associate with her. He could see where they had been mended, and there was a newly washed look about them.

'What have you been doing with yourself?'

She said: 'I am going to be a nurse with the Army of Liberation.'

'You would make a good nurse,' Landon said. But he felt a stab of jealousy. He was jealous of the Army of Liberation that might take her from him. He did not want her to be a nurse. He did not want her to go with the army. 'Is that really what you would like to be?'

'I have to do something.'

164

He saw that too. She had to live and she wanted to serve. She was a patriot. But he was no patriot and he had no urgent desire to serve Alvarez. He would have liked to say to her: 'Come away with me. We'll leave this country.' He felt that he hated Anagua and everything about it. Everything except the girl, whom he loved. And yet, owning nothing, how could he take her away? It was out of the question. He had nowhere to go. He too must serve Alvarez.

'If I were sick,' he said, 'I should like you to nurse me, Anita.'

'If you were sick,' she answered, 'I should wish to nurse you. I should not wish anyone else to do it.' She spoke seriously, as though this were something that she wanted him to know.

He began to answer her, and heard the scream of the bombs falling.

'Get down!' he yelled. And he seized her and flung her to the ground and himself beside her, all in one reflex movement that was for him the natural reaction to the once familiar whistle of bombs.

He put his arm over the girl's head, trying to shield her, and the bombs straddled the street, two falling on one side and two on the other, with the open street like a dividing line between them. The ground vibrated with the shock and racket of the explosions, and the blast seemed to smash against his eardrums, deafening him. Something hard and unyielding struck him on the left shoulder, numbing it; a shower of dirt and debris rained down upon him and the girl; and then it was over, and there was a strange, breathless hush, like a pause in the action of a play.

He took his arm away from the girl's head and raised himself to his knees, rubbing the numbed shoulder.

'You're not hurt, Anita?' he asked.

She sat up also, looking dazed and bewildered. It occurred to him suddenly that this was perhaps the first time she had heard a bomb falling.

She said: 'They came so quickly. There was no time, no time at all.' Her voice reflected her bewilderment. This was something she had not imagined.

'But you are not hurt?'

She shook her head. The dust lay upon her thickly, covering her clothes and her hair. Dust hung in the air like a mist. But she was unhurt.

'My ears,' she said. 'They feel strange. There is a ringing noise in them.' She put her hands to her head, as though to keep out the sound.

'It's the effect of the blast.'

Now that his anxiety for the girl was quietened he had time to look around him. The house on the left was no more than a heap of rubble. On the other side of the street an outer wall was still erect; but even as he looked it swayed uncertainly for a moment and then collapsed inward.

He heard a child screaming, a thin, terrifying sound. He went to look for the child and found it crushed under a fall of rubble, only the head showing.

'It's all right now,' he said. 'I'll get you out.' He spoke in English, forgetting that the child would not understand. But it would have made no difference either way.

He began to dig with his fingers, flinging aside the lumps of brick and mortar. The girl helped him, and the child stared up at them, weeping.

Landon felt that there was accusation in the child's eyes and he was glad when they no longer stared at him, no longer wept, when they were closed for ever. For the small body, when they uncovered it at last, was a thing that had been broken beyond the skill of surgery.

It was the girl who wept now, but silently. He looked at her across the small crushed body and said: 'This is the price of liberty. This is the sacrifice to El Aguila.'

15

TIME TO PART

'I WANT A boat,' Landon said. 'I want one that's big enough and seaworthy enough to take me away from here.'

Alvarez looked at him in some surprise. 'You wish to go away?'

Landon took a cigarette from the silver box on Alvarez's desk and lit it. He lowered himself into a chair and stared at Alvarez through the cigarette smoke.

'The time has come for us to part.' His voice was a little hard, a little bitter. That was the way he felt. 'I don't want any more of this revolution, no more at all. I want to get right away.'

Alvarez also took a cigarette and leaned back in his chair. There was a scar on the left side of his head where the bullet had grazed him; it was visible through the close-cropped hair. His ear too had healed, but the top was gone; it looked slightly ragged, as though a rat had been gnawing it.

'You have altered your mind,' he said. 'I thought you were going to accept employment in Anagua. That was what you said only yesterday. Why this sudden change of plans? Has something happened?'

'No, nothing has happened. It's just that I've had enough. I want to clear out.'

And yet it was not true that nothing had happened. The bombing had happened – and the child's death. It was the sight of the crushed child that had finally sickened him of the whole wretched business. He knew that this one would not be the last; there would be other children crushed under the wheels of the revolution. It might be in the sacred cause of freedom; it might be worth the sacrifice if you took the wide view. But he could no longer take the wide view, and he wanted no more of it. He wanted to get away, and he wanted a boat.

'Where will you go?' Alvarez asked. He did not sound greatly interested.

'I don't know. Anywhere. Does it matter?'

Perhaps he would sail across the Pacific to New Zealand or Australia or one of the countless islands. Anywhere would be better than these damned Latin-American states where they were forever fighting and bickering. Best of all would be the healing peace of a great ocean.

'No,' Alvarez said. 'It does not matter.'

'And you will give me a boat?'

'It is the least I can do for you. You have done much for me, and through me for Anagua. Even if you are now unwilling to come with me further you have earned this reward. I promised you a boat long ago.'

He paused, leaned forward, and signed some papers with rapid strokes of the pen. There was much business calling for his attention and he had little time to spare.

Still writing, he began to speak again. 'Colonel Costa had a yacht. Costa has fled. You may have heard.'

'No, I had not heard.'

'It is so. He slipped away during the night. He stole a jeep and bluffed his way through the road block. No doubt he is heading for Zamora; he may well be there by now. His possessions naturally are confiscated by the Army of Liberation. The yacht is yours. I will make out an order to that effect. Also an order for provisions. You will wish to prepare for a long sea-voyage no doubt.'

Landon began to express his thanks, but Alvarez stopped him.

'There is no need for thanks. You are being paid; that is all.' Suddenly, unexpectedly, his features relaxed their usual stern expression and became more human. It was as though he were revealing briefly a side of his nature that was normally kept hidden away, concealed by the mask of the relentless reformer. This was an altogether gentler, less single-minded man. 'Mr Landon,' he said, 'what is your honest opinion of me?'

Landon hesitated. It was not an easy question to answer. 'I—'

Alvarez spoke for him. 'You think I am hard, self-centred,

unfeeling.' He lifted a hand. 'Do not trouble to deny it. I know. And that, of course, is how I must inevitably appear to you, to the world. You think I have no love in me perhaps. And yet if I did not love my fellow-men I should not be the person that I am. I should not be in this present position. There are easier ways of life than that of a liberator. Mr Landon, sometimes I envy you—'

'Envy me?'

'I envy you your lack of involvement. You are free. You are not held captive by an idea, a faith. You can take a boat and go. I cannot do that – ever. For me there is no boat, no release, except perhaps by the martyr's gate – the cross – the firing squad – the hangman's noose—'

Landon shifted uneasily in his chair. He did not wish to hear these revelations of Alvarez. Alvarez was a man he had never greatly liked, a man he never could have loved. And he had no desire to see this other side of the picture.

Alvarez himself seemed to realize this. This mask slipped into place again; the face became stern, impassive. 'But this is of no interest to you.' He pulled some papers towards him with a gesture of impatience, as though angry with himself for the moment of weakness. 'Does Pete go with you?'

'Yes.'

'Of course. He has no stake in this country either.' He paused momentarily, and when he spoke again there was a slight change in the inflection of his voice. There was a hint of disapproval in it. 'Are you taking the girl – Anita Romero?'

Landon met the cold stare of Alvarez's black eyes and answered as coldly: 'She has refused to come.'

Alvarez nodded. 'As I should have expected. She is Anaguan. This cause is hers.'

The yacht that had belonged to Colonel Costa was in the basin with a number of other sailing craft. It was a sloop of about twelve tons, with neat, trim lines, and from its appearance seemed almost new. Landon went down to the harbour to supervise the provisioning and to check up on the gear. Pete went with him, happy at the prospect of leaving Anagua.

'I've had as much of this country as I ever want. I'll be glad to be pushing on.'

'You're a restless soul, Pete.'

Pete chuckled. 'Restless. Sure thing. Damn restless. Like you, Mr Landon.'

'Not like me,' Landon said. 'I'm getting old and tired.'

Pete gave a snort of derision. 'You ain't old. You got a lot of life ahead. Plenty time.'

'Not enough time. Not half enough.'

Landon was pleased with the appearance of the sloop. It looked seaworthy enough to sail anywhere in the world, even round Cape Horn. In the lockers were charts and navigating instruments – everything that would be needed. There was enough accommodation – more than enough – and all that remained was to stock up with provisions and cast off.

'Good, hey?' Pete said, tapping the boards with his knuckles. 'Damn good. That Costa knew how to pick a boat.'

Landon had forgotten about Costa. He wondered how much the colonel had paid for his yacht – if he had paid. Well, that was not a thing to worry about. Costa would never have the sloop back even if Landon did not take it. Costa would be lucky if he saved his own skin when Alvarez caught up with him.

Pete said musingly: 'I have never been on the Pacific. It'll be a new experience. Australia – now, that's a place I always did wanta see.'

'We may not get to Australia.'

'Sure. We get there in time. What you think?'

Landon did not answer. He was thinking about the girl. He knew that it was because of the girl that he was not completely happy about leaving, not happy as Pete was. If the girl had been coming also, then it would have been different. But the girl was not coming, and he could not make her do so.

'Let's be going,' he said curtly.

They left the yacht basin and walked back along the waterfront.

'There's the *Southern Voyager*,' Pete said. 'Still unloading. I hear they been having more trouble. They didn't shift that cargo so fast after all.'

'Too many accidents.'

'That's right. Enthusiastic but not skilful. That's the way of it.'

The *Southern Voyager*'s derricks were working. There were few shore cranes in Santa Rosa; none that could lift heavy tanks. Landon could see what looked like an armoured car swinging out over the pier. He wondered whether they had got down to any of the ammunition yet, the high-explosive shells that would be stowed in the lower parts of the holds.

He did not have much time for wondering, for when they were a hundred yards away from her the *Southern Voyager* suddenly exploded.

It was like the volcano again; it was a man-made volcano erupting at the touch of some fuse, some trigger that had set the whole tightly-packed load of cordite and T.N.T., of shells and cartridges and mortar bombs, bursting out of the steel prison of the ship.

There were two detonations, the second following so closely upon the first that they sounded almost as one. The *Southern Voyager* seemed to burst open like a rotten fruit, and the armoured car that had been swinging from the midships derrick was caught like a leaf in a whirlwind and flung up and away, to fall with a crash unheard against the background storm of the exploding cargo on to the roof of a dockside storehouse.

A vomit of black smoke gushed upward with streaks of crimson flame dancing and flickering around and within it. Bullets from the cargo began to fly in all directions, the tracers brilliant as shooting stars against the gloomy backcloth of the smoke. The foremast was torn away at deck level and fell across the pier, crushing a man beneath its iron weight.

On the surface of the water a thousand dropping fragments made an intricate pattern of splashes and concentric ripples that flowed into one another, mingling and struggling, until the whole area was dimpled and pock-marked and corrugated by this falling hail of tortured metal. The bridge of the ship was no longer anything that could be accurately described as a bridge; it was a grotesque tangle of twisted steel interlaced with burning timber. The holds were belching craters of fire and smoke.

With the first blinding flash and hammer of the explosion Landon and Pete dropped flat on the ground. The blast came in two waves, like a sudden, red-hot wind. It came and passed over them and was gone; and after it came the minor sounds – the crackle of the small-arms ammunition, the clatter of falling debris, and a strange, frightening noise that turned out to be a man screaming.

Pete lifted his head cautiously. 'By God,' he said, 'that was some crack-up. Just take a look at that ship now.'

Under its pall of smoke the *Southern Voyager* was settling down in the water, lower and lower. Then she heeled slowly over, away from the pier, until what had been her starboard rails were just kissing the surface. And in that position she remained while the fires burned inside her and every now and then something erupted violently like a small echo of the first destroying explosion.

Landon got up. 'We'd better see if we can help.'

Pete got up also – reluctantly. 'Not much we can do there, Mr Landon.' He watched the flying tracers apprehensively. 'We could maybe get ourselves killed though.'

'Come on,' Landon said.

They went forward cautiously and found a man crouched against the wall of a shed. He looked dazed; he was groping in the air with his right hand as if searching for something, perhaps something solid and tangible to grasp, to hold on to in a disintegrating world.

'Mr Anderson,' Landon said. 'Earl.'

The American stared at him without recognition. His eyes seemed unable to focus; his lips were trembling. Landon put a hand on his shoulder, and Anderson shivered.

'Pull yourself together,' Landon said. 'You haven't been injured, have you?'

'Injured?'

'Nothing hit you?'

'I don't know. I don't know what happened. Something cracked open. I—'

He began to touch himself with his hands as though feeling for an injury. Then he seemed to brace himself, making an effort at self-control.

'You're Harvey Landon, aren't you? What happened? Tell me what happened?'

'The ship blew up.'

'God!' Anderson said.

'Where were you? What were you doing?'

'I was coming away. I'd just come ashore. I didn't see—'

'You'll be all right,' Landon said. 'Just take it easy. You'll be fine.'

He was fairly certain that all Anderson was suffering from was the shock.

He heard a fire-engine coming, heralding its approach with a clanging bell. An ambulance screamed past.

'They don't need us now,' Pete said. 'We best be on our way.'

'They might be able to use some help,' Landon said. 'Come on.'

He went towards the burning ship and Pete followed, grumbling.

'It was sabotage, of course,' Alvarez said. 'It may even have been planned by Costa before he left. I blame myself. I should have been more careful with that man.'

Alvarez was in the room that he had made his administrative office for the period of his stay in Santa Rosa. But he was not sitting at the desk; he was striding backward and forward across the room. He was in a fever of anger and frustration.

'It is almost a total loss of the cargo. We have lost the teeth of the revolution.'

'But some of it had been unloaded,' Landon said. 'You will have that.'

Alvarez stopped pacing and rested his hands on the desk, leaning towards Landon, who was seated on a chair and smoking.

'Do you know how much we have saved out of the entire ship's cargo? I will tell you. One light tank, two 25-pounder guns, and three mortars. All the rest was either still in the ship or in the sheds adjoining the pier. Those sheds, as you know, also blew up some time after the ship.'

Landon had heard that this was so, and he was thankful that he and Pete had left before it happened. Many others had been killed.

'For those two guns and three mortars,' Alvarez said, 'there is of course no ammunition. It is a great help in our fight with Valdez. Do you not think so?'

Alvarez left the desk and began pacing again. Landon felt sorry for the man. He had been through so much; he had overcome so many setbacks; and now this final blow had fallen. For this shipload of arms he had made the hazardous journey to the United States; for this he had bargained with Cranefield; and now it was gone, destroyed in one swift, terrible blast as though it had never been.

Alvarez said vehemently: 'We will find the men who did this thing. They shall be punished. I will see to that.'

His thin face was dark with anger and hatred against the saboteurs. If they were caught it was obvious that they could expect no mercy.

'How will you find them?' Landon asked.

'I do not know. I only know that they will be found.'

He turned suddenly. 'You were there. You were down by the pier.'

There was something almost accusatory in the way he said it.

Landon took the cigarette out of his mouth. 'You don't think I blew up the *Southern Voyager*, do you?'

Alvarez turned away again. 'No, I do not suspect you. You had no reason for doing it, no motive.'

'Otherwise you might have suspected me?'

'I did not say so.'

'My opinion is that you'll never find who did it now. They may even have been killed in the explosion.'

'No,' Alvarez said. It was obvious that he did not wish to consider that as a possibility. He wanted someone to punish. 'Men who blow up ships do not blow themselves up also.'

'There is no accounting for fanatics. They do very strange things.'

'No, no, no,' Alvarez said. 'These men are still alive. These saboteurs will be found and they will be punished. You may rest assured of that.'

Three men were found. Alvarez had insisted and his subordinates had found the men to assuage his anger. What did it matter whether they had or had not been concerned in the blowing up of the *Southern Voyager*? They protested their innocence, but that was only natural; one did not expect confessions. So long as one had some bodies to weight the hangman's noose, what else mattered? So long as Alvarez was appeased.

Therefore, three men hung that night from the gallows, and a thin black cloud drifted across the town from the still-smoking arms ship.

And Valdez moved fast to crush the insurrection.

16

ZAMORA ROAD

LANDON HAD BEEN to look for the girl again, but he had not found her. She was not at the house and no one there could tell him where she had gone. He came away angry and frustrated. Tomorrow he and Pete would be sailing away from Santa Rosa in the sloop that had once belonged to Hernando Costa, and he wished to say good-bye to Anita Romero before he went.

He wished to do more than that; he wished to make one last attempt to persuade her to come also. In the face of all his previous urging she had remained adamant, dedicated to the revolution; but perhaps the loss of the *Southern Voyager* would have shaken her resolve. It was so obvious that the revolt now had no hope of success, that El Aguila was beaten, and that it was only a question of time before his forces would be driven out of Santa Rosa and back into the interior, to San Quinton, the jungle, and the mountains, perhaps, indeed, to utter extermination.

Landon wanted to explain to the girl; he wanted to demonstrate to her that to leave now was the only sensible course, that it was ridiculous to remain in Santa Rosa, hanging on the bedraggled skirts of a hopeless cause. Surely she must see the sense of such an argument, must agree to come away with him.

'I must stay,' she had said. 'You can go where you please, but I must stay here. This is my country.'

He had argued, but all his arguments had broken upon the quiet strength of her resolve. Finally he had become angry, his voice had risen.

'What has Aguila done to you? Has he bewitched you? Don't you see that to follow him is to go to your death? Have you forgotten the crushed child?'

She had shivered at the memory. The child's death had been too recent.

'No, I have not forgotten.'

'That's how it will be with you. You will be crushed too.'

She had turned away from him then. 'If it must be, it must. I am not afraid.'

No, she was not afraid. But he was – afraid for her. And now he could not find her, could not make this last effort to persuade her to leave Anagua.

He decided to search for her. He would search the whole town if need be. He would search all day and all night, but he would find her. It was unthinkable that he should leave without seeing her once more.

He walked through the hot afternoon streets, through the grinding traffic, the dust, and the crowds of dark-faced, sombre people. It occurred to him how seldom an Anaguan looked happy. Perhaps the sadness of the old days was still in them, a time before the coming of the Spaniards, when human sacrifices were offered upon the altars of the gods, and priests with sharp stone knives cut out the pulsing hearts of their living victims. Blood had always flowed freely in Anagua. Perhaps it always would.

Landon wandered down to the waterfront and saw again the wreck of Alvarez's hopes. The *Southern Voyager* was a tangle of scorched and twisted iron, a junk heap of a ship resting upon the bottom alongside the charred piles and blackened boards of the pier. Her holds gaped to the sky, the hatch edges as jagged as a ripped-open tin can, and over it all was the acrid, penetrating odour of the fire that had at last burned itself out. It was the bitter odour of defeat.

Nobody appeared to be working amid the wreckage of the ship and the waterside sheds. It was as though all this had been abandoned, had been written off as a dead loss. Perhaps in among the debris were still the remains of men's bodies left to rot with the rotting hopes of the revolution.

As he moved away a man touched his arm, and this man too appeared to him as a symbol of abandoned hope, of rottenness and corruption, of defeat and decay. The ragged clothes stank, or perhaps it was the body inside the clothes. The man was skin and bone; there was no bridge to his nose; it had collapsed in upon his face; his eyes had a white, half-blind look about them, and his skin seemed to have been corroded.

With a gesture of loathing Landon wrenched his arm away from the clawed hand. The man's voice came like the whistle of wind through a hollow tube.

'Money, señor. For charity's sake, a little money to save a starving man.'

Landon reached in his pocket and threw the beggar some coins. They rattled on the ground and he dived with an eagerness that was itself repulsive to pick then up.

'A thousand thanks, señor. May Christ bless and protect you from all harm.' He gave a jerk of his thumb in the direction of the wreckage. 'As he has not protected some. As he has not protected the cause of El Aguila, the holy cause, as you might say.'

'El Aguila may yet win,' Landon said.

The beggar shook his head, breath whistling through the nostrils of the corrupted nose. 'No, he will not win now. It is Valdez who will win. The Sergeant will prune the Eagle's claws.' He chuckled as if he found the idea amusing. Then suddenly he looked sharply at Landon. 'You are the Englishman who came with Alvarez. That is so?'

'It is so.'

'Go away, Englishman. This country is not for you. You will not grow fat on the blood of Anagua.' He stabbed a finger again at the twisted skeleton of the *Southern Voyager*.

'Ask them. Ask the Yanquis. If you can find one who is still alive.'

'I did not come here to grow fat,' Landon said.

'Why did you come?'

'What is that to you?'

'Nothing, nothing. Have you a cigarette, señor?'

Landon threw him one, and he caught it deftly and lit from Landon's match. The smoke came out through the wreckage of his nose, from two holes that looked as though they had been bored in his face. He grinned at Landon like a wolf.

'Why are you angry, Englishman?'

'I am not angry.'

'You are angry because you know that El Aguila cannot win. And therefore there will be no reward for you. That is why you are angry.'

'I looked for no reward.'

'That is not true. Every man looks for his reward, but the reward is not always money. For some it is love, for some revenge, for others power; for a few it is the hope of life everlasting in the world to come.' A ghastly smile seemed to hover about his twisted lips. 'Some man blew up this ship. Perhaps he had his reward, perhaps not. Perhaps he simply loved to see destruction because he himself had already been destroyed. Who can tell?'

Landon stared into the opaque white eyes and saw nothing there, no hint of any meaning that might lie behind the apparently random words.

'What do you know about the explosion?'

'I? Nothing, señor. What should I know except that three men have been hanged. Is not that enough?'

Landon turned away from him, impatient with himself for troubling to exchange words with this piece of human garbage. He had no time to waste. He must find the girl. What did it matter to him who had blown up the *Southern Voyager*?

'Go away, Englishman,' the beggar said. 'Go away before it is too late.'

Landon said: 'I'm going. You don't need to trouble your head about that. I'm going just as fast as I can get out.'

As he walked away he thought he heard the beggar chuckling. But he did not look back.

It was a little while after that Valdez's aircraft came – the first wave of the assault on Santa Rosa. Landon heard the engines, then an anti-aircraft gun firing spasmodically, like a man with hiccups. He saw some tracers going up, pale in the afternoon light. They looked as though they might have come from guns on the southern fringe of the town.

Bombs began to fall, but they were a long way off. It could be that the attack was being made on the barracks or the defences along the road to Zamora. It was impossible to tell for certain.

Traffic came to a standstill. Drivers stopped their vehicles, got out, and stared up into the sky. Some people ran into their houses;

others came out; all appeared uncertain what to do. Alvarez and the Army of Liberation had been far too busy to spend time on instructing the citizens of Santa Rosa even in the elements of air-raid drill. As a consequence every one did what he thought was best, and the result was confusion.

Landon began to run. He felt a desperate urge to find the girl. An army truck came round a corner and ground its way up the street, going slowly because of the congestion of people staring into the sky. Landon saw that the truck was full of Alvarez's men armed with rifles.

The truck drew to a halt level with Landon. A man yelled from the cab, and he saw that it was Pete.

'Jump in, Mr Landon. Hurry now.'

He went to the door of the cab and saw that with Pete was Captain Ortega, one of the officers who had come from Oxaca. Ortega was a thick-set man with a uniform that always looked too tight for him. He had a florid complexion, a heavy jowl, and a thick black moustache that he was for ever smoothing back with his stubby fingers.

Ortega said: 'Will you come with us? Valdez is advancing along the Zamora road.'

Landon hesitated, thinking of the girl. The driver let in his clutch and the truck began to edge forward.

'I'll come,' Landon said. He put his foot on the step and hauled himself up. He was still thinking of the girl.

There were already four men in the cab, but he squeezed in somehow. It was as hot as a furnace, heat beating up from the engine in waves. Sweat started to dribble down his face and his shirt stuck to him.

'Glad we found you,' Pete said. 'Looks like we got a fight on our hands before we leave.'

'What armour has Valdez got?' Landon asked.

It was Ortega who answered. 'Reports mention tanks and armoured cars.'

'How many?'

'Twenty – thirty – but one does not have to believe everything one hears. For myself, I do not think Valdez could gather that number so soon – not on this side of the country.'

'And you're going with rifles to stop these tanks?'

'We have some bigger guns,' Ortega said. 'We are not men who look for miracles.'

'Do you think you can stop Valdez?'

'Who knows? Either we stop him or —' Ortega drew a finger across his throat and laughed, as though he found considerable amusement in the prospect of having his throat cut. 'Valdez has not a forgiving nature.'

'Do you know where the bombs have fallen?' Landon asked.

'They tried to hit the barracks, but they did little damage. They are not brave, those pilots. They keep very high.'

The truck came out of the town and on to the Zamora road, a wide, concrete motorway that wound its way along the coastal strip between the mountains and the sea. If Valdez was indeed coming he would have to come that way.

About a mile beyond the town they came to the road block. Here everything pointed to the haste with which the defences had been prepared. Until the loss of the *Southern Voyager* had upset his plans Alvarez had been thinking only in terms of attack, of pressing on to Zamora without delay. He had scarcely considered the possibility of having to defend Santa Rosa against Valdez's troops. The road block, therefore, had been set up in a desperate hurry and was not all that could have been desired.

There were some iron stakes driven through the concrete, some barbed wire, some sandbags, and a few hastily planted mines. As far as Landon could make out the main defensive armament consisted of an old German field gun, a British 17-pounder anti-tank gun, some 20-millimetre automatics, a few mortars, and two bazookas. In his opinion the guns had been badly sited and a screen of sandbags had been thrown up round them in a very amateurish fashion. All in all, the situation looked far from promising.

'Who is in command here?' Landon asked.

'Colonel Cainas,' Ortega said. 'This has been all very much of a last-minute operation. We have had to improvise.'

They tumbled out of the cab of the truck and the riflemen jumped down from the back. The soldiers did not fall in; they stood about in little groups, smoking and arguing among themselves, often pointing in the direction of Zamora, from which Valdez's forces would come. Drill was not a strong feature of the Army of Liberation.

Landon saw Colonel Cainas approaching. He looked cheerful. Landon could see nothing for him to be cheerful about.

'Señor Landon,' Cainas said. 'I thought you had deserted us.'

'I left it too late. I should have gone yesterday.'

'Your loss is our gain. Never mind. When this little trouble is over you will be able to sail away in your nice new boat to wherever the fancy takes you.'

'Doesn't that depend on which way the trouble ends?'

'We do not envisage the possibility of defeat,' Cainas said.

He turned to Ortega and began to give orders. The men dispersed, moving away to take cover.

Cainas spoke again to Landon. 'Would you care to take command of the 17-pounder? My men are very inexperienced, and it is a British gun.'

'If you wish,' Landon said.

Pete went with him. He knew nothing about artillery, but he liked to stay close to his captain.

'You and me, Mr Landon,' Pete said, 'we're a couple of damn fools. We got no stake in this rumpus. What's the bonus in dying a hero's death for El Aguila?'

'I have no intention of dying. That isn't the object of the exercise.'

'Nor me,' Pete said. 'But it could happen.'

The 17-pounder was on the left of the road; it had a split trail dug into the hard ground and a sixty-degree traverse. There was a steel shield that looked very comforting.

'Nice gun,' Pete said.

Away beyond the road-block towards Zamora the road curved inland round the bluff of a hill. At this point Valdez's tanks would be forced into a narrow way with no room to manoeuvre on the landward side and with a steep drop towards the sea on the other. It was here that the 17-pounder was intended to engage the attackers.

Landon recognized the man in charge, an N.C.O. named Ansaldo. He also was one of those who had come from Oxaca and he had been rapidly promoted to the rank of sergeant. He was a young and earnest man, but his knowledge of guns was limited, and it was obvious that he was relieved to see Landon.

'It was said that you had gone, señor.'

'Not yet. I had business to complete.'

'I am glad,' Ansaldo said.

Landon examined the gun. It was ready for action; the gun team had not done too badly. Then he looked for the ammunition. He counted twelve rounds laid out ready for use.

'Where is the rest of it?'

Ansaldo wrinkled his forehead. 'The rest, señor?'

'The other ammunition. Surely this isn't all.'

'It is all, señor.'

'God Almighty!' Landon said.

Pete whistled softly. 'That's twelve tanks – if you kill one with each round.'

Landon glanced at him sourly. 'You're the one who's expecting miracles. If we get one tank with the whole twelve we'll be lucky. I wonder how many rounds the field gun has?'

'Six rounds, señor,' Ansaldo said.

'Nice work. When we've fired off our lot we can pack up and go home.'

'We got no home,' Pete said softly.

'Maybe we won't be needing one after this day's work.'

'Valdez is not strong,' Ansaldo said. But there was no conviction in his voice. He seemed to be trying to encourage himself, but without much success.

'How do you know how strong Valdez is?' Landon asked. 'We haven't even had a reconnaissance plane out. Who brought the report of Valdez's tanks?'

'We have scouts along the road.'

'Did they say Valdez was not strong?'

'I do not know what they said. I am only a sergeant. They do not bring their reports to me.'

'It's a damn pleasant situation, whichever way you look at it,' Landon said. Pete was right, dead right: they were two fools, sticking their heads into this when the sloop was there waiting to take them away. They could have been at sea by now, beyond the three-mile limit. They could have finished with Anagua. Yet here they were, waiting for Valdez to blow them to pieces. It just didn't make sense.

He lit a cigarette and tossed one to Pete. The sun was like the open door of a furnace and there was no shade. The sweat made rivers down their faces and the sea looked like a glimpse of paradise, tantalizingly close.

'I wish they'd come,' Pete said. 'Get it over with.'

'They'll come.'

'Could be they've broken down – or gone back home.'

'Could be. But it won't.'

The aircraft came first. They were old Mustang fighter-bombers. It looked as though Valdez had no jet planes; perhaps he had grudged the money to pay for them.

The Mustangs were more venturesome than the earlier bombers; they came in low and strafed the gun positions. The 20-millimetre Oerlikons fired back, but it was such hopelessly wild shooting that it made Landon sick to look at it. He lay flat on the ground behind a low wall of sandbags and he could hear bullets ripping into the bags.

Sergeant Ansaldo let out a yell of pain as a bullet hit him in the left arm just below the elbow. Another man made no sound when he was hit; he would never make any sound again. The bullet took him in the back of the head and came out between the eyes, and it made a bad mess of the face. That was two gone from the 17-pounder team, and they had not started to use the gun yet.

Ansaldo's face poured sweat and his lips were compressed in a thin line of agony. The dead man lay with his shattered face kissing the ground; Landon could see the hole in the back of his head where the .50 calibre bullet had gone in. It looked a big hole, but it was nothing like the one on the other side. There was blood staining the soil, and some other, greyish matter mixed with the blood.

Landon said: 'Are you hurt badly, Sergeant Ansaldo?'

'It is my arm.'

'You'd better get away back. Have it seen to.'

'It is not bad. I will stay here.'

'You can't fight a gun with a smashed arm. I'm giving an order. Get back.'

Sergeant Ansaldo hesitated a moment, then began to drag himself away.

Landon glanced at the dead man. 'This one isn't going to be any trouble. No trouble to anybody.'

The Mustangs swept round in a wide circle and came in again. There were three of them. This time they dropped small bombs – very inaccurately. Landon could feel the earth drumming under him, but there was no other discomfort from the bombing.

He heard Pete again. 'Them boys couldn't hit an eighteen-hole golf course.' He laughed derisively. 'They should take lessons.'

'It's harder than it looks,' Landon said.

It was like gunnery. People who had never tried the game thought you could hit a target first time – smack-bang – just like that. But it never worked out that way; there were too many factors to take into account, too many ballistic problems to solve. When your target was moving it was a thousand times more difficult.

The sun was moving out over the sea when the first armoured car came round the bluff. The bluff was half a mile away and the armoured car was coming fast. The 17-pounder was already loaded and the car moved into the sights like a toy. It approached obliquely, with the angle widening as it came nearer. They fired one round and were behind it. The smoke came curling back from the muzzle and the smell of burnt cordite was sharp in their nostrils. They rammed another round into the breech and fired again. The second round missed also; the gun rocked back on its carriage with the slam of recoil; and that was ten rounds left.

The field gun fired one round and blew a hole in the side of the hill, half-way up.

The armoured car must have been travelling over the concrete at top speed. Whoever was driving it had his foot down hard on the accelerator and meant to slam the car through regardless of any hazard. Landon wondered what the men with the bazookas were doing; they ought to have been able to take this boy. He could hear the stammer of the Oerlikons, and there was a scatter of tracer whipping across the road, but it was not having any appreciable effect on the armoured car.

'Pretty,' Pete muttered. 'Damn pretty.'

'And useless.'

The car came on, its own machine-gun chattering. There was no check in its speed, no indication that there had been the slightest pressure on the brakes. It was like a projectile mounted on four spinning wheels flung at the defences, a battering-ram of steel and rubber that would burst a way through and carry on under its own irresistible momentum into the very streets of Santa Rosa.

It struck the iron stakes that had been driven into the road, and the entire front of it was beaten in like a tin can under a sledgehammer. The back jerked up and the car went over the stakes in a somersaulting motion, over and over and over, until it came to rest at last with its wheels in the air and still spinning. It began to burn then, and the flames came up and engulfed it. They could feel the heat of the fire as far away as the 17-pounder, beating outward in dull red waves. There was no sign of life in the wrecked car. There was no foot on the accelerator now.

'What you think he done that for?' Pete asked. 'You think he was mad – or just wanting to die like a hero?'

'He may have been scared,' Landon said. 'Men do queer things when they're scared. Maybe he didn't see the road-block. Maybe he didn't see anything.'

Pete chuckled. 'First time I ever see an automobile climb over a fence.'

The tank was more cautious. It came round the bluff slowly, like a man peering round a corner to make sure that his creditors are not waiting for him. The front of the caterpillar tracks appeared first, and the muzzle of the gun; then the barrel, the turret, and the rest of the tank. It swung with the stiff, jerky motion that track steering imparts to a vehicle, straightened out, and began to advance down the half-mile stretch of concrete that led to the road-block.

The field gun fired one round and missed. The shell hit the bluff and brought down a shower of earth and rock. From the distance it looked like smoke.

The tank came on, and another one eased itself round the bluff, halted, and began to fire.

Landon could see the puff of smoke that came from the muzzle as the gun fired. He heard the whine of the shell and the heavy crump as it landed and burst somewhere behind him. The tank gunner had overestimated the range, but if he knew his job he would soon bring it down. Landon decided to take the second tank and leave the bazookas to deal with the first.

It took three rounds to get on to the target, but the third one was a beauty. A burst of black smoke seemed to grow suddenly out of the side of the tank, and when it had cleared they could see that the gun barrel was no longer pointing towards the road-block but had been twisted up into the air like a stove-pipe. They were not going to have any more trouble with that one.

'Seven rounds left,' Pete said.

Seven rounds – and the first tank still coming on, slowly but steadily, with a kind of inevitability.

Landon asked angrily: 'What in hell are those bazooka boys doing? Admiring the scenery?' The tank stopped.

'Don't fancy the look of them stakes,' Pete said.

'Who would?'

Landon heard at last the whoosh of a bazooka. The tank remained unscathed.

'Good God! What do they want to aim at – a house? They have a sitting bird and they can't hit it.'

'Maybe we better take him,' Pete suggested.

'You tell me how to give this gun ten more degrees of traverse and maybe we'll do just that.'

He wiped the sweat off his face. It was running into his eyes so that he was unable to see clearly. He looked towards the bluff and saw a third tank appear. It looked heavier than the other two, probably a cruiser; it was hump-backed, stubby, with a rounded turret.

'Could be an old Sherman,' Landon muttered. It was that type. And the gun would probably be a 75 mm.

He yelled orders. The 17-pounder swung on to the tank and fired – once – twice. The tank moved clear of the bluff and edged off to the left-hand side of the road. A fourth one and then a fifth came round the bluff.

The tanks brought their guns to bear on the road block and began to fire. The 17-pounder ate up its remaining five rounds and scored one hit on the fourth tank.

'We get out of here now,' Landon shouted. 'Fast!'

The shells from the tanks were beginning to burst far too near to them now. Before long it looked as though the whole defensive position would be blown sky-high. It was time to go.

The gunners hesitated. They looked scared and bewildered. Landon snarled at them.

'Get to hell out of here.'

They began to crawl away from the gun, keeping close to the ground. A shell splinter hit the shield with a clang and skidded away to imbed itself in a sandbag.

Landon thumped Pete's shoulder.

'Come on, Pete. The party's over.'

Wriggling like snakes, stomachs to earth, they began to move back from the gun position. It was not, Landon mused, a heroic way of doing things, leaving your gun and crawling away to safety – if there was safety anywhere. But this was no time for heroics; he had done as much for Alvarez as he felt called upon to do; he had fought his gun until the gun had died on him, and that was enough. The only sensible thing to do now was to take avoiding action, to save your own skin. Nobody was going to benefit from bits and pieces of Harvey Landon scattered over the battlefield – least of all Harvey Landon.

To hell with it, he thought. To hell with the whole, damned, crack-brained business.

They had progressed about a hundred yards when a shell landed plumb on the 17-pounder, and that was the end of the gun. It had certainly been time to leave.

Landon was feeling painfully exposed. He felt like a snail that has lost its shell. The cover was sparse; rocks, scrub, little else. He began to make for the hilly ground away to his right. Perhaps he and Pete could go to earth over there; it was the only chance.

He no longer had any doubt that Valdez's army would take Santa Rosa; the road block was smashed and the tanks were moving up; he could hear the intermittent crackle of their machine-guns, filling in the gaps between the thunder of the bigger guns. But perhaps if he and Pete could get to the hills and hide themselves they might be able to sneak back when things had quietened down. They might be able to take the sloop and escape. It would not be easy, but it might be possible.

Then he thought of the girl in a town filled with Valdez's troops, and doubts assailed him again.

He was still crawling towards the hills, still turning over vague plans in his mind when the world disintegrated in the blast and flaring crimson of a shell-burst. Suddenly there was a black pit opening in front of him, and into that pit he fell headlong.

17

VALDEZ

THERE WERE TWO other men in the cell with Landon. One of them was Pete and the other was Cranefield's prospector Anderson.

Landon had a bandage round his head and a throbbing pain in his temples. He felt washed out; he felt like something the tide had thrown up on a beach, something vomited up by a sick dog.

Pete's left arm was bandaged above the wrist and he had a criss-cross of sticking plaster on his left eyebrow. Anderson appeared to be unscathed, but crumpled. He had taken no part in the battle.

One wall of the cell consisted of iron bars stretching from floor to ceiling, a barred door in the middle fastened with a massive lock. Through the bars could be seen part of a corridor, and on either side of this were other cells, all occupied, all overcrowded.

A small barred window with no glass in it, high up on the other side of the cell, allowed air and a little light to filter in. With the help of Pete, Landon had been able to see out of this window. The view was not particularly pleasing: a dusty, pounded yard like a barrack square and on every side of it, closing it in, plain, whitewashed buildings with more barred windows.

This was the Santa Rosa gaol.

There were two bare wooden bunks, one above the other. Anderson was sitting on the lower one, his head in his hands, his shoulders hunched. The men had been in the gaol for three days and on each day they had heard the crackle of a machine-gun coming from the yard. Each day had seen a reduction in the population of the prison.

'I could use a cigarette,' Pete said.

He was leaning against the wall, his shoulders pressing against the cold stone. His shirt was torn and an expanse of black chest was visible. Watching him through half-closed eyes, Landon thought again what a tough boy it was; tough and young and virile. Too bad that all this toughness and youth and virility should have to be mown down by the bullets of a machine-gun. Today, tomorrow, the next day.

A gaoler strolled down the corridor, keys jangling at his belt. He had a skin almost as dark as Pete's but there was nothing black about his nose; it was parrot-beaked, and the lips below it were thin.

Landon went to the bars and called softly: 'Hey, gaoler!'

The man approached without haste. His walk was all insolence. 'Gringo!'

He spat, and the spittle missed Landon only by inches.

'What you want, gringo?'

'Cigarettes.'

The gaoler laughed, mocking him. 'No cigarette for prisoners.' He spat again, narrowly missing Landon on the other side. Perhaps the third time he would hit his mark.

Landon pulled some money out of his pocket. They had taken away his watch, his revolver, Pete's sheath-knife, everything except his money. By some whim they had allowed him to keep that, perhaps to tantalize him. They knew that he would never be able to use it.

He fluttered the wad close to the gaoler's nose and watched the man's eyes glitter.

'This for cigarettes.'

'It is against regulations.'

'Regulations were made to be broken. You could use this money, a man like you.'

The gaoler glanced over his shoulder, then looked again at the money. He licked his lips; his tongue was as brown as a leather strap.

'Very well, gringo.'

He reached down into the pocket of his greasy shirt and pulled out a crumpled packet. There were nine flattened cigarettes in it.

'These for the money.'

'And matches.'

'Matches also.'

It was about fifty times the value of the cigarettes, but Landon paid. Money was no use to him now; it was just so much paper. He took the cigarettes and the matches, and the gaoler went away, stuffing the notes into his hip pocket. The keys jangled at his side.

Landon tossed a cigarette to Pete. He caught it in his left hand, stuffed it in his mouth and lit it from Landon's match. He sucked smoke into his lungs.

'Tastes good.'

Landon touched the American's shoulder. 'Want a cigarette, Earl?'

Anderson shook his head without looking up.

'Have it your own way,' Landon said. 'But you ought to shake yourself out of that mood. It won't do you any good.'

'Leave me be,' Anderson said.

'He don't like being shut up,' Pete said. 'Maybe it's a new experience. How about you, Mr Landon. You ever been inside the cage before?'

Landon lit his cigarette and the throbbing in his head seemed to ease a little. He leaned against the bunks, facing Pete across the narrow cell.

'Too often,' he said. He remembered the gaol in Santa Ana where Vargas had blown the wall in and they had got away on horseback. This cell was luxurious compared with that one. But this time there was no Don Diego to haul him out. This time it looked as though he was in for keeps.

He flicked ash on to the floor. 'I've been in worse accommodation – and better.'

'You think they mean to shoot us? You think we'll be stuck up against a wall for that goon with the machine-gun to practise on?'

'Could be.'

'I never thought I'd ever be dummy for a greasy machine-gunner. You don't think they could maybe run out of ammo before they get around to us?'

'They won't run out of rope. I think I'd rather have the machine-gun.'

'Me, I'd be happy without either. If you'd really like to know my personal preference, it'd be to die of old age in a nice soft bed, yes, sir.'

'I'll tell the gaoler. Perhaps he can arrange it.'

Anderson took his head out of his hands. 'Why don't you guys let up?'

'We just naturally like to talk,' Pete said. 'We don't know how long we'll be able to.'

'Then talk about something else, can't you?'

'The trouble with you,' Pete said, 'is you let yourself get depressed. I'd say you ain't never had it tough before. Now, Mr Landon and me, we're old hands; we been in plenty of trouble, so we're used to it. We don't let it worry us none.'

'Not much,' Landon said. 'Not more than a dose of arsenic in the belly.'

Anderson said: 'They won't do anything to me. They wouldn't dare. I'm an American citizen. I'll demand to see the American consul.'

'I don't think they run to one in this town,' Landon said. 'Or if they did, he's probably taken a powder.'

'I'm an American citizen,' Anderson repeated, as though the mere repetition of the words might act as a charm to save him.

Landon allowed smoke to ooze out of his mouth and drift away towards the barred window with its little patch of sky, tantalizing them.

'I'm a British citizen. So's Pete. But we're not leaning very heavily on that. When you take part in a revolution and the revolution folds up you have to take the consequences. No good howling American or British then. No good pulling the Stars and Stripes or the Union Jack out of your pocket. You're on your own, pal, you're on your own.'

'I didn't fight for Alvarez.'

'You came with the arms ship. It adds up to the same thing. You didn't really get down to that prospecting, did you? Somehow I don't think you're ever going to now. Cranefield had better try and make a deal with Valdez.'

He smoked half the cigarette, stubbed it out carefully, and put the unused half away.

'If you're not using that bunk I think I'll get some sleep.'

'Okay,' Anderson said. He got up and began to pace up and down the narrow confines of the cell, hands in pockets, shoulders hunched.

Landon swung himself on to the bunk, closed his eyes, and went to sleep.

He had no idea what time it was when they woke him. The cell door was open, the gaoler was standing beside it, and two armed guards were outside.

'You,' the gaoler said. 'The Generalissimo wants to see you. Pronto.'

Landon took his time. He yawned, stretched himself, rolled off the bunk, and pushed his fingers through his hair.

'Hurry!' the gaoler snarled.

Landon looked at Pete. 'If I don't see you again, Pete, thanks for everything.' He put out his hand and Pete grasped it in his own engulfing paw.

'You'll see me again, Mr Landon. Sure you will.'

Anderson gave a short hysterical laugh. 'What makes you so sure?'

'Pipe down,' Pete said.

Anderson moved away from the cell door and pressed himself against the far wall, as though afraid that the guards might take him also. He gazed at them with scared, fascinated eyes.

Landon went out of the cell and the door clanged shut behind him. As the guards marched him away he heard the jangling of the gaoler's keys.

Landon had heard so much about Valdez that he had fallen into the habit of feeling that he knew the man. He had a picture of the dictator in his mind, a picture built up partly from descriptions given by others and partly from his own imagination. The picture was vivid and clear – and it was almost completely false.

Valdez was not as he had imagined.

For one thing, he had fair hair and blue eyes, and no one had told Landon that. Therefore, he had naturally supposed that Valdez would conform to the Spanish-Indian type common in Aflagua, whereas this man sitting behind the desk might have been a German.

Valdez was fat – grossly, even obscenely, fat; the flesh bulged from him everywhere in great folds. He was wearing a fine silk shirt, and the shirt was stained with dark patches of sweat. It was unbuttoned to the waist, and Valdez's chest and stomach were visible, smooth and hairless as a baby's skin. On chest and stomach lay the tattoo of a naked woman; she seemed to be standing in the opening of the shirt like a prostitute standing in a doorway. When Valdez moved the flesh quivered and the woman appeared to ripple sensually, voluptuously, as though inviting attention.

Valdez's hair was cropped so closely that the scalp was visible beneath it. His face was the colour of an old brick, and its entire surface was pock-marked with little cavities, as though a woodpecker had been at work on it, delving for food. There was a vertical scar in the exact centre of his upper lip; it went all the way up the nose. Perhaps, Landon thought, some patriot had once tried to slice the face in halves. Under the scarred lip the teeth were far too white and far too even to be anything but false; indeed, there was much about this face that gave the impression of falsity.

Valdez grinned at Landon like an overfed wolf, baring the white, even teeth. But there was no friendliness in the smile.

'Señor Harvey Landon?' Valdez said. He had a hoarse, croaking voice; it was the kind of voice one might have expected from an educated toad.

'That is my name,' Landon admitted. He was aware of the armed guards standing behind him, barring any way of escape, watchful that he did not attack the Generalissimo, whom his enemies called the Sergeant.

'You have given me much trouble,' Valdez croaked.

'There might have been more.'

'Naturally. That was your intention, of course. Valdez was to be deposed. Valdez was perhaps to be hanged. But the old fox is not so easily caught. Why did you help Alvarez?'

'Does it matter why?'

'No, it does not matter. But the reason it is not difficult to divine. You are an adventurer, Señor Landon, a soldier of fortune. You sell your services to anyone who will pay you. We have heard of you. You were involved with Don Diego Vargas in the Central Republic. Vargas was hanged. Has it ever occurred to you that you have a bad habit, señor?'

'What bad habit?'

'The habit of choosing the wrong side.'

'Unfortunate – not bad.'

'You are a soldier of misfortune perhaps.'

'Perhaps.'

'There is no perhaps in this case. You realize, of course, that we shall execute you.'

'No trial?' Landon said.

Valdez laughed, and the woman inside the shirt quivered as though she too were laughing.

'Forgive me, Señor Landon, but it is very funny. You say that so seriously. It is as if you really believe that we should go to the trouble of setting up a court, of bringing witnesses, counsel perhaps – all such nonsense. And for what purpose? To tell us something that we know already – that Harvey Landon is guilty of assisting a revolt against the legal government of Anagua. No, my friend, we need no court of law to tell us that we may shoot a traitor.'

'I am not a traitor. I owe no allegiance to Anagua. Nor any to you.'

'It makes no difference,' Valdez said.

'Then why have you brought me here? What point can there be in this interview?'

Valdez wiped the sweat from his face with a fine large handkerchief.

'May I not satisfy my curiosity? I have heard of you. I wished to see the Englishman. I shall be one of the last to see you.'

'Do you think it would be wise to execute a British citizen without trial?'

'How do I know that you are British? Have you a passport? If so, please show it to me.'

'You know I have no passport.'

'If you have no passport you have no visa, and therefore you are an illegal immigrant. How am I to be sure that you are British? Anyone might tell that tale.'

'You know it's true.'

Valdez shrugged. 'Possibly. But it makes no difference. Who do you think will tell the British Government that you have been shot in a gaol in Santa Rosa? What action would they take even if the information did leak through? None. They have more important things to worry them than the fate of some obscure adventurer who has gone poking his nose into matters that do not concern him.

Those who dabble in the politics of Central America must expect to take the consequences.'

'Have you heard me complaining?' Landon said.

'You ask for a trial.'

Valdez took a cigar from a box on the desk, lit it with a match and leaned back, puffing smoke. The breasts of the woman tattooed on his chest rose and fell in rhythm with his breathing.

'Tomorrow,' Valdez said, 'we execute your friend Alvarez. I feel sure that you will wish to witness the execution, and I have, therefore, arranged that you and Pete and the American shall be allowed to do so.'

Landon did not answer. He stared at Valdez but said nothing.

'On the following day it will be the turn of the American; after that, Pete; finally, yourself. You will observe that I am honouring you by leaving you until the last.'

'So that's an honour.'

'Most certainly. We did not honour Cainas so much. He has already been shot.'

'You ought to shoot Costa too. He's a nice, sweet double-crosser.'

'Colonel Costa is loyal – to me,' Valdez said. He said it lightly, but there was a warning glitter in his eyes which seemed to say that this was no topic of conversation on which to venture unwarily. This was dangerous ground.

Landon said, staring at Valdez and ignoring the danger signals: 'Or to his sister.'

Valdez seemed to stiffen. He leaned forward, resting his thick fingers on the desk. 'What was that?'

'They say in Santa Rosa that Costa runs with his sister's legs. They say he rides on the shoulders of the Sergeant's whore.'

Landon would never have believed that a man as gross as Valdez could possibly have moved so quickly. He came round the desk like a bull, dragging the big automatic pistol from the holster on his belt. Landon tried to dodge, but the guards seized and held him. The barrel of the pistol struck him on the right cheek and then on the left, and the pain rushed up into his eyes. He felt the sting of blood flowing, and saw Valdez, his face aflame with rage, lift the automatic to strike again. And then the blackness came over him again like a dark cloud from which there was no escaping.

*

Landon awoke to the companionship of pain. At first he kept his eyes closed, just fighting the pain. It was easier not to open the eyes. But in the end he had to do so. Even then he could not see clearly; something seemed to have been pushed up under each eye like a small bolster. He did not realize immediately that these strange hillocks of flesh were his swollen cheeks.

He was lying on his back on the lower bunk in the cell, and Pete was leaning over him. Even with blurred vision he could see the expression of concern on Pete's face. There was anger there also – and pity.

'You awake now, Mr Landon?'

'I'm awake, Pete.'

His throat was so dry he could hardly bring the words out; they seemed to stick somewhere along the line, as though they had been rusted in.

'They treated you bad, them bastards.'

'Yes, Pete, they treated me bad.'

His face was stiff; it was as if cement had been poured over it and allowed to set. Under the stiffness it ached with a dull, throbbing ache like a dozen rotten teeth. His lips were thick, blubbery – as thick as Pete's. He put a hand to his face and felt the open gashes and the congealed blood.

'I was a damn fool,' he said. 'Just one damn fool.'

It had been madness to provoke Valdez; there had been no reason to do so; it could not help him. He had done it on an impulse; the words had come as if by their own volition. And they had touched a nerve in Valdez. By God, they had done that sure enough.

'Why did they beat you up?' Pete asked.

'It was Valdez. He didn't like something I said.'

'I'd like to beat him up.' The bunk shook under the fierce grip of Pete. He was one big powerful slab of man and he was very angry. Landon could imagine Valdez in that grip. Valdez would need his guards if Pete ever laid hands on him.

Anderson moved into Landon's line of vision.

'Did you get any information? Did you hear what they intend to do with us?'

Landon tried to grin, but nobody could grin with a face set in cement; it was one of the impossibilities.

He said: 'They're shooting Alvarez tomorrow. We're to be spectators.'

'Oh, God!'

'They were sure to do that,' Pete said. 'He'd be a dangerous man to leave lying around.'

'And us?' Anderson said in a strangled voice.

'We get the same treatment. Valdez believes in equal shares for all. In some ways he's a Marxist.'

'No, no, no. He wouldn't dare to do it. I'm an American. They can't shoot an American citizen. They can't—'

'You should have gone looking for that uranium somewhere else,' Landon said. Anderson made him sick with his whining. When you went in for games like this you had to take what came to you; it was no use howling about the rules.

The sweat was pouring down Anderson's face, but it was not because of the heat.

'When? Did they say when?'

Landon did not spare him. 'You, the day after tomorrow; Pete, the next day; myself, last. Valdez likes to drag it out. I think he enjoys watching. It's a kind of entertainment. If he had to be hauled away from the flesh-pots of Villanova you must expect him to make somebody pay. We happen to be the unlucky ones.'

Anderson buried his face in his hands; his shoulders trembled. 'No, it can't be. Something will happen, something.'

It was the child's outlook. Such things could be done to others, yes; but one's own body was sacrosanct.

'The only way out of a mess like this,' Landon said harshly, 'is the way you make for yourself.'

'That's so,' Pete said. 'That surely is so.'

He moved away from the bunk and began to prowl round the cell, tigerish in his lithe muscularity. Tigerish – and caged.

It was like the molten heat of a steel foundry in the prison yard. Valdez did not have his executions at dawn; he waited until the sun was up. And under the hard white glare of the sun Alvarez had come to the end of his road.

Landon, Anderson, and Pete stood with their hands manacled behind them and guards on either side. They stood bareheaded in the sun and the sweat dripped from them in great beads like oil.

Valdez was sitting on a chair with a kind of canvas awning to shade him. With his fleshy stomach and the rolls of fat at his neck, he looked like a gross, debased representation of Buddha. At his elbow was Colonel Costa, smiling.

'That snake,' Pete growled. 'Alvarez should have put a halter round his neck when he had the chance.'

One of the guards jabbed a rifle butt in Pete's side. 'Silence, you!'

Pete looked at the guard as though printing the man's face on his memory. But he said nothing.

They brought Alvarez out and marched him before Valdez. He stood there erect. There was dried blood on his face, and one of his arms hung limply at his side, as though he had no more power over its movements. It was plain that he had not been handled gently by his captors.

Valdez looked at him with his wolf's grin, baring the too-white teeth.

'So – The Eagle has had its wings clipped. It cannot fly any more. It will never fly again. Such a pity.'

Alvarez said nothing.

'Do you have any last words?' Valdez asked. 'Some message perhaps that you would care to leave to posterity. There is no hurry. Marcos is a patient man; he will wait.'

The man squatted down by the machine-gun spat on the dusty ground of the prison-yard. He did not look patient; he looked morose and sullen, his skin almost black. The number two on the gun touched the ammunition belt as though caressing it. He chuckled softly.

Still Alvarez said nothing.

Valdez took out a handkerchief and wiped the sweat from his face. 'No? No final words of wisdom? No instructions to the people on how to get rid of Pancho Valdez? Since you yourself have been so successful, it would be a pity if the method should be lost. And why not tell us how to lick the gringo's feet?'

He was trying to provoke Alvarez, but Alvarez remained aloof, refusing to be drawn. He stood with the sun beating down on his greying head and his mouth closed in a firm thin line. It was Valdez who was provoked. Suddenly he leaned forward and spat in Alvarez's face. The spittle ran down Alvarez's cheek, but though his hands were free he made no attempt to wipe it off. He merely stared contemptuously at Valdez and still uttered no word.

Valdez yelled: 'Take him! Shoot him!'

Alvarez turned and looked at Landon. His head bent forward in a slight bow.

'Adios,' he said.

Then they were hustling him away to the wall.

They did not blindfold him. He stood erect, proudly staring into the muzzle of the machine-gun. Marcos put his hands on the gun and looked at Valdez, waiting for the signal. Valdez brought his right hand down in a chopping motion, and the machine-gun began to crackle. Dust flew from the wall behind Alvarez and his shirt fluttered. A row of holes appeared in his chest. He fell sideways, rolled over on to his face, and was dead.

The machine-gun stopped firing, and Valdez got up from his chair.

He spoke to Landon. 'The entertainment is over.'

They had to drag Anderson out of the cell. He screamed and fought with the guards who came to take him. In his terror he shouted to Landon and Pete to save him.

'They can't kill me. I haven't done anything. Tell them I'll give them money. I'll do whatever they want. I'll work for them. Tell them. They can't kill me; they can't do it.'

The guards forced his hands behind his back and tied them with cord. He became limp suddenly. They took him, one on either side, and he went out of the cell with his feet dragging. The door clanged shut behind him and the key grated in the lock.

'I don't think he wanted to go,' Pete said. 'He'll find they can kill him. He should have done his prospecting some other place. This country just ain't healthy.'

He was silent for a while. Then he said: 'You got any cigarettes left, Mr Landon?'

Landon took the last one out of his pocket, broke it in halves, and gave one half to Pete.

'You could call me Harvey,' he said.

Pete shook his head. 'No, Mr Landon; no, sir. I like it the way it is.'

'Please yourself.'

They were smoking the cigarette when the machine-gun chattered briefly.

'Mr Anderson,' Pete said. 'He'll be doing his prospecting some other place now.'

The swelling under Landon's eyes had gone down a lot, but his face was still stiff and sore from the beating that Valdez had given him, and his head ached. He sucked smoke into his lungs and loved it. This was the last cigarette. It looked as though it might be the last he would ever smoke. Enjoy it, Harvey, enjoy it.

'We have to get out of here,' he said.

He lay on the lower bunk and Pete lounged against the wall opposite.

'And we have to get out tonight.'

Pete blew smoke through his nose and watched it drifting away in a blue-grey cloud.

'You got any ideas?'

'Maybe,' Landon said.

18

BREAK OUT

LANDON SWUNG HIS feet to the ground and stood up. He touched Pete who was lying on the upper bunk.

'Awake, Pete?'

'Sure thing. I didn't sleep neither.'

There was a little light coming into the cell from a lamp in the corridor outside. It was past midnight. At the end of the corridor a gaoler sat on a chair, dozing. The keys of the cells hung on a steel ring hooked to his belt. It was the man who had sold Landon the cigarettes.

Pete dropped lightly from the upper bunk.

'Ready now?'

'Ready,' Landon said.

He went to the door of the cell and rattled it gently. Pete stood on one side, close to the wall, in the angle between the wall and the bars. There was deep shadow where he stood and he was almost invisible, his black skin blending with the darkness.

The gaoler did not stir.

Landon rattled the door again, a little more vigorously. The gaoler lifted his head. Landon made a hissing sound with his lips and pushed one hand through the bars. In his fingers he held all the paper money that he had left. He fluttered the notes like a signal flag.

The gaoler saw the signal and got up, yawning. He walked down the corridor with a slow, waddling gait, and the keys jangled softly at his waist. He was wearing a cartridge belt with an automatic pistol in a leather holster. It was eighteen hours since he had shaved, and the black stubble was pushing through, giving his face a shaded look.

He reached the cell and stood there, away from the bars, his feet apart, hands resting on hips. He stared at Landon.

'What you want, gringo?'

'Cigarettes,' Landon said.

He could hear Pete breathing, and he hoped the gaoler would not hear, would not peer into the darkness on his left. He had to hold the man's attention. He fluttered the notes.

The gaoler came a little nearer. Landon drew the notes back so that the man could not snatch them.

'Cigarettes.'

'You don't get cigarettes where you go,' the gaoler said, and chuckled hoarsely, enjoying his own joke. 'Too much fire perhaps.'

'Perhaps. Time to think about that later. I'm asking for a cigarette now. Here's the money.'

'Suppose I come in and take the money.' He patted the automatic at his side. 'I have it for nothing then.'

Landon hoped he would come in. That would make it all so easy. But he knew that the man had no intention of opening the door of the cell, of exposing himself in that way. He was too wary.

'You wouldn't want to cheat a man who has to die,' Landon said.

The gaoler laughed again, softly; there was mockery in his laughter. 'You think not, gringo?'

He put a hand in the pocket of his shirt and pulled out a paper packet of cigarettes. It looked like the same crushed packet that he had sold Landon on the previous occasion. He held the packet close to his chest like a crafty card player with a good hand.

'The money, gringo.'

'The cigarettes,' Landon said, keeping the wad of notes away from the bars. There must be no quick snatch. Everything had to go according to plan.

The gaoler came closer. He held out his right hand, rubbing the fingers, one against another. The cigarette packet was in his left hand.

'No games, dead man. The money—'

He was close enough now; he had walked into the trap. Pete's arm came through the bars like a black snake, hooked itself about the gaoler's neck and tightened. The gaoler's back pressed against the bars and the black arm choked back what might have been a cry. The gaoler's hands clawed at the arm, trying to loosen it, but the arm was like a ship's hawser; it did not give an inch. The gaoler's mouth sagged open as his lungs gasped for air and no air came through. He gave a last convulsive jerk like a puppet on a string, and then he had gone, and it was only the empty body that was left there hanging on Pete's arm.

'Who's the dead man now?' Pete whispered.

Landon reached through the bars and unhooked the ring of keys from the gaoler's belt. Pete took his arm away, and the man slumped to the floor. Landon found the right key, unlocked the cell door, and swung it open.

'Come on, Pete.'

The two men stepped out into the corridor. They listened. There was no sound, no indication that anyone had taken alarm.

'We'll get the others,' Landon said.

He began to move along the corridor, going with the keys from one door to another, wakening the prisoners.

'Rouse yourselves. This is a break out.'

Men who had been condemned to die needed no urging. The magic word was Freedom. They came out of their cells and stood silently in the corridor, waiting for the next move. The gaoler lay where he had fallen, not stirring.

Landon stooped down and took the automatic and cartridge belt. He fastened the belt round his own waist, took the pistol out of the holster, and saw that it was loaded.

'What now?' Pete asked.

There were thirty-five men and Landon knew many of them by sight. They were Alvarez's men and some of them had come from Oxaca, some from San Quinton. Two had been with him when they captured the launch on the Rio Chico. They were all desperate men, their desire to escape sharpened by the daily chatter of the machine-gun and the knowledge that they also were on the list for execution.

'The guard-room,' Landon said. He spoke to the men softly but urgently. 'We will take them by surprise. They may be sleeping. Are you ready?'

A low murmur answered him. He could sense the tension in them, the sudden return of hope. If they could escape from the gaol these men might disappear, might melt into the interior of Anagua where Valdez could never find them. The hope burned up fiercely in them like a fire suddenly fanned from near-dead embers. It seemed to blaze from their eyes.

'Ready.'

There were six men awake in the guard-room. They were playing cards at a long table on which the remains of a meal still lay scattered. These men were awake but they were not ready, and they had no time to reach for their weapons before the prisoners were upon them.

Some of them got to their feet; some of them dropped their hands on to pistol butts; some cried out briefly before the cries were strangled in their throats. They were clubbed and throttled and cast aside. For these prisoners whom Landon had released were not men but animals, jungle beasts whose cage door had been left open. They were savage and ruthless.

There were other gaolers sleeping in a dormitory adjoining the guard-room. Many of these did not even wake; they were killed in their sleep. The tide flowed over them and went on, rolling to the outer doors, armed now and irresistible, a tide of bitter, angry men with the blood-lust in them and the light of freedom visible ahead.

Landon was no longer their leader. He no longer had any control over them. He stood aside and allowed the flood to sweep on; he stayed close to Pete and followed.

They came out into the prison-yard where Alvarez had been shot. There were a few lights burning, and in a kind of concrete tower were two guards with a machine-gun and a searchlight. The searchlight came on suddenly, dazzling the escapers. They halted for a moment, huddled together, hesitating, confused by this white beam that had caught them and was holding them like moths transfixed by the collector's pin.

Then the machine-gun began to fire, stammering in short bursts like a man cursing. Men screamed, clutched at chests, fell twitching. The group scattered, running for cover. A siren began to wail, giving warning that there had been a gaol break.

A hoarse shout went up: 'To the gate! The gate!'

They ran across the yard under the white glare of the

searchlight. The machine-gun spat at them, picking them off. Some fell, but the others ran on.

Landon and Pete watched the beam and moved round the perimeter of the yard – the long way, but the safest. They came at last to the gate behind the first rush of prisoners. There was a guard-room above the gate, forming an arch under which they were able to take cover. A sentry attempted to halt them; he lifted his rifle, fired one round, and was shot through the throat.

The escapers crowded under the arch where the searchlight could not find them and the deadly fire of the machine-gun could not reach. Some of them had found axes, and now they began to hack at the wicket in the main gate, splinters flying from the stout timber.

The siren went on howling.

Some of Valdez's soldiers, still only half awake, clattered down the stairs from the guard-room over the gate and were picked off one by one as they appeared. The ground under the arch became slippery with blood, while the shrieks and groans of the wounded mingled with the wailing of the siren and the sullen thudding of the axes.

From across the yard came the flash and crackle of rifle fire, and bullets ricocheted off the walls. The men under the arch piled dead bodies for a defensive wall and fired back with the weapons they had captured. They had to hold the arch until the gate was down.

The axes beat faster, frenziedly; the iron-bound wicket held.

In the shadows under the arch it was impossible to tell how many were still alive. Out in the yard the dead lay like heaps of discarded clothing. Here and there a wounded man was dragging himself painfully along, trying to reach some kind of shelter from the bullets that hummed and whined across the dusty square. But for these poor wounded there was little hope of escape.

The siren died suddenly, and the desultory crackle of rifle fire and the crashing of the axes sounded all the louder for the lack of this competition. Landon heard the sudden pounding of feet and saw a dark mass of riflemen rushing across the yard. Some stumbled and fell, cut down by the fire of the prisoners, but a dozen or so reached the wall of dead bodies and came to grips with the defenders. A savage hand-to-hand struggle developed, in which rifles were used as clubs and men clawed and gouged with bloody hands.

Landon emptied his automatic at such close range it was impossible to miss. A man fell against him, blood spurting from his shattered head, and the blood ran down Landon's face until he could taste its saltness on his lips. His body rebelled against the indecency of it; his stomach tried to bring up food that was not there and he retched. He wiped his mouth on his arm, trying to wipe away the slime and the disgust.

He felt someone dragging at his left shoulder. And then Pete's voice was in his ear – urgent, hoarse, throaty.

'The gate is down! Come away!'

He turned and stumbled over the bodies of the dead and wounded men, and went through the shattered wicket with Pete at his heels, a rifle swinging from Pete's hand. They hesitated only a moment in the street outside, then turned to the left and ran, keeping close against the wall. Other men ran with them, but they were apart; for this was no longer a combined force but a company of stragglers, each one for himself.

They had gone perhaps a hundred yards when a bullet hummed past Landon's head, struck the wall, and ricocheted with a shrill screech. He had an impulse to drop to the ground and lie still, but he knew that there would be no escape that way; the only possible course was to keep driving on.

Then they saw the armoured car. It came round a corner and halted in the middle of the road. It was about fifty yards ahead of Landon and Pete, and there were buildings on either side of it. There was no exit for them that way.

The car had been driving with sidelights only. Now the driver switched on his head-lamps and the whole street was illuminated by a flood of light. A dozen men tried to melt into brickwork as the machine-gun on the car opened fire.

Landon heard Pete's yell. 'This way! In here!'

And then Pete's hand was slamming him into what appeared to be a black tunnel, but was in fact a narrow alleyway between two rows of houses. They went down the alleyway fast, plunging blindly into the darkness, instinctively moving away from the whining bullets.

Landon was sweating; he felt sick in the stomach; his head throbbed with the pain of his wound and the beating that Valdez had given him. But he forced his body to go on. There was no time for weakness.

They met no one in the alleyway, and the houses showed no light; the people in them might all have been dead. Most certainly they could not be sleeping, for the siren would have awakened them. Perhaps they were being discreet; perhaps they had had enough of fighting and wanted no more of it.

The firing of the machine-gun stopped suddenly. They heard the armoured car grinding up the street in low gear, as though it were moving warily among the dead. Glancing back Landon could see the headlights shining past the entrance to the alleyway. He ran on.

It was a wall that stopped them. It stood across the alleyway, joining up with the walls on either side. They had came to the end of a cul-de-sac.

Pete cursed softly. 'A trap! A damned trap!'

Landon was searching the wall with his hands, feeling in the darkness for a way through. Suddenly he came upon a break in the flat surface. He called to Pete.

'There's a door here.'

He found a handle and turned it. He tried the door both ways, pushing and pulling, but it did not open.

'Locked!'

'Stand out of the way, Mr Landon,' Pete said.

He lifted his rifle and smashed at the door with the butt. The door was solid; it did not budge. He beat on it again more fiercely. They could hear the armoured car drawing near the other end of the alleyway. At any moment a searchlight might be turned on them, and after the searchlight would come the bullets, hissing down at them between the close and prisoning walls. They had stumbled into a trap sure enough, and it looked like being a deadly trap.

Pete beat a tattoo on the door. It was enough to have aroused the entire neighbourhood, but not a light glimmered out from the dead walls, not a chink. And the door gave no hint of opening. Pete lowered the rifle despairingly.

'Maybe there's a window.'

And then they heard a movement inside the house, and a sound as of a bar being lifted. The armoured car reached the end of the alleyway and stopped. The door of the house creaked open on protesting hinges. They heard a voice speaking to them; it was an old, thin voice and it held a note of urgency.

'Quickly! Come inside!'

They went into the darkness and heard the door swing shut behind them; they heard the bar being replaced in its sockets.

'This way,' the voice said, and a hand tugged at Landon's arm. He allowed himself to be drawn away from the door and Pete followed. The air was heavy and stale; it was like going into a tomb.

'Take care,' the voice said. 'There are steps here.'

The steps felt like worn stone. Landon went carefully, probing with his feet and counting the steps. There were eight.

They came to the bottom and the voice said: 'Stay here. Do not move.'

Landon heard the owner of the voice going back up the steps. He heard another door close, then feet again on the steps. Someone brushed past him. There was the scrape of a match, a candle flared up, died down, and began to burn steadily as the wax melted. The room came into view; it was small, sparsely furnished with a table and some plain wooden chairs. Pete was standing with his rifle butt resting on the floor and his hand on the barrel; he blinked in the light and shuffled his feet. From somewhere, a long way off, came the muffled sound of knocking.

The candle was resting in a china candlestick on the table. By the table stood a woman – very old, very wrinkled.

She said: 'You come from the gaol? You escaped?'

'Yes,' Landon said.

'I heard the siren and the shooting.' She peered at Landon, her eyes strangely brilliant and glittering in the candlelight. 'You are the Englishman. I have seen you with El Aguila.'

'El Aguila is dead,' Landon said.

She nodded her head. 'So I was told. That dog Valdez killed him, as he killed my sons also. Some day Valdez will roast in hell for the crimes he has committed. We had hopes that El Aguila would succeed in liberating this poor country, but it was not to be; it was not God's will.'

'There will be another liberator.'

'Perhaps. Some day. But I do not think I shall live to see it. I am too old. That is why I have dared to shelter you. If they kill me it will be nothing; a few more years will do the work for them anyway. And I remember my sons; they were such men as you, señor, and they were beaten as I see you have been beaten. And then they were shot, as one might shoot a mad dog.'

There was a sudden loud hammering. The house vibrated.

'They are at the door already,' the woman said.

Pete lifted his rifle and held it slanting across his chest.

'You will not need your gun,' the woman said.

Landon said urgently: 'Is there a way out at the back? We must get away.'

The old woman was calm. She seemed to have thought it all out.

'I will hide you,' she said.

To Landon the idea did not sound attractive. He had no wish to be caught in the house, to be drawn out like a winkle on the end of a pin.

'It would be better to go.'

'No.' The woman was firm. She put her hand on his arm, restraining him. It was as though she would have calmed him with her own calmness.

The thudding on the door became louder. They could hear men's voices.

'They will be here in a moment,' Landon said. 'Where can you hide us?'

He could see no way out of the room except by the steps down which they had come; no other door, no window. Already it was beginning to look as much a trap as the blind alley. The woman took the candle off the table and moved to the far end of the room. On the floor Landon saw what he had at first supposed to be long wooden packing cases. Now in the candle-light he saw that they were coffins. There were two of them and they were new.

'These are for my sons,' the woman said. 'I am to have the bodies tomorrow. Tomorrow these will go to the grave, but tonight they must serve the living.'

'I did not realize that your sons had been so recently killed. I am sorry.'

'It is as God willed.'

When she had spoken of the killing he had supposed that it was something that had taken place in the distant past, perhaps in some earlier revolution. Now he realized that it had probably taken place only that day, that he had in fact heard the machine-gun that had mown down this woman's sons in the prison-yard.

'I am sorry.'

He could smell the new wood of the coffins where the saw had cut it. It was a clean, sweet smell that had no business with death and corruption.

He said to the woman: 'You cannot mean that we should hide in these coffins?'

'Of course.'

He did not like it. Surely Valdez's men would not omit to look in there. They would be found at once.

The woman seemed to read his thoughts. 'They will not look inside a coffin. They will be afraid to do so. It would be a kind of sacrilege. They may not fear man, these dogs, but they fear God. At least, they fear what God may do to them. Get into the coffins.'

There was no time to lose; the outer door would not hold much longer. The whole house shook under the blows that were raining upon it.

Landon spoke to Pete. 'We'd better do as she says. There's nothing else for it.'

Pete looked at the coffins and did not like the plan either. 'It's a bad omen,' he said.

Landon raised the lid of one of the coffins. 'Get in.'

Pete lay down in the coffin, the rifle beside him. It was fortunate that the old woman's sons had been big men. There was just room for Pete, no more. Landon put the lid back in place, and the woman laid a small ivory crucifix upon it.

'They will not touch this,' she said.

Landon got into the other coffin, and the woman closed the lid over him. He felt immediately stifled; he had an urge to leap out again but he conquered it. He lay in the close darkness of the coffin and heard the old woman shuffling up the stone steps. He heard the hinges of the door squeal as she opened it. Then there was a moment's silence, a cessation of hammering on the outer door, and after that a sudden clatter of feet and a hubbub of voices.

He caught snatches of words. 'They came into the house. We know. Where have you hidden them?'

Then it was the old woman's voice, fearless. 'No one has come into the house, none but you beasts.'

'Guard your tongue, old woman. You are a lying hag. Perhaps we shall cut out your tongue so that you can tell no more lies. How would you like that?'

'Some day you will be hanged,' the woman said. 'You have the hanging look.'

The man swore and shouted to the others to search the house from top to bottom. He was obviously the officer in charge of the party, and he was angry. Perhaps a little frightened also by the happenings at the gaol. Someone would be punished for that night's work. Valdez would demand scapegoats.

Landon could feel the sweat oozing out of his body and soaking his clothes. He felt unable to breathe, and he had a wild notion of jumping out of the coffin and attacking the officer. But that would have been madness. He could hear the sound of his own breathing and imagined that it must be equally audible to anyone outside the coffin. Every moment he expected the lid to be pulled off, exposing him. He was nagged by a ridiculous fear, not of the consequences of discovery, but of the ignominy of being seen in such an absurd situation.

He heard the officer's voice again. 'What are those?'

And the woman answered clearly and defiantly. 'They are coffins.'

'What is in them?'

'The dead bodies of my sons – murdered by Valdez.'

'You are sure of this?' The officer sounded only half-convinced.

'Naturally I am sure,' the old woman said. 'But if you think there are live men hiding in them why do you not open them and look?'

There was a pause, silence except for the sounds of the men searching other parts of the house – throwing open doors, turning furniture over.

Then the officer said: 'There were three of them. Three men could not hide in two coffins.'

Landon wondered whether he really believed there were three or whether this were simply a tale to cover up his own fear, his reluctance to desecrate the coffins.

'I have seen no men,' the woman said.

Landon heard again the clatter of heavy feet, then a man panting.

'We have looked everywhere, Captain. There is no sign of them.'

The officer cursed savagely. 'The hag must have shown them a way out. We will deal with her later. Is there a back way?'

'There is a back way, Captain.'

'Then go. Quickly. We have probably lost them now. The old witch! May she suffer the torments of the damned!'

'It is you who will suffer,' the woman said.

Landon heard the men going away. He heard a door slam. Then there was silence. He listened to his own breathing and the thumping of his heart. He waited for the old woman to give some sign that it was safe to come out of the coffin, but there was no sound except a slight scraping, as of someone shuffling his feet on the floor, and a gentle cough. Surely, he thought, she will tell us to come out. She must know that we are suffocating.

Then he heard the sound of footsteps approaching the coffin. The lid shifted slightly; a line of light showed through and there was fresh air.

The woman's voice said: 'They are gone.'

Landon pushed the lid back and stood up, breathing deeply and wiping the sweat from his face. The woman moved to the other coffin and lifted the lid. Pete came out grinning; the sweat was dripping from him also.

'Tight fit, Mr Landon. I've had nicer beds.'

'Not many as useful,' Landon said.

He stretched his limbs. 'I thank you, señora,' he said. 'You are a very brave person.'

'Not brave, señor. Only bitter. Where will you go now?'

'To the harbour.'

'You will have to leave by the back of the house. It is not far.'

'I think I know the way.'

'Perhaps you should wait a little longer. Valdez's men will still be sniffing.'

'No,' Landon said. 'I think—' He stopped speaking suddenly. He heard the door at the top of the steps creak open. A man came slowly down the steps. He had a revolver in his right hand and he was wearing the uniform of the Anaguan army.

'You will stand perfectly still,' he said.

The woman swung round, staring at him, her eyes wild, her lips twitching.

'How did you get here?'

'I did not leave. We are not utter fools. You were clever, but not quite clever enough.'

Pete made a movement and the revolver threatened him. The soldier's face was lean and hard; his fingers curled about the trigger.

'Drop that rifle,' he said.

Pete opened his hand and allowed the rifle to clatter to the floor. Landon's hand moved towards the pistol in the holster at his waist and the revolver switched its menace to him.

'Don't touch it, gringo. Raise your hands above your head.'

Landon's hands went up slowly, and he watched the soldier, waiting for any sign of relaxation of vigilance, a moment when the man might be off his guard. He seemed to be alone, the only one left behind; but he was being wary; he kept his distance from the two fugitives so that there was no chance of rushing him. If they tried that he could kill them both, and perhaps he even wished that they would rush him, so that he might have an excuse for shooting them.

There was a pause. The three men and the old woman stood like figures in a tableau, scarcely moving. The candle guttered on the table, the open coffins lay on the floor, as though the dead had recently arisen and left their graves agape behind them.

It was the woman who moved first. With a sudden scream of anger and frustration she flung herself at the soldier, her fingers clawing at his face. He swung the revolver and fired twice, one shot following so closely on the other that the crack of the second came while the sound of the first was still echoing in the confined space of the room.

The woman clutched at her chest and fell to the floor. The man who had shot her hesitated just a fraction of a second too long. In that brief moment of time both Landon and Pete were upon him. He tried to swing the revolver round at them, but Landon grabbed his wrist and pushed it aside. Pete wrenched the revolver out of the man's grasp and shot him between the eyes with his own gun.

It had all taken less than half a minute, and the soldier and the woman were dead.

Pete held the smoking revolver in his hand and looked down at the dead bodies. He made a clicking noise with his tongue. It might have been disapproval.

'We better get down to the harbour – fast,' he said.

Landon hesitated. 'I must find Anita first.'

Pete's head jerked up. He stared at Landon unbelievingly. 'Find that girl? You can't do that.'

'I have to. I can't go off and leave her here.'

'You were going to do just that before. Remember?'

'It was different then. Alvarez was alive. Valdez hadn't captured Santa Rosa.'

Pete picked up the fallen rifle and slung it over his shoulder. He stuffed the revolver into his pocket and took ammunition from the soldier's belt.

'How you mean to find her? Where you going to look?'

'I don't know.'

'You go looking around for that girl,' Pete said, 'and all that happens is you get yourself back in the lock-up waiting for the machine-gun to get to work on you.' He put his hand on Landon's shoulder, talking earnestly. 'We gotta be away from this town before daylight. If we don't do that we're dead pigeons. That ain't going to help Anita none. Don't you see that?'

'I suppose you're right,' Landon admitted. He knew that Pete was simply looking at things in a realistic light. There was no hope of finding the girl. He did not even know whether she were still in the town, whether she were alive.

'You bet I'm right,' Pete said. 'We get down to the boat damn fast, hey?'

'I suppose so.'

'Maybe some day you come back for Anita.'

'Maybe. Some day.'

But he knew that there would be no coming back – ever. If he left Anagua it would be for good and all. There would be no return journey.

'Better be on our way, Pete.'

19

ONCE ABOARD

THE SLOOP WAS where they had left it. There was no light showing. There was no light on any of the yachts in the basin.

'Maybe we're lucky,' Pete whispered.

They had had to avoid two sentries, but the sentries had been drowsy and it had not been difficult. Now all that remained was to get the sloop out to sea. That might prove to be a more difficult task – especially if there should be anyone on board.

Landon went first. There was no moon, but in the starlight the mast and rigging of the sloop showed faintly. Landon stepped softly on to the deck and lowered himself into the cockpit. The sloop rocked slightly.

He heard Pete drop from the quayside and land on the deck, and again the sloop rocked, the fenders squeaking softly between boat and quay.

'Quiet, Pete.'

As he moved towards the companion leading down into the cabin he thought he detected the sound of a furtive movement and the hissing of breath sharply drawn in. He pulled the automatic out of its holster and slipped the safety-catch off. The door was not fastened; he pushed it open gently and went down into the utter darkness of the cabin. He could see nothing, but he could sense that he was not alone. He remained perfectly still, the automatic gripped in his right hand, and the deck moved under his feet as Pete dropped down into the cockpit.

He heard Pete's voice, sounding hoarse. 'You gone below, Mr Landon?'

He made no answer, but now there was a sudden movement in

the darkness of the cabin, and he knew that someone had come very close to him; he could hear the sound of breathing. He jabbed at the sound with the pistol and felt the muzzle touch something that yielded to the touch. He heard a gasp.

'Don't move,' he said. 'Stay just where you are, and if you try to shout I'll blast you to hell.'

'Harvey!'

It was the girl's voice – Anita's. He lowered the pistol, reached out his hand, and touched her face.

'You!'

He could not understand it. He had thought he had lost her, that he would never see her again. And she was here.

His fingers stayed where they were, touching her face, and she did not move.

'Anita,' he said.

Pete came softly down the companion and into the cabin. His voice was worried.

'Mr Landon – you here?'

'I'm here,' Landon said. 'Anita is here too.'

He slid up the safety-catch on the automatic and thrust the weapon back in its holster.

Pete said wonderingly: 'Anita?'

Landon put his hand on the girl's shoulder. He could see now the vague outline of her face.

'How did you get here?' he asked.

She said: 'I heard the prison siren, and the guns. I knew that someone must have broken out. I hoped that it might be you and I was sure that you would come to the boat. So I came also.'

As she said it, it sounded so simple, as though she had taken the only possible action. She had come where she knew that he would come.

'You know that Alvarez is dead?'

'Yes,' she said, 'I know. Everyone knows.'

'They didn't arrest you?'

'I am not important. They had enough men to arrest; they did not trouble about the women. I was able to hide.'

'You wish to go with me now?'

'I wish to go with you.'

'I shall not come back to Anagua.'

'There is nothing left in Anagua for me. There is no more hope for the revolution now that El Aguila is dead. We are without a leader.'

'Why do you wish to come with me, Anita?'

'Because I love you,' she said. 'There is no other reason.'

For a moment there was silence in the cabin. Then, suddenly, they heard the tramp of boots on the quay, coming nearer.

'It is the sentry,' the girl whispered.

They waited, listening to the approaching tread of the sentry's boots. The boots drew level with the sloop and halted. The three in the cabin made no movement, no sound. They could imagine the sentry standing above on the quay and looking down. Had he noticed something that had aroused his suspicions? Would he come down into the yacht to investigate? Why did he not move on?

A light flared, showing through the glass of the skylight. It flickered twice and went out. Landon felt the tension flowing out of him: the sentry had merely stopped to light a cigarette. After a while he belched loudly, spat into the water, and began walking again. The sound of his boots died away in the distance and Landon said: 'Time to be moving out.'

They cast off and pushed away from the quayside, listening to the soft chuckle of water sliding along the planks. Pete was the propelling force with a long pole that reached to the bottom. There was no auxiliary engine, and if there had been they would not have dared to use it; they had to be silent, remembering the sentries.

Landon held the tiller and they moved gently towards the entrance to the basin, a narrow gap between two concrete breakwaters that curved towards each other, separating the basin from the bay. Beyond the bay was the open sea – and freedom.

The sloop came softly up to the entrance, and the bows encountered some obstacle that yielded a little way and then held. The sloop stopped moving. It lay between the concrete jaws of the breakwaters and would go no farther. Pete thrust on the pole and could make no headway.

'Something there, Mr Landon. Something there.'

Landon said impatiently: 'Get along for'ard and see what it is.'

Pete went quickly and was back again as quickly as he had gone.

'It's a net, Mr Landon. Stretched right across.'

Landon swore briefly. Valdez's men had not been so careless with the yachts as he had fondly supposed. Perhaps this was Costa's idea. Costa had an interest in keeping the yachts in the basin. Now the sloop lay helpless and exposed, for though it was dark, it was not so completely dark that a man whose eyes had become accustomed to the gloom could not detect the outline of a yacht.

'A knife, Pete. We'll have to cut the net.'

'They took my knife,' Pete said.

'I'll find one,' Landon said. 'You'd better get for'ard again and hang on to that net. We don't want to drift back.'

He stumbled down into the cabin, searching in the dark. He found a table knife with a sharp, pointed blade. He climbed out of the cabin and joined Pete in the bows. Pete was lying down and holding the net. Landon began to hack at it with the knife. The net was tough and there seemed to be no end to it; it was like trying to lop off the arms of an octopus. He thought of a fly caught in a spider's web.

'It's giving,' Pete said.

But now they were coming to the lower part of the net, and Pete could not pull it up high enough for Landon to reach it.

'I shall have to go over the side,' Landon said.

He lowered himself over the bows, took a deep breath, and dived under. He felt for the net, gripped it with his left hand, and slashed at it with the knife in his right hand. When he was forced to the surface for lack of air the net was still holding.

Pete leaned over the bows. 'How's it going?' he asked anxiously.

'Maybe next time,' Landon said.

'It better be. I think maybe somebody's coming. I seen lights.'

Landon went down again, slashing desperately with the knife. He felt the net give way at last, the two halves drifting apart. He dropped the knife and came to the surface, gasping for air, his lungs burning. Pete reached down and pulled him up on to the deck as easily as he would have lifted a child.

'We better get away quick now, Mr Landon. They're coming.'

Lights were flashing on the quayside; men were shouting. There could be little doubt that the sloop had been spotted.

Landon hurried aft and found that already the girl was using the pole. He took it from her and thrust at the breakwater, and the sloop moved out of the basin and on to the rippling water of the bay.

From the quay came a sudden spurt of red flame and the crack of a rifle. A bullet whined past and was lost in the night. Pete dived into the cabin and came out with the rifle. He took aim at a shadow moving on the breakwater and fired.

Landon said sharply: 'Hold it, Pete. You won't do any good that way. Better hoist the sails. We need to move.'

Pete put the rifle down and did as he was told. The girl helped with the sails; her father had been a fisherman and she was as much at home in a sailing-boat as were Landon and Pete.

More rifles had opened fire from the quay and men were running along the breakwater. Landon could hear bullets ricocheting from the surface of the water, and once there was a thud as one embedded itself in the boards. But the sloop was moving into darkness, and the firing became wilder.

The mainsail went up like a bird unfolding its wings. A breeze filled it and the sloop began to move faster. The rifle fire dwindled and died away, and now there was only the sound of the mast creaking and the water chuckling at the bows.

Ahead two beacon lights marked the two headlands on either side of the entrance to Santa Rosa bay. Beyond those lights was the open sea.

'We going to make it,' Pete said, and there was exultation in his voice.

Landon was cautious. 'We're not out of the net yet.'

Out in the bay the wind was fresher and they began to scud along. The headland lights were closer, one on the starboard bow, one on the port. The sloop ran between them, and the sea opened in the darkness to take the little boat into its keeping. It was the wide Pacific stretching before them.

'We made it,' Pete shouted. 'We made it.'

Yet the sound of his voice had scarcely died away when they heard the beat of the diesel engine coming up astern.

'You spoke too soon,' Landon said.

Pete looked back, but there was only darkness, picked out by the lights ashore. And then there was a moving light, two lights, red and green, marking the approach of the pursuing launch.

'It's them all right,' he said. 'But we got no lights. They never find us.'

But at that moment the searchlight was switched on, cutting a silver path across the surface of the water. It swung from left to right like a long white arm, and it caught the sloop and held it, fixed to the end of that arm, unable to shake free.

'It was a sure thing you spoke too soon,' Landon said.

He could see the girl's face in the white glare of the searchlight, and it was the first time he had seen her clearly since she had gone from him before the coming of Valdez. She was wearing a shirt and blue jeans as she had on the long journey from the Caribbean coast, and her black hair was swept back from her forehead and tied with a ribbon. However much she might change with the passing of the years, that, he thought, was how he would always remember her. And then he thought bitterly that there might not be any passing years; for the launch was coming up fast and the searchlight was on them and there was no way of eluding it, no way of getting more speed from the sails, more speed to outstrip the diesel.

He spoke to Pete: 'We gave them a good run, Pete. It just wasn't quite good enough.'

'We ain't finished yet,' Pete said.

He picked up the rifle and crouched down in the cockpit. He put the butt against his shoulder and fired into the blinding glare of the searchlight.

'Missed!'

He tried again. Again it was a miss. The sloop was dancing on the sea and making accurate shooting almost impossible.

'I'll get them bastards yet.'

He pressed the trigger again and the bolt slid forward with a metallic click.

'Empty, by God!'

He pulled a clip of cartridges out of his pocket and rammed it into the magazine. A machine-gun spat at them from the launch and bullets swished into the water. One went through a window of the cabin and half a dozen more crashed into the timbers.

'Get down, Anita, down,' Landon yelled, and when she was slow in obeying him he seized her arm and pushed her down below the level of the gunwale.

The launch was much nearer now, overhauling fast.

'I get him this time,' Pete said. 'By God, I get him this time.'

He settled the butt of the rifle hard against his shoulder and squeezed the trigger. The butt thrust back in recoil and the searchlight went out suddenly, leaving the sloop in utter darkness.

'You did it, Pete. You did it. You smashed their light.'

'They don't find us now,' Pete said. He stroked the rifle affectionately. 'You did your stuff, boy. I'm awful glad I brung you along.'

They sailed on westward. After a time the sound of the launch died away and one by one the shore lights went out like stars fading with the coming of the dawn.

The girl came and stood beside Landon at the tiller, and Pete sang softly to himself. The water gleamed with phosphorescence and all around them was the glittering reflection of the stars.

'Where we heading?' Pete asked.

'Westward,' Landon said.

'What's westward?'

'Australia.'

'I never been to Australia,' Pete said, and he began to sing again.

Landon put his free arm around the girl's waist. 'And you, Anita, would you like to go to Australia?'

'Wherever you go,' she said, 'I like that too.'

'Australia it is then.'

The wind lay in the sails and the sloop moved on over the gently heaving surface of the Pacific Ocean.

Pete went on singing.